WANT, NEED, LOVE

Also by Niobia Bryant

Published by Dafina Books

WANT, NEED, LOVE

NIOBIA BRYANT

Kensington Publishing Corp.

http://www.kensingtonbooks.com

DAFINA BOOKS are published by

Kensington Publishing Corp.
119 West 40th Street
New York, NY 10018

All Kensington Titles, Imprints, and Distributed Lines are
available at special quantity discounts for bulk purchases
for sales promotions, premiums, fund-raising, and edu-
cational or institutional use. Special book excerpts or
customized printings can also be created to fit specific
needs. For details, write or phone the office of the
Kensington special sales manager: Kensington Publishing Corp., 119 West 40th Street, New York, NY 10018,
attn: Special Sales Department, Phone: 1-800-221-2647.

Dafina and the Dafina logo Reg. U.S. Pat. & TM Off.

ISBN-13: 978-0-7582-8718-2
ISBN-10: 0-7582-8718-6
First Kensington Mass Market Edition: December 2014

eISBN-13: 978-0-7582-8719-9
eISBN-10: 0-7582-8719-4
First Kensington Electronic Edition: December 2014

10 9 8 7 6 5 4 3 2 1

Printed in the United States of America

*For my eighth-grade teacher
who made it clear she didn't believe in me . . .*

Thanks for the motivation.

Prologue

1994

"I will not teach my kids to lie or keep secrets from their mother."

Henri Ballinger's words bounced off the glass of the storm door as he leaned his tall and solid frame against it. He eyed his wife, Olivia, sandwiched by their two youngest daughters, Shara and Reeba, on the bench swing hanging from the strong limb of an oak tree. Their eldest, Mona, laughed and pushed them with strength. He curved his full lips into a smile, wishing he was out there with them enjoying life—and not dealing with the inevitable.

"It's always been done this way, Henri. You know that," his sister Winifred said from behind him, her southern accent slightly more pronounced than his.

"Yes, Henri. It is *the* way," Millicent agreed, sounding identical to her twin.

He turned to find them both standing in the center of the kitchen, their eyes filled with trouble, as they stared at him. He was their senior by just nearly six years, but once they had burst onto the scene and learned how to speak well enough to boss him around, they had. With age they had learned to finesse what they wanted from him.

Like now.

Henri shook his head and turned to look back out the door. "They will need the love and support of their mother as they come to grips with their gift—"

"She will never understand," Millicent stressed.

Henri ignored them as he left the house and stepped onto the rear porch. His mind was made up. There was no need to give them hope of changing it.

The women in his family, dating as far back as the late 1800s, were gifted with the ability to predict a person's one true love. There were no great explosions, lightning strikes, or rituals involving animals and wildness, just a brief premonition or instinct that could be mistaken as trivial if the woman didn't know better.

Henri rested his dark eyes on each of his daughters. Like his great-great-grandmother Aimee Guilliame, his grandmother Etienne, his mother Love, his sisters and countless cousins and aunts before them, his daughters had to be taught about their gift via their Creole heritage, and the preciousness of protecting it. Honoring it.

Usually they hid the gift like an amusing secret from those who married into the family. Vague references to it. Shared secretive glances.

"Look at Mommy, Daddy," Mona called over to him.

He chuckled as his wife threw her hands high into the air and flung her head back as she laughed with the spirit of a child. His heart swelled with love for her. It was a love he knew she returned just as deeply.

Henri wasn't going to tarnish it with secrecy. He was going to break tradition.

With a smile still spread across his handsome face, Henri stepped off the porch and headed across the yard to his family.

Chapter 1

"Hey . . . double or nothing."

Mona pouted her plump lips after mouthing the words along with the Omar Epps character in her favorite scene of *Love and Basketball,* when Sanaa Lathan's character played him one-on-one for his heart. It was one of her all-time favorite romance movies. She had been sixteen years old when it was released and had foolishly thought she was deeply in love with her first boyfriend, Warren Michaels. Her affection for the movie lasted much longer than her childish adoration of Warren.

"Awww," she sighed as the characters kissed. Twirling one of her tight ebony ringlets of hair around her pinky, she lay back among the dozen full-sized pillows on her queen-sized bed. Pillows that almost fooled her into forgetting that one side of her bed was consistently empty as she slept. Nude. Alone. Empty. Consistently.

"A freaking born again virgin," Mona muttered,

confident that a solid eight months without sex had earned her that title.

Freeing her body of her cotton sheets by kicking them away with her long, shapely legs, she reached down to lightly pat the top of her cleanly shaven mound. "You're the dick whisperer," she said. "I'm not sure what vibes you are throwing out to make the penises behave, but you have them well trained to not be naughty with me. Too trained."

With one last pat, Mona rolled off the bed and rose high up onto her toes as she stretched her five-foot-eight-inch frame and tilted her head back far enough for the tips of her long spiraled hair to stroke the middle of her back. Mona wasn't a lover of the length, which was high maintenance, but it reminded her of time well spent with her mother. The hours she spent brushing her mother's hair and greasing her scalp as they talked about her day at school. It was a ritual she would love to replicate with her own daughter one day and so she kept it long. One memory of many she hoped to leave behind once she was gone on to heaven too.

The death of her mother and the subsequent illness of her father not long after had led Mona back home to Holtsville. Pushing aside a poignant feeling of sadness at the loss of her mother, which instantly drew in the emptiness at her father passing away not a year later, Mona padded across the dozen area rugs she had layered across the bedroom floor. Each had a bright floral pattern, and somehow the varying colors worked, making her all white bed linen seem like a cloud floating above a garden. Her mental peace on earth.

As she went through the normal motions of preparing for her day, she was constantly aware of the singleness of her life. The lone washcloth in the shower. A single toothbrush in the cup holder on the left-hand corner of the double sink—of which only one was used. For breakfast just one slice of wheat toast with a fried egg and a cup of lemon tea. A closet with nothing but her eclectic mix of business attire for work and hippy chic garb for play.

Everything was a constant reminder of her "only the lonely" status.

Her first boyfriend was just one of several heartbreaks scattered on the bumpy road to "happily ever after." And despite that fact she was a hopeless romantic who wanted nothing more than to be in love. She was still hopeful.

Finally dressed in a red cotton pantsuit that emphasized her tall and slender frame with fullness at her breasts, hips, buttocks, and thighs, Mona slipped into animal print kitten heels. She grabbed her matching briefcase before leaving the modest but comfy two-bedroom cottage she'd been renting for the last few months upon her return to the small rural town of Holtsville, South Carolina. The early spring air was rich with the smell of the towering trees, grass, and wildflowers of her surroundings. Mona was not an "earthy, dig your feet in the dirt, sigh over cute furry animals" type of woman. At all. She preferred paved roads to dirt ones and sidewalks to grass lining the roads, but even she couldn't deny the allure of the southern quiet being broken up only by the sounds of nature.

She came down the steps of the wraparound porch

and opened the back door of her red VW bug with a white convertible top. The heart-shaped logo she used for her business, Modern Day Cupid, was on the doors and trunk. She shook her head at the irony of being a professional matchmaker who couldn't find a love of her own. That little nugget *stayed* stuck in her craw almost as much as her little vibrator stayed pressed to her—

"*Bzzzzzz . . .*"

The vibrating of her iPhone interrupted her thoughts. She knew it was an e-mail and didn't bother to check it as she reversed down the paved driveway and started on the main road leading into the heart of rural Holtsville. She drove by the many houses and mobile homes that were far outnumbered by the amount of towering trees, fields overrun with farm animals or waist-high grass, or abandoned homes covered in wild ivy.

Mona smiled and shook her head at the memory of those first months after her family moved there from New Orleans, Louisiana, when she was just ten. In her young eyes rural Holtsville made metropolitan New Orleans look like New York in comparison. It wasn't the type of town you moved to for opportunity. Relocating to Holtsville meant that either you grew up there or left behind family there; otherwise you wouldn't know it even existed.

Holtsville was her mother's hometown, which she'd left behind to attend Xavier University in New Orleans. It was there she met and eventually married Mona's father, a native of the city. And it was there they remained for the next fifteen years, until her father fell in love with the laid back pace and the small town familiarity during a two-week summer visit one year.

Two years later they were off to Holtsville.

Mona pulled to a stop at a red light, chuckling at how miserable she had been in those first few weeks after the move. She had ached for everything they left behind in New Orleans. She even threatened to run away—threats her parents smartly paid no mind to. "Just a little drama queen," she muttered as she checked for oncoming traffic before turning onto the main road through Holtsville.

She briefly contemplated stopping at Donnie's Diner for a good home-cooked breakfast made with plenty of butter, but pressed on toward Walterboro instead. Mona hadn't hired a receptionist yet—as she had in her previous office of five years in Columbia—so along with her matchmaking duties she had to make sure she was there to answer the phones. *One more thing on my to do list.*

"Driver, roll up the partition, please," she sang along with Beyoncé's song on the radio. Mona quickly ate up the fifteen miles to the neighboring larger city where the office for her business was located.

Main Street of downtown Walterboro was still reminiscent of the older days of five and dime stores and small mom and pop shops, even with the inclusion of a restaurant and bar. It could easily be the backdrop for a 1960s movie, the narrow street just wide enough for one-way, one-lane traffic.

Mona pulled her convertible into a corner parking spot. As she reversed to get closer to the curb, she spotted a tall man in a three-piece suit casually leaning against the hood of a dark gray BMW. Her foot paused on the brake pedal when he turned his head toward her vehicle. The mirror aviator shades he wore looked good against his dark complexion and gave the tailored suit an edge that made her pulse race a little.

"Child, please," she warned herself, focusing her attention on parking her car.

As she climbed from her VW and walked around to the passenger seat to remove her briefcase, she gave the man a brief glance. He looked down at his watch and then pushed off the car to walk closer to the glass front door of her storefront office.

She closed her passenger door and frowned a bit when he swore and turned away from the storefront in anger—not the usual laid back nature of potential clients looking for love. Sliding her briefcase in the bend of her arm, she walked up to him giving him a more thorough evaluation from the top of his jet black fade, to his chiseled dark-skinned features and the firm fit of his suit on his body.

"I'm Mona Ballinger. Can I help you?" she asked, coming to a halt by where he paced on the sidewalk.

He stopped and turned to face her. She was almost five foot eight, but he easily towered over her by another six inches, even though she was in her kitten heels. "You own this business?" he asked, his voice deep, masculine, warm . . . and tinged with annoyance as he removed his shades.

Mona lightly gasped at the sight of his dark brown eyes surrounded by long and full lashes that no hundred-dollar tube of mascara could replicate. *Well damn . . .*

"Yes," she finally answered with emphasis as she stiffened her spine and locked her knees.

"Hmph," he said, using his striking eyes to take her in from head to toe.

Mona arched a full, shaped brow as he made her feel somehow inadequate, like she didn't meet up with his expectations. "Listen, it seems you have all day. I—on the other hand—do not," she said, stepping to the side to then move past him.

The hell? Mona worked the key to the front door free from the others dangling on her Coach key ring.

"A matchmaker who breaks up relationships?"

Mona glanced at him over her shoulder as she pulled the glass door open. "Do you want to explain who you are and what you want?" she asked. "I'm trying my best not to be rude, but since you're so fluent with it I'll just get on your level."

He reached out to press the door open wider for her. "It's funny you have no idea who I am, but you advised my fiancée to end our engagement," he said.

Mona acknowledged his gentlemanly move with a brief nod of her head. "And who is your fiancée?" she asked as she walked inside the renovated flower shop that housed her one-room office. She strode across the hardwood floors and placed her items on the white-painted wood desk in the center of the room, set atop a large red area rug.

"Are you ruining so many relationships that you can't keep up?" he asked.

Mona turned and faced him, one hand pressed above the curve of her hip and the other against the edge of her desk. He stood there with his arms crossed over his chest, his very presence seeming to shrink the size of the already small interior of the office. "It's not my job to find just anybody for someone," she said. "I want him or her to be with . . . the *right* person."

He shook his head and released a chuckle filled with sarcasm. "You're taking 'modern day cupid' too seriously, ya think?"

Mona's face became pensive as she repositioned her body to lean back against the edge of the desk. She studied the handsome man and then eyed his luxury vehicle through the glass window. The looks. The arrogance. The wealth. Crossing her legs at the ankles, she nodded in sudden understanding. "So Carina did take my advice?" she asked, picturing him with the pretty, fair-skinned pediatrician.

He was Anson Tyler and he fit every description his former fiancée had given about him last month as she sat with Mona in the lounge area of Modern Day Cupid. Of course Mona had asked why an engaged woman would even seek out the services of a matchmaker and the woman admitted that she was ready to end the relationship.

His face stiffened with anger. "Your advice based on what?" he asked, his voice flushed with his annoyance at her.

Mona purposefully pressed her lips together and gave herself a five count to think before she spoke. She and her younger sisters, Reeba and Shara, had a gift of premonition and a sixth sense about love inherited from the female lineage of their ancestors, said to date back to the days of slavery. Although she could distinctly remember reaching over to touch the other woman's hand and having a clear vision of her with another man, Mona didn't tell him the basis of her certainty that a forever love was not in the cards for him and Carina.

And Mona was *never* wrong. But she wasn't going to tell him that. "Listen, Mr. Tyler," she began, rising to move around her desk to take her seat in the white, leather, tufted club chair. "Please believe that I do not take what I do lightly. I have nothing to gain by the end of your relationship, and this confrontation you are trying to have with me is pointless. I'm sure the end of a relationship—particularly an engagement—is not easy, but the end of marriage is worse. You two were not meant to be together."

Anson walked up to her desk and, bending his tall frame to press both his hands against the top of the desk, loomed over her. "Who in the hell do you think you are?" he asked.

She leaned back in her chair and crossed her legs as she tilted her head to the side and locked her eyes with his. "I *know* exactly who and what I am," she told him confidently.

He stared at her.

She met his stare even as she forced her body to remain relaxed, when she in fact was a bundle of nerves.

His eyes shifted to her left hand. "Do you have a man of your own, Ms. Ballinger?"

Mona hated that her gaze shifted away from his for even a millisecond and that her face revealed just enough to elicit a knowing look from him. Running her hands through her curls, she sat up in her chair and began shifting items around on her desk. "No, Mr. Tyler, I don't," she said, fingering an ink pen with her logo imprinted on it. "But I believe in love. I respect love. I want people to be happy in love. I want it for myself and I want it for every client who hits me up on social media or my Web site or walks through that door. So, I'll give you the same advice I gave your . . . Carina. The same advice I gave Carina."

He snorted in derision as he rose and wiped his mouth with one strong hand.

"Take some time. Gain some perspective. And when you feel ready to move on I will be more than happy to match you up—"

"Here the hell we go," Anson balked, throwing his hand up in the air. "Destroy a relationship and then pick up two new customers for this sham you're running."

Mona jumped to her feet, sending her chair toppling back with a *wham.* "Get out," she snapped, pointing one red spike-shaped fingernail at the door.

"No problem." He turned and stalked to the door.

"What you need to deal with is what doubts brought her through that same door you're about to walk out of," she said, her cold voice filling the silence as she glared at his broad-shouldered back.

He paused with his hand gripping the handle.

Mona's chest was still heaving with anger and indignation. "Your fiancée came to a matchmaking company, Mr. Tyler, on her accord. I didn't seek her out. She was supposed to be in the midst of her happily-ever-after. What brought her here? Now you go somewhere and deal with that reality you're running from."

He looked over his shoulder at her. His eyes were

filled with the truth of what she'd said, and Mona felt regret for her harshly spoken words.

"Go to hell," Anson said, his voice soft but filled with meaning.

Her regrets evaporated. "I have been there for the last ten minutes."

With long strides he walked through the door, slid on his shades, and moved to his car. Moments later his vehicle took off down the street.

Mona shook her head as she turned and bent to set her chair upright. She dropped down into it and pressed her elbows into the top of her knees. "Well, that's a first," she drawled before releasing a deep breath.

In college, Mona had discovered that she had a natural instinct for matchmaking her friends. Her gift of premonition had just been a confirmation that she had been right. Among her family they all liked to joke that they were descendants of Cupid, and the Ballingers used their strong intuition to ensure that those who were worthy were gently nudged toward their one true love. In time, people she didn't even know would come to her for help in finding love. What began as her helping out friends became a hustle to make ends meet and then a small business that she aggressively expanded when she graduated from college. With the combination of her personality, her belief in love, her gift, and the marketing and business skills she'd acquired in college, the business was a success.

She truly loved love. To have someone question that and her integrity shook her a little bit.

Not that it was the first time.

Mona leaned forward in her chair and picked up the gold gilt frame holding a photo of her parents, her twin aunts, and her sisters. She smiled softly. Her Aunt Millicent, whom they all called Millie, had pleaded to take the photo right after the "big talk," when Mona and her sisters had learned of their gift.

That day her aunts had also stressed the importance of keeping it all a secret from people not in their family. Something Mona had never quite understood. They didn't do voodoo or root or spells. They were not witches. They had no superpowers. They couldn't read crystal balls or change the future. Hell, they didn't even know what to do with a tarot card.

They were just able to see a clear image of a person happily in love with someone else. And if they had not been trained to detect it they would have thought it was just their imagination working overtime. Two-second visions that were a snapshot out of someone's life. That's all. No biggie.

So why the secrecy?

Mona shifted her eyes to her middle sister, Reeba. Unlike her youngest sister, Shara, who was off traveling around the world, Reeba lived in Holtsville as well, but Mona spoke to Shara more. Reeba felt that Mona was disrespecting their ability by making money with it. It took nothing but a blow of wind for them to flip a happy-go-lucky convo into a full-blown argument. Nothing at all.

Sighing, she sat the frame back among the few others filling the front left corner of her desk. Her intentions were—and would always be—the best. It was up to others to believe that. The words she spoke to Anson Tyler had been the utmost truth.

I know *exactly who and what I am.*

She sighed as she readjusted her chin in her left hand and used the other one to scroll through the documents displayed on the touch screen of her computer. The pictures and profiles of the men who had submitted their info to Modern Day Cupid were in the hundreds. She had three times as many women also seeking her matchmaking services. Everyone was looking for love.

And they weren't the only ones.

The only problem was, like every other woman in her family, Mona could not use her intuition to help herself or anyone else in the family make that love connection. After a string of horribly disappointing relationships, she was beginning to believe that her ability to help others was so strong that she drew anything *but* the "right one" to herself.

She reached over to strike her inner wrist where she had the word "Believe" tattooed. It symbolized her belief in herself. In her business. In her dreams. In love.

But above all she absolutely believed in "the one." That folks were meant to be in a special relationship. How could she not when her gift was a testament to that? And so she had to believe in it for her clients as well as herself.

Chapter 2

Focus, man. Focus.

Anson cleared his throat, sat up straighter in his chair in the waiting room of the two-story corporate offices of Jamison & Jamison Contractors, Inc., and rearranged the papers inside the leather folio he carried. He was ten feet from a very important business meeting, and his disappointment over Carina ending their two-year relationship and his annoyance at the woman who advised her to do so was just a hindrance. And Anson was always about his business. He had no choice. Failure was not an option.

His life was the epitome of hard-knock. Both parents lost to a drug addiction that left him and his younger brother, Hunter, with memories of living from pillar to post with plenty of missed meals in between. A surprise visit from social services had underscored the squalor, the filth, the lack of necessities. The neglect. He didn't know what stung more deeply—his parents' neglect or their inability to get their acts together after losing their children. As a twelve-year-old boy he could have forgiven them anything if they had just shown up and reclaimed their children.

Anson took a deep breath, hating that the pang that came with the memories was still so sharp after more than twenty years.

He was well aware that his past and the fact it was still stuck in his craw fueled his desire to succeed and never go back. He'd fought hard to turn his life into a success story after being aged out of the foster care system at eighteen. There were many battles he'd had to fight and defeat to gain custody of his brother and raise him while working two jobs and attending first community college and then Clemson University. During that time, and even many years after he'd graduated with his Bachelor of Architecture, they had survived on the very basics. Oodles of Noodles and Dollar Store groceries had been their lifesavers. They'd worn clothes until they were threadbare. He had held his little pickup truck together with metal coat hangers and duct tape. They had come through it . . . thankfully together.

Started from the bottom—now we're here.

The song lyric from Drake's "Started from the Bottom" was his anthem. Now fourteen years later after earning his degree, he was a successful architect who also owned a dozen small businesses. He was far from the days of wondering where his next meal would come from and sometimes he would sit back and be amazed at the wealth he'd accumulated. His brother, Hunter, had earned his doctor of medicine from Morehouse School of Medicine in Atlanta and had been accepted into their surgical residency program there as well. Anson couldn't be more proud.

All of his plans had come to fruition.

Except for his desire to be married and start a family.

An image of Mona Ballinger's face filled with anger as she ordered him out of her office replayed in his mind.

Curly-headed troublemaker.

"Right this way, Mr. Tyler."

Anson looked up at the tall, full-figured secretary before rising to his feet and smoothing the front of his clothing. He picked up his monogrammed leather portfolio where it leaned against his chair before he followed her past her station in the metal building housing the offices of Jamison & Jamison Contractors. He cleared his throat and straightened his double-knotted silk tie just before she opened the double doors and stepped aside to allow him to enter the large conference room.

Devon and Deshawn Jamison both rose to their feet from their seats at the conference table and extended their hands in gestures that were as identical to each other as their DNA.

Anson firmly shook each hand. "Good morning, gentlemen," he said, his voice deep and serious. "I know you're really busy and I appreciate the opportunity to meet with you about this new business venture."

Devon and Deshawn briefly glanced at each other and smiled before reclaiming their seats. "Nice suit . . . Junebug," Deshawn quipped, pushing up the sleeves of the lightweight plaid shirt he'd tucked into well-worn denims.

Anson stiffened.

Devon chuckled.

Anson eyed them both before he too smiled.

While Anson had been in college he worked as a laborer for the men sitting before him. In fact it was during those summer days and the fall nights and weekends that his love of architecture was born. These two men who were his senior by just eight years had become his mentors of sorts. He looked up to them, admired them, and appreciated not just the work and skills he'd acquired from them but the time and effort they took to guide him on and off the work site.

Now here he was interviewing to be the architect for their expansion into multimillion dollar commercial properties across the East and Southeast. "This is an important meeting. I just wanted to show you both I respect you and the next level you're approaching in your business," Anson said with a slight tug of the knot of his tie as he lightly cleared his throat. "I would never want to disrespect either of you by strolling in here with anything less than what I bring to every meeting and interview."

Anson lived by the mantra: "Nothing personal. It's just business."

"And we appreciate that, Anson," Devon said. The elder of the twins by minutes, he reached for the portfolio and unzipped it.

Anson sat back as they flipped through his organized documentation of his architectural work over the last decade. He was extremely proud of everything from the rough drawings and blueprints to the prints of the completed construction of the buildings. There were also several features in regional architectural magazines and an award or two for his innovation.

Anson was not just a former worker looking for a handout. He was a talented architect looking to bring just as much to the table as the opportunity they offered. He'd worked to establish himself. He'd made plenty of sacrifices. This was his legacy.

All three men looked up as the double doors to the conference room opened and two women came in, smiles on their faces. Anson rose to his feet.

"We're in a meeting, babe," Devon said, looking on as his wife, Chloe, came straight to him to press a kiss to his lips.

"With Junebug? Puh-*lease*," Anika said, before going around the opposite end of the table to kiss her husband Deshawn as well.

And then they both came back around the table to hug Anson close. First Chloe, the former supermodel who was still tall and svelte and gorgeous, looking far younger than her forty years.

He turned as Anika playfully swatted his arm before hugging him, her thick and shapely frame womanly and soft. Anson had nothing but respect for either woman. Like their husbands of more than a decade, the women had also nurtured him and given him invaluable advice over the years.

"How's my house?" Chloe asked, leaning against the edge of the table.

Anson smiled. "*My* house is just as beautiful as

it was when you sold it to me three years ago," he countered.

"Ladies," Devon interrupted to end their casual conversation in the middle of their business meeting.

"How's Carina?" Anika asked, turning the portfolio so that she could flip through the pages.

Anson stiffened. "We're not together anymore," he admitted after a pause.

Both Chloe and Anika made sad faces. "Ohhh," they said.

"We'll have to find you someone new," Anika said, looking over at Chloe.

"You know what, I have somebody in mind," Chloe said.

"Who?" Anika asked.

Anson bit back a smile as Devon and Deshawn shared a brief glance before each moved around the table to lightly touch his wife's lower back to gently guide her toward the door.

"Dominique, the shampoo girl at the beauty shop," Chloe said.

"Nooooo, no no no no," Anika insisted with a wave of her hand. "She cut her last boyfriend with a razor blade. Forty-five stitches across his back."

"What?" Chloe gasped, her eyes widening. "Why didn't you tell me about it?"

"You know I don't gossip."

Both women paused and then broke out into laughter.

The men each kissed their wife's cheek and then stepped back to close the double doors.

"You're lucky we have a meeting of our own," Anika said with a feigned hard stare at Deshawn.

"This is rude," Chloe added.

The men continued to close the doors.

"Bye, Junebug," both women said just seconds before the doors shut.

Anson chuckled.

"Don't laugh . . . You're in for a string of bad dates," Devon said, going back around the table to turn the portfolio toward him to continue his perusal.

"*Real* bad," Deshawn added dryly, running his hand over his low cut that was lightly sprinkled with silver.

Anson held up his hands. "The last thing I need is another matchmaker—or two—in my life," he said. "Trust me on that. Help a brother out."

"I'll control my wife," Devon said, taking his seat.

"Say what?" Deshawn balked. "Ms. Ex-supermodel turned business mogul with a dozen different product lines banking millions every year?"

"And you can do something with tough as nails Anika flying around the country giving domestic violence seminars where a part of the program is martial arts training and selling pink Tasers in the lobby?" Devon countered.

Deshawn laughed. "My baby tough as nails, boy," he admitted.

Anson looked at the two men, both married for well over a decade, with kids. Stability. Love.

He wanted that.

He thought he'd been close to it with Carina.

Maybe not a deep, soul-searing love, but a sincere

caring and concern and a desire for her to be his wife and bear his children. He'd been so close to the family he wanted. He still wanted that. He didn't like detouring off his plan. Not at all.

Devon tapped a page of the portfolio with one strong finger as he looked over at him. "What was your inspiration for the design of this gymnasium in Summerville?"

Anson loosened the knot of his tie as he sat up straighter in his chair. He was ready to get back to business. The resolution of his personal life had to wait. For now.

Hours later, Anson was in his media/game room watching the NBA playoffs and sipping a snifter of his treasured bottle of seventy-year-old brandy when the doorbell sounded. He slid the crystal into the cup holder of one of twenty leather recliners before the hundred-foot projector screen as he rose to his feet in nothing but the low slung pajama bottoms he wore.

He started to check the surveillance cameras he'd had installed just last month, but padded barefoot across the polished hardwood floors to the front door instead. Anson opened the extra wide entry door and started in surprise to find Carina standing there. He eyed her as she smiled and breezed past him to enter the spacious foyer of the uniquely designed single level home.

What now?

Anson closed the door and slowly turned to face

her. The few days since they last spoke or he'd seen her had done nothing to dull her prettiness and lessen the curves of her thick frame in the white wrap dress she wore. "How can I help you?" he asked, crossing his arms over his bared chest.

Carina giggled lightly and ran her hand across her eyes as if to see clearly. "Why so rude, Anson?" she asked, leaning against the wall as she rested her eyes on him.

"The last time I called, you made me feel I was harassing you and then hung up on me," he answered with ease.

Carina kicked off the gold-tipped heels she wore and walked over to wrap her arms around his waist and rest her head against the deep groove between his pectorals. "I was trying to be strong and you call-ing made me weak," she said.

He felt her words blow gently against his chest. "Allowing some woman with an agenda to change your mind about us when she didn't even know us was already a sign of weakness," he said, reaching behind his back to unclasp her hands and push them back down to her sides.

Carina took one step back and eyed his bared chest and the way the pajama bottoms hung low on his hips and clung to the length of his member. "I missed it, Anson," she admitted softly, untying her wrap dress and exposing the sheer bra and thong panties she wore beneath it as she reached to take his inches into her hand.

He gripped her hand tightly.

She looked up at him with a lick of her lips.

"Just *it* or me too?" Anson asked.

"Sex wasn't our problem, Anson," she said. "Right?"

He stiffened as his eyes searched hers.

"Your fiancée came to a matchmaking company, Mr. Tyler, on her accord. I didn't seek her out. She was supposed to be in the midst of her happily-ever-after. What brought her here? Now you go somewhere and deal with that reality you're running from."

He hated that the words of the meddling matchmaker came back to him in that moment. He hated it because there was a lot of truth in what she said. Truths that his ex-fiancée just confirmed.

"I didn't know we had any problems," Anson admitted.

Carina's eyes shifted away from him.

Anson took a step back from her. "Would have been nice to be clued in before you went looking for a love connection elsewhere."

She looked back at him and smiled softly as she took a step toward him. "Listen, I just thought we could have a little fun . . . for old time's sake," she said, stroking one of his nipples with her index finger.

Anson caught her hand. "I don't do dick on demand for anybody," he said.

She arched a brow and stepped back from him to let the dress fall from her shoulders to a puddle at her feet. Striking a pose, she looked deeply into his eyes, daring him. "So you don't want this?" she asked after a moment, her voice disbelieving.

Anson's head below his waist stirred to life, but he forced the head on his neck to remain in control. "Yes . . . but I want everything that comes with it and

I just realized everything else is not available, and maybe never really was."

Carina sighed and bent over to pick up her dress and pull it on. "Look, Anson, I had a long, stressful day at my practice and I just wanted to relax a little bit. That's all."

He shrugged one broad shoulder. "That's not enough."

"Fine," she said, securing the dress with jerky movements that revealed her agitation. She bent to scoop up her shoes.

He stepped aside as she moved toward the front door.

"Good-bye, Anson," she said over her shoulder.

"Why did you go to the matchmaking service?" he asked just as she opened the door.

She paused and hung her head low, as if she wished she had made it out the door before the question could have been asked. "Don't, Anson," she pleaded.

"Do, Carina," he insisted with censure.

She turned. "You're cold. Distant. Unreachable," she said, her eyes filling with tears. "Even in bed— as good as it was physically—there is a part of you that is closed off to me emotionally and I can feel it. There is a shield around your heart. And it made me feel less than. Lacking. Wanting more than a wet ass from you, Anson. More than a big house and the white picket fence and the two kids and a dog. I wanted to feel loved, not *acquired* like a business."

Anson crossed his arms over his chest and frowned deeply at her critique.

Carina eyed him up and down and shook her head as if she found him lacking. "It's not all about your plan, Anson, and until you realize that, or find the woman who makes you forget it, you will continue in a long line of meaningless relationships or wasting the time of another woman like me who wants more than just to be respected for her career. I am a woman, Anson," she finished with emphasis.

His eyes squinted and his brain raced to dissect everything she said. To find any meaning between the lines.

"Say something," she almost screamed, her frustration with him obvious.

"We were together for two years and you felt this way the entire time and said nothing?" Anson asked, his voice hard and cold . . . and distant.

Carina shook her head. "What happened to you to make you so coldhearted?"

He brushed away what he saw as feigned concern. "Was the trip to the matchmaker your first time looking elsewhere for this love you claim I didn't have?"

Her shoulders slumped and she looked defeated by his words. "No," she admitted.

Anson's eyes hardened as he stared at her.

Carina held up her hands. "You gave me no choice, and if you really are honest about us, you didn't love me, and in time I realized I didn't love you either," she said, turning and exiting his house.

Anson stood there long after the lights from her car flashed across the windows of his home as she reversed and left his yard. His life.

It wasn't anger and jealousy that left him rooted in that spot. The woman he'd been in a relationship with for the last two years, whom he'd proposed to just two months ago, had admitted she'd cheated and she had no use for him outside sex. He was waiting to feel the classic signs after receiving such news.

Those feelings never rose in him. He didn't even care to find out the details of her infidelity. The "who, what, when, where, and why" of it was futile to him. She was untrustworthy. Period. Point blank.

"What happened to you to make you so cold-hearted?"

Anson walked out onto his porch, leaving the front door slightly ajar. He took a seat on the padded bench lining the rails and extended his legs to cross his ankles as he looked up at the night sky beginning to fill with stars. He and Carina were done. He could admit that he had no deep and profound love for her, but he'd expected the same faithfulness he'd given to her. Their sex life had been heated enough, but had it been the best sex he ever had? No. The type of soul-searing connection that all those foolish romance novels proclaimed existed? Never.

Although he'd been successful in business, his personal life had been a run of one-night stands and meaningless relationships. In Carina he'd thought he'd found the ideal candidate to wed and settle down with. Someone who understood the importance of career focus and the "American dream."

His architectural firm and other small business ventures were his priorities. He'd seen too much and came through too much to ever go back to having wish sandwiches for dinner and living pillar to post. He doubted that he would ever meet the woman who'd make him put love before financial security.

Chapter 3

Two weeks later

Mona sat her iPad down on the sofa beside her and wiped her face with her hands, wishing it was that easy to wipe the fatigue away. Pulling her bare feet up onto the sofa, she wrapped her arms around her legs and settled her dimpled chin in the groove between her knees. Through her bright pink spectacles she looked off into the distance at the rain pelting against the window. She was exhausted and briefly closed her eyes as she took a deep breath. . . .

"No," she cried out, sitting up straight and looking around bewildered.

Her heart was pounding and she was relieved to still be in her living room. She wiped her eyes with her fingertips as she pressed her feet to the floor.

"Not another one," she moaned.

Over the last couple of weeks she had been plagued by brief visions that alluded to the faltering health of Anson Tyler, the angry ex-fiancé of her current client, Carina. Mona was determined to forget the irate man and their whole confrontation, but the dreams plagued her. They were just flashes lasting no more than a second or two, but in each one he was injured—by fire, by illness, by drowning, and so on. This time he had fallen off the cliff in true Wile E. Coyote getting played by the Road Runner fashion from those Looney Tunes cartoons. She'd never had such a vision and didn't know if it was a true premonition or her just taking out her frustration because he'd questioned her motivation in her business. She took the integrity of her business very seriously and hated that it had been questioned.

That had to be all it was.

Rising to her feet, she jumped around and rolled her shoulders. "Wake up, Mo. Wake your butt up, girl," she kept saying, even squatting to playfully box the air with her tiny fists.

Moving her successful boutique matchmaking services to a smaller town should have meant downsizing, but if anything business was booming even more. In the last few weeks she had more than twenty new clients complete the initial online sign up for her services adding to the already large base of clients in varying stages of receiving her amenities, from the required interview either in person or by FaceTime to one-on-one coaching or image consulting, prior to her searching her database for matches.

And she still had to make time for the purely business end of it. The paperwork, the advertising and marketing, the bills, the collection of past due accounts.

"Fuuuuuuuuck," Mona said, tilting her head up to the ceiling and childishly kicking her feet.

Giving herself a mini time out for her mini

tantrum, Mona sat on the sofa for a few moments and just breathed. Slowly and deeply. "I need help," she said, hating the anxiety that was consuming her and hating even more that she had to humble herself and ask for assistance.

Mona rose and walked across the cozy and intimate living room to slip her bare feet into a pair of rubber boots, pull on her trench coat, and grab an umbrella from the white milk can umbrella holder she kept by the front door. Spring showers in the Southeast came often and that night was no exception.

With her car keys in her fist, Mona stepped out onto the porch and opened her umbrella before dashing down the stairs to her vehicle. Luckily the night rain was gentle and she barely got wet before unlocking and opening the door and sliding onto the leather driver's seat. She gripped the wheel tightly as she steered, but it wasn't for fear of losing control on the wet road. It was tension. Plain and simple.

With one last turn down a long, muddy, dirt road, Mona looked out at the white two-story home that her mother had inherited from her father upon his passing. It was where they'd lived once they moved to Holtsville from New Orleans, and upon their father's death the house was willed to Mona and her sisters.

Only Reeba resided there now. Shara was off seeing the world, and Mona had found her own place after the animosity stewing between her and Reeba made the house tension-filled and stressful.

"Am I crazy?" Mona wondered aloud as she parked the car and reached for her umbrella on the floor of the passenger side. "Watch how quick this shit go left."

Mona got out of the car and hurried up the brick path leading from the driveway to the front stoop. As she stepped onto the porch, the front door opened and Reeba stood there behind the screen.

All of the Ballinger girls resembled each other, and ever since they were just chubby toddlers, people mistook them for triplets. Same build. Same bronzed cinnamon complexion most people accomplished with high end cosmetics. Same jet black hair reaching their midback.

As Mona stood before the screen door it was almost like looking at a mirror reflection save that Reeba wore her hair bone straight and parted like Pocahontas. "Hey, sis," Mona said, reaching for the door handle as Reeba stepped back to allow her entrance.

"Where you going in this weather . . . dressed like that?" Reeba asked with a smile, eyeing Mona's bright yellow pajamas and fire-engine red rain boots with a hot pink trench with a ruffled bottom.

"I need to dress up to come see you?" Mona asked, moving over to the crackling embers in the fireplace. She rubbed her hands together and enjoyed the warmth of the fire.

"You want some tea?" Reeba asked, turning to head back to the large kitchen at the rear of the house.

"Not without a splash of amaretto." Mona removed her trench and boots before padding behind her sister.

"One Mama's special coming up," Reeba said,

picking up the copper teapot on the stove to fill with water.

Mona smiled as she looked around at the warm and bright decor that easily rivaled the dark rainy skies outside the many windows lining the walls. "You haven't changed anything," she said, moving over to the fireplace once used for cooking to stroke her mother's cast iron pot.

Many winter nights her mother had lit the fire and they'd all sat around it as she made cocoa. Not from necessity, but because she knew her girls loved the idea of a fireplace in the kitchen.

"Why would I?" Reeba asked. "It's not just my home . . . I'm just the only one who never left."

Mona stiffened. That was true, but she didn't understand why Reeba made her feel guilty about it. Her love for the small town had been long to come, as it had for Shara. Reeba, like their father, had clung to it instantly and upon graduation had chosen to stay, attending the College of Charleston and commuting every day to campus.

"There's nothing wrong in either of our decisions on where to attend college and live after graduation, ReeRee," Mona said gently, referring back to her childhood nickname to diffuse the far too familiar tension she felt rising between them.

"I was speaking of after Daddy died."

Mona glanced over her shoulder. "I thought I was doing you a favor by moving out," she said.

Reeba just shrugged before turning with two steaming cups to sit on the large island in the center of the kitchen. "Once again you were wrong," she said with a twist of her lip. "But you always see and do things your way . . . regardless of anything else."

"How is the air up there on that high horse?" Mona asked.

"Peaceful," Reeba returned with ease.

Mona plopped down onto one of the bar stools and pulled her cup and saucer closer to stir. "I can't believe I even considered asking you to come help me at Modern Day Cupid," she balked, the spoon hitting sharply against the porcelain as she created a mini whirlpool in her tea.

Reeba dropped her spoon. "What?" she gasped sharply in disbelief. "Girl . . . please. I wouldn't dare walk foot in that place, far less help you with pissing all over family traditions."

Mona released a heavy breath. "I don't see why you or the aunts get to tell me what I do with the gift *God* gave me."

"That God gave to generations of women in our family who have all respected the way things are done," Reeba snapped.

"I respect it as well, maybe more so because I use it for what it is intended rather than hide it like it's something to be forgotten or forgiven." Mona rose to her feet and held up her hand. "Just forget I even brought it up."

"Mona—"

"No," Mona said forcefully. "I should be able to ask my sister to help, but that's my dumb-ass fault for thinking that."

"Sure was."

Mona had moved to the door, but paused and turned. "You don't even know you're wrong. You're so caught up in this supposed indignation that you're not even using common sense. And as much as I respect the college education we both have, it is that common sense that I leaned toward more."

Reeba arched one full, shapely brow. "So I don't have common sense?"

Mona shrugged one shoulder. "Not if you think a business that has been thriving in the black for the last three years is all dependent upon me touching everybody who comes through the door and hooking them up with the person I see in that vision," she said, her tone as tight as she felt. "I have clients across the country. Some I have never met in person. Some I am not able to lay hands on. My database is only made up of people who come to me for a match. I am successful because I built a network of professionals who want to cut out some of the chase in falling in love."

Reeba shook her head and looked down into the tea she continued to stir. *Clink-clink. Clink-clink.*

"Now every so often do I have two people in the database and I'm able to touch one of them and see a vision that they are meant to be. Yes. And every time it happens I feel honored and blessed to help them connect, but that's less than three percent of the business I do. Most times it's just me doing the work outside the premonitions and I still have a more than seventy-five percent success rate," she snapped. "So this assumption that my business is all about the use of my gift is *bullshit.* It would be nonsensical and I shouldn't have to tell you that, Little Sister All High and Mighty Think She Know It All *and Don't.*"

They both jumped as a potted plant fell from one of the windowsills.

Reeba rose to pick it up. "Mama and Daddy don't like your tone either," she said.

Mona felt some of the tension from her shoulders ease. "Maybe they don't like that you don't respect your elders," she countered, walking back into the kitchen to grab the dustpan and brush set from the pantry by the back door.

"Twenty-three months does not make you my elder," Reeba said, reaching up from where she squatted to take the set from Mona.

"Two years older plus a minor in marketing in addition to the same business degree we both have . . . does make me your elder, boo. Sorry, but you need to go on ahead and swallow that nugget of truth."

Reeba dumped the dirt back into the pot and righted the roots of the plant before sitting it on the edge of the island. "I still don't absolutely agree with you, Mo," she said, looking up with some emotion in her eye that let her know their estrangement bothered her just as much.

"Fine, you don't have to. You don't have to agree with me, but stop judging me for making money on my visions and for leaving home," Mona said.

Reeba made a face. "I could care less y'all heifers flew the coop. It just made me the favorite," she boasted.

Mona arched a brow. "Hmph. You were the only one to get a new car when you graduated high school."

"For the commute, that's all. For the commute," she said, pouting her lips playfully as she nodded.

Mona laughed. "You full of it," she said, reclaiming

her seat at the island. "And put some more amaretto in my drink."

"Chick, please. This is your kitchen too and not the bar at the club," she said, reclaiming her seat as well. "You better handle your handle."

Mona rolled her eyes, but moved over to the cabinet over the counter to remove the bottle of liqueur. "All we need is Shara and some nut cake," she said.

"Well, Shara is in Thailand this week, but I got the nut cake," Reeba said, taking the lid off the round metal can in the center of the island. "Thank God one of us knows how to cook Mama's recipes."

"Forget the recipes. I wish we had her luck in finding the right man to even feed some good soul food—and other *things*—to," Mona said, retrieving a cake knife from one of the metal canisters filled with utensils lining the counter by the stove.

"You were just whining about not having time to run your business," Reeba said. "So when would you have time for a relationship?"

"I would make time," Mona said, handing her sister the knife and setting the two saucers she retrieved next to the can.

"Not me. I'm too busy trying to find a new job," Reeba said.

And that was another part of the reason Mona thought her sister might jump on the chance to help work with her—she had been laid off when the call center where she was a supervisor closed down last month. Mona didn't bother to broach the subject again.

She fell silent as she sipped her tea and broke pieces of the cake off with her fingers to nibble on.

"Have you ever had visions that had nothing to do with love?" she finally spoke into the silence, her thoughts filling with Anson.

"Not really."

Mona looked over at her sister sharply. "Not really . . . or no?" she emphasized.

Reeba looked like she struggled with the answer at first. "No," she finally answered with emphasis.

Mona squinted her eyes and pressed her elbows against the top of the island as she peered at her sister.

"What?" Reeba asked, sitting up straight and looking affronted.

Mona leaned in closer toward her with an even harder stare.

"Okay, once or twice. . . . It just felt like if I would think of someone I hadn't seen in years, then within days—weeks at the most—I would cross their path whether in person or online. I always thought it was odd," Reeba said. "But it could just be a coincidence . . . or not."

Mona nodded and rose to her feet. "I gotta go," she said, pinching the last few crumbs from her plate to suck from her fingers.

"Everything okay?" Reeba asked.

Mona nodded again.

"If you can't or won't talk to me, then call the aunties," she suggested, placing their cups and saucers into the deep cast iron sink.

Aunts Winifred and Millicent were the keepers of the family history and still resided in Baton Rouge, Louisiana, in a small but beautiful mansion on a converted plantation. But Mona wouldn't call them.

Not now. It had been weeks since she'd last called her beloved aunts and for that she was ashamed.

Mona was back in her rain boots and trench and headed out the front door before Reeba had time to leave the kitchen. She rushed to her car, just remembering she forgot her umbrella as the light rain wet her. She hurried to close the door and rev the motor to life before blasting the heat and waiting for the chill to leave her. Then she reversed down the drive and onto the unpaved road.

"But it could just be a coincidence . . . or not."

Mona drove out to the main road toward Chloe Bolton's old residence. In the days after Mona's clash with Anson Tyler, she had done what anyone naturally did in the age of social media—she researched him online. Although she found him on LinkedIn, Facebook, Twitter, and About.me, it was the before and after pictures on his company's Web site that revealed that he lived right in Holtsville in the house she could tell was obviously the former home of Chloe Bolton.

What person in Holtsville didn't know exactly where the supermodel's home was? She was a worldwide celebrity living in a small southern town. Of course, Mona had driven by the sprawling home to take a gander.

So she knew where he resided and that's where she was headed.

It wasn't until his home first came into sight and she saw that every window was dark that she glanced at the time on the dash and paused. It was nearing nine o' clock. That wasn't late. Sometimes she didn't go to bed until one or two in the morning, but it was rude to stroll up to someone's home without warning. "And I'm in pajamas," she muttered, shaking her head at herself. "Come on, Mona. Get your shit together."

She braked and then put her car in reverse to back down the dead end road. She didn't even want to chance being seen turning around in his driveway.

Hitting the gas, she started the car in reverse.

THUD!

Mona gasped and slammed on the brakes, her eyes darting up to the rearview mirror that she hadn't been using. "What did I hit? What did I hit?" she kept repeating frantically as she put the car in park and scrambled out the door to race around it.

She screamed out at the sight of Anson on the ground, his face twisted in pain. She dropped to her knees beside him as the rain continued to pelt their bodies. "Oh my God. I'm so sorry. I didn't see you. I'm so sorry. Are you okay?" she said, her words running together.

"Shut. Up." He forced the words through clenched teeth.

Mona opened her mouth to say something, but thought better of it.

"Call. Ambulance."

"Okay," she said, snatching off her pricey trench coat to ball up and ease beneath his head to cushion him from the asphalt road.

She rushed back to her car, but then paused and turned back. "I don't have my phone with me," she admitted.

"Pocket."

Mona lifted the pocket of his running pants, which were plastered to his leg, and scooped her hand in to retrieve the phone. She jerked it back as she accidentally brushed against his member.

He moaned in pain.

She knew he needed help and had no time for being shy. Arching her brow, she dug her hand back in his pocket and grabbed his phone. Shielding it from the rain, she quickly dialed 911.

"I am so sorry, Anson," Mona said with just her head peeking through the curtains of the examination room of Colleton Medical's emergency room department.

Anson's jaw was tight as he lay in the hospital bed with his left wrist in a brace and his right foot in a cast. He continued to stare at the cabinets lining the wall and paid her no mind as she walked into the room and stood by his bedside table. She could tell that the hours he spent awaiting treatment hadn't helped his anger toward her cool off.

"I told them I was your sister," she said.

He glared at her.

Mona licked her full lips and fought back the urge to yawn. It was nearly one in the morning and she had been sitting in the waiting room on a chair that should have been meant for torture. The candy she'd purchased from the vending machine barely did anything to kill the taste of coffee and sleep clinging to her tongue. She was wet. She was cold. She was exhausted.

She didn't dare reveal that though. At least she hadn't been hit by a car, resulting in a sprained wrist and broken ankle.

"I just want to apologize again," Mona said. "I didn't see you, Anson."

His lips thinned until the smooth caramel complexion of them blanched a shade.

She knew he was itching to tell her something, but he was fighting to keep the words from flowing out of his mouth.

"Of course, you should send me your medical bills and I'll cover them," she said. "Umm . . . you . . . know the office address."

Anson released a heavy breath that was brimming with his anger—and probably continued dislike of her.

Mona felt flushed with guilt. "Carina said you were an architect. I hope you're right handed."

"Be quiet," he said, as he struggled to sit up on the edge of the bed and swing his injured foot around until it hung off the bed.

"Huh?" Mona asked, stepping forward with her hands outreached to help him.

The look he shot her made her freeze like a mime.

"Be quiet," he repeated. "And go away. Matter of fact . . . stay away. You have single-handedly done more to screw with my life than anyone I have had the displeasure to meet."

Mona gasped in shock.

"First you ruin my personal life," he said, glaring at her over his shoulder. "And then you stalk me—"

"Stalk?" she repeated in disbelief.

"Stalk," Anson repeated with emphasis, his brown eyes lit with anger. "How did you know where I live? What were you doing there? Who throws a car in

reverse and hits the gas without looking over their shoulder? What do you have against me?"

Each question was delivered with an ever-increasing level of bellicosity.

Mona opened her mouth and then shut it. She wisely figured it wasn't the time to regale him with the idea that she came to warn him of something based on premonitions that might be nothing more than dreams.

But why would I dream of him?

Because he's fine.

Mona felt her cheeks warm as she admitted that Anson Tyler was indeed a fine-looking man. Very dark and delicious, like Lance Gross or Blair Underwood. Very fit. Very fine.

"Then you hit me with that stupid little car and take me out of commission for the next six to eight weeks."

Mona's shaped brows dipped above her pert nose. "It was an accident—"

"YOU. HIT. ME. WITH. YOUR. CAR."

She jumped back and grimaced.

"Just get out. And stay away from me," he said, sounding tired as he lay back on the narrow hospital bed and covered his eyes with the forearm of his uninjured arm.

"Can I offer you a ride home?" she asked.

Anson raised his forearm just high enough to look at her in exasperation. He reached across his chest to hit the button to call the nurse.

"Yes. Can we help you?" a voice said through the intercom in the room.

"Security, please," he said, covering his eyes again.

Is he going to press charges? Can the hospital security keep me here until the police come? Should I run?

"It was an accident, Mr. Tyler," Mona insisted, already backing out of the examination room.

She literally jumped when she lightly collided with someone entering the room.

The security guard sidestepped and held back the curtain to enter. "Is there a problem here?"

"She lied to get back here. She's not family," Anson said without uncovering his eyes.

"Ma'am," the guard said.

Mona eyed him. He was her height and only about twenty pounds heavier. *I could take him. Easily.*

But instead of making a scene she just walked out of the room ahead of him.

Chapter 4

Brrrrnnnggg . . .
Brrrrnnnggg . . .
Brrrrnnnggg . . .
Brrrrnnnggg . . .
Propped up on pillows in the middle of his king-sized bed, Anson stirred from his sleep He was completely lost to time and place, and the brightness of the morning sun still streaming through the windows of the expansive suite surprised him.

Had a full day passed or was it just later in the same day? He had no clue. "Damn pills," he muttered.

Brrrrnnnggg . . .
He reached out and patted the bed beside him until he felt the coolness of his phone. Swiping his finger across the touch screen, he raised the cell to his face. "Yeah," he said, his voice still filled with his interrupted slumber.

"So you running into cars now, big brother?"

Anson chuckled at the sound of his younger brother Hunter's voice as he reached for the remote sitting on the bedside table topped with caramel-tinted leather trimmed in copper studs. "No, cars are running into me. Well, one car. Driven by one curly-haired she-devil who's like a thorn in my ass since the first mention of her name," he said, grimacing as he shifted his cumbersome foot atop the pillows.

"Is she fine?" Hunter asked.

Anson flipped through the digital satellite channels. "Who?"

"The curly-haired she-devil," Hunter said.

"That's irrelevant," Anson countered, tapping the remote against his thigh in the white track pants he wore.

"Looks are never irrelevant, and because you said that I know she's fine. Next question is just how fine?" Hunter said. "Enough for me to drive down from Atlanta?"

Anson thought about Mona and he could clearly remember the day he confronted her at her office and how the first sight of her climbing from her car in that red suit had made him forget that he was angry at her. She was even more beautiful when her eyes were lit with anger as she told him to get out of her office. Pretty caramel brown skin and jet black hair that was vibrant in the red suit she wore, which showed off her tall figure with her wide hips. Bright eyes. Full pouty lips. Long lashes. Dimpled chin.

On a scale of one to ten, when it came to beauty Mona Ballinger was a strong nine—he favored a thicker build. When it came to her being a nuisance she was a twenty on that same scale . . . and climbing.

"No woman is worth you leaving Morehouse

School of Medicine, Dr. Tyler," Anson said, not trying to hide his pride.

"What about you?" he asked. "Can I come check on my big brother?"

"Nope. You focus on school. I'm straight," Anson said. "I'm gonna work from home for a week or so, and my office manager, Malik, is going to make sure the office runs smoothly until I can maneuver this foot better."

"You need a woman's touch . . . and that's doctor's orders."

Anson bent his good leg. "I thought you were a surgical resident, not orthopedics."

Hunter laughed. "Actually I don't need a medical degree—"

"From Morehouse," Anson interrupted.

"—to know a man needs a woman to baby him back to good health."

Anson shook his head. "I've had my fill of women between Carina dumping me and Mona plowing into me," he said. "Good riddance to the opposite sex."

"Wow. You switched teams, dude?" Hunter joked.

"Let me correct that," Anson said with a chuckle.

"No need. Just jokes. Just jokes."

"Whatever," Anson said dryly.

"So tell me what exactly happened last night."

"I doubted Mother Nature—and the weatherman calling for a seventy percent chance of rain—and went to look at the Jamison house right down the road from me. They want me to update it—"

"Did you get the contract?" Hunter asked.

Anson's gut clenched. "They have to meet with

the rest of their board first and that won't be until later this week."

"Cool."

"So I walked there. It rained. I waited for it to let up. Got tired of waiting and walked home. I spotted the car sitting a little ways down the road from my place, but I had no clue she would suddenly throw it in reverse and hit me."

"Damn. You think she did it on purpose?"

"No," Anson admitted begrudgingly. "Still . . . she did some damage. I don't want to see her face ever again."

Ding-dong.

"Shit," he swore, using the remote to switch to the channel he'd reserved for his video surveillance. "Someone's at the door."

"I gotta go. We're about to do afternoon rounds," Hunter said.

"A'ight. Call me later," Anson said.

He dropped the phone and squinted his deep set eyes as he spotted the top of an unmistakable mass of curls. "Is this woman crazy?" he muttered, waving his hand dismissively as he sat the remote down and turned back to the television to watch SportsCenter on ESPN.

Ding-dong.

Anson ignored her and her persistence with his doorbell. He just wanted her to go away. "What's next?" he muttered, wondering if he needed to get a restraining order to keep the she-devil from continuing to disrupt his neat and orderly life.

Ding-dong. Ding-dong. Ding-

"Shit," Anson swore, reaching to pick up the

crutch leaning against the side of the bed. "God forgive me for what I'm thinking right now."

Ding-dong. Ding-dong. Ding-dong.

He maneuvered off the bed and used the crutch under the arm on the same side as his injured ankle to hobble from the bedroom and down the long length of the hallway of the sprawling house to finally reach the front door. The constant ringing of the doorbell accompanied his uneven gait.

Ding-dong. Ding-

"Hold on. I'm coming," he yelled, even though the door was too thick and the house too solid for her to hear him.

Reaching forward with his good hand, Anson opened the front door and then sidestepped it, using the tip of the crutch to nudge it back wider.

Mona took in Anson standing there glaring at her and she grimaced as she bit her bottom lip. "Hi, Anson," she said, with a small wave that she didn't bother to finish.

He just glared at her standing there with her hair up in a topknot and huge black shades covering nearly half of her face. She was wearing oversized coveralls and a tank with bright pink Converse sneakers, and she looked as childish as she was acting.

"Do I have to call the police?" he asked.

She held up both slender hands. "No, you do not. I felt so bad for *accidentally* backing into you at night . . . while it was raining . . . and you were wearing dark clothing," she emphasized. "So I thought I should at least bring you a goody basket because

I know you don't . . . have . . . a woman . . . in your life anymore. Sorry about that too. Ummm . . ."

Now if that don't beat all . . .

Mona bent down and lifted up a huge basket blocked from his sight by the other door. "I did assume someone was here with you and I was just gonna leave it, but I guess you're alone?" she asked.

"Miss Ballinger. Please. I am begging you to respect that I am a gentleman and the last thing I would want to do is to curse you or use my one good hand to touch you in a way that would finally help it sink in for you that I really don't want to see you or be near you or even pass by you in the street."

Mona looked pained. "That's extreme," she said. "Plus you need help, and since I'm the one who harmed you—*accidentally*—I'll have to help you. . . . Even though I'm really busy at work and would have to juggle some things and—"

"You do realize you're trespassing?" he asked tightly.

Mona stepped forward with her basket and it pushed against Anson's unrelenting build as he remained locked in his position. She kept pushing gently but consistently.

Anson's eyes widened as he felt his crutch shifting from beneath him and had no choice but to hop back and right it under his arm. "The hell?"

Mona eased right past him and stepped into the foyer, setting her basket down to reach out to help steady him.

"No," he snapped.

"But—"

"No."

"I could—"

"No!"

Mona acquiesced and stepped back.

Once he felt secure in his stance, Anson lifted the crutch and pushed the front door open even wider. "You have ten seconds to step out of my house or you will be arrested for trespassing, Miss Ballinger."

"Listen, Mr. Tyler," she said, pushing her shades up atop her messy topknot. "I live five minutes from here and I am the one who hit you—"

"Accidentally," they said in unison, hers with emphasis and his with sarcasm.

"Let me help you. Please," she finished, looking up at him with bright eyes filled with pleading.

He stiffened when she blinked her long lashes like a Disney cartoon. Anson pushed aside his thought that she looked adorable. So did puppies and they had to be trained how to behave as well.

"Do you want to go to jail?" Anson asked.

The complacent look on her narrow face disappeared and her docile eyes lit with fire. "It only works if you call the police, and you won't call because you need my help. So shut up and show me where your kitchen is," she said, picking up the basket and turning to look around his home before walking away from him.

"Miss Ballinger," he called behind her.

"This is gorgeous, Mr. Tyler," she said over her shoulder before disappearing into the dining room on the left.

Anson bit his bottom lip, hung his head back, and closed his eyes as he released the heaviest of breaths.

"You don't see houses like this in Holtsville," he heard her say, her voice echoing.

He had never felt so frustrated in his life. Ever. Not in foster care. Not in his struggle to get his brother out of the system. Not while working and attending college full time. Not setting up his business. Not even in the final minutes before a deadline while he was still feeling inspired and wanting to make changes to his plans. Nothing. Ever. Never.

Closing the door with his crutch, Anson tottered behind her into the dining room, but she was no longer there. At the sound of noises from the kitchen, he came around the long length of the ebony wood table and pushed through the swinging doors connecting the dining room to the kitchen.

She was unloading the items from her basket onto the top of the stone island. She looked up at him and smiled, revealing twin dimples deep enough to lose the tip of a finger. "This kitchen is straight off HGTV or something," Mona said, shaking her head in wonder. "Was it like this when Chloe Bolton had it or did you change it?"

Anson felt throbbing in his foot and moved over to sit down on one of the linen-covered high chairs surrounding the island. Propping the crutch against the chair behind him, he grunted as he elevated his foot onto the chair in front of him. "Do you know my social security number and bank info too?" he asked around a grimace.

Mona came around the island to help raise his leg and gently set it on the chair. She patted his knee comfortingly before moving back to her basket of goodies. "Do you want me to get your pain pills?" she asked.

Anson sniffed the air at the faint scent of something light and fruity. It smelled good and he knew it had to be her scent. It was just the fragrance a man wanted to find at a woman's pulse points. Her neck. Her wrists. The valley of her breasts and the meeting of her thighs . . .

"Here you go," she said, setting a plate beside his elbow.

Anson cleared his throat guiltily and pushed away his thoughts as he looked down at the thick and meaty club sandwich with a Styrofoam cup of broccoli and cheese soup on the side. He recognized both from Donnie's Diner, the local restaurant in Holtsville. He liked that it was takeout and not something she concocted. He was hungry and his stomach grumbled in protest.

"May I?" Mona asked.

Anson looked over his shoulder to find her with her hand paused by the handle of one of the double doors to his oil-bronzed refrigerator. "Now you ask permission?" he said before taking a huge bite of the sandwich.

She waited, poised like a robot, as she looked at him.

"Go ahead," he said finally, surprised that he felt like chuckling.

Mona nodded her thanks and opened the door. She pulled out a pitcher filled with red liquid. "Let me guess. Cherry Kool-Aid," she said.

"Tropical Punch."

"Same difference."

Anson lifted the cup of soup and sipped some of it with the plastic spoon she'd provided as he watched her pause by the glass front cabinets and look over her shoulder at him for permission. He nodded.

She pulled two highball glasses down and filled both with the drink. "Mighty fancy house to have Kool-Aid in the fridge," she said, coming over to sit a glass beside his paper plate.

"You seemed to spot it like you were familiar with it," he said.

"Growing up in New Orleans with three kids who stayed thirsty, my mama kept plenty of Kool-Aid. There was always a pack or two in the pantry, and who didn't have sugar?" she said, before taking a deep sip. "Much cheaper than cases of soda or juice."

Anson thought back to how there were times when his parents didn't waste the money to make sure a staple like sugar was in the house. Most times they drank water, and sweetened Kool-Aid was a rare treat. But he didn't share that with her. Plus those days were long gone and he hated that his thoughts still dwelt on his tough past.

"You okay?"

Anson looked over his shoulder again and was surprised to see her sitting on the edge of the island with her feet in the chair and her plate in her lap. His brows dipped at her buttocks pressed against the top of the island. "Are you against sitting in chairs?" he asked.

Mona shrugged one shoulder. "I like following my gut and my gut said hop up on this island. So I did. Life is more fun being spontaneous," she said.

"And was it spontaneity that led you to my house last night?" he asked, his annoyance with her rising again and brimming along the edge of his voice.

She opened and then closed her mouth. "Umm. Uh. See . . . what had happened was . . ."

Anson leaned back in his chair and eyed her as she struggled to find the words.

"I was going to apologize and then I changed my mind because I hadn't really paid attention to what time it was," she said as if off the cuff, and then smiled like she approved of what she came up with.

The look he gave her was filled with disbelief.

"What other reason would I have to go to your house?" she scoffed.

Anson held up his hands and shrugged.

Mona looked offended. "Listen, Anson Tyler, I am the modern day cupid and true love is my commodity. The last thing I need is to stalk down and obsess over a guy who bullied me on first sight. The size of your ego is amazing. I don't know where you find the strength to carry that mofo around."

She was annoyed and he liked it. "I'm just saying first you end my relationship and then I catch you sitting outside my house. . . ."

"I didn't end your relationship—your fiancée did," she reminded him. "I didn't know who you were. And if you had stayed in your own life without colliding it with mine—"

Anson sat up straighter. "*I* collided with *your* life?" he asked.

"Bad choice of words, but you *know* what I mean."

Her eyes were brighter than diamonds as her anger surfaced.

Anson kept his face straight. "I've had women do crazy things to get near me. That's all I'm saying. Don't feel bad you're not the first woman to want to see what Anson Tyler is all about."

"Negro . . . please," she snapped.

He just held up his hands, enjoying egging her on. *She deserves it for all the hell she put me through.*

"And you were in your pajamas?" he asked, sipping the rest of his soup directly from the cup.

"You're not my type, Mr. Tyler," Mona said, focusing on her sandwich.

"Good-looking, educated, employed black man," he said. "Then what is your type?"

"Light-skinned, good-looking, educated, employed black men," she countered with a "so there" look.

Anson waved his hand at her dismissively. "Yeah, right. Shemar Moore or Blair Underwood?"

Mona climbed down off the island and began cleaning up.

"The dude off *The Game* or the dude off *House of Payne*?" he asked as she leaned in to pick up his plate.

"Pooch Hall?" she asked.

"Nah, the other one," he said, shifting in his seat to eye her. "The one who was married to the white girl."

"Coby Bell," she said, searching and finding the garbage pail to dump their used paper products.

"That's the one."

Mona checked the sink and picked up a sponge from the dish rack. She put it under the faucet and the water flowed automatically. She jumped back a bit in surprise. "Ooh, that's fancy," she said.

"Any light-skinned man and Idris Elba?" Anson called over to her with another challenge.

"Sounds like you really sat around and marinated on this before," she said, giving him a mean side-eye.

"Don't throw shade to detract from the fact you know the automatic allure of the light-skinned brothers is played out," he said.

"Touchy much?" she asked, moving over to stand beside him, with one hand braced on the back of his high chair.

Her face was just a foot away from him and his eyes took her all in. She really was remarkable with her high cheekbones and pouty lips on her slender face. She was just as alluring with her hair up and in overalls as she was striking in a bright red business suit with her hair down around her shoulders like a wild mane.

His heart literally skipped a beat.

No, no, no, no.

"Getting whacked by a car and hopped up off pain pills usually makes me touchy and grouchy," he said, looking away from her.

"Honestly I came here to set things straight, and I'm sorry again for hurting you," she said with sincerity.

He forced himself to not look at her again.

In truth, he had occasionally thought of her since the day they argued at her office. Previously his thought had snidely been that she probably used her good looks to help lure foolish men into her business who were seeking a relationship with a woman who looked like her. He hadn't felt any desire for her though . . . until now.

Shit.

"Okay," he said, his tone with her back to cold.

That sweet scent of her filled his nostrils and he

hated that his male instinct was to inhale and let the aroma burst in his chest.

She hit you with a car. She hit you with a car. She hit you with a car.

"You know you really should let me hook you up with someone—other than me," she said, platonically rubbing his broad shoulders before she moved away to wipe down the top of the island with the damp sponge she left sitting there.

"You could find a woman for an ugly dude like me?" he said slyly, reaching for his crutch.

"You're not—"

He chuckled as she caught herself and swallowed back the rest of her words. He glanced over at her and she looked like she wanted to chuck the sponge at his head. Using his crutch, he maneuvered to his feet. "Dark and fine like good aged wine and it will only get better with time," he boasted.

"Oh no you didn't," she said with a wince.

"Oh yes I did," Anson countered.

Mona just shook her head.

"Listen, I'm still not a hundred percent sure why you came to my home last night, or why you even know where it's located when we never met before I came to your office," he began.

Mona opened her mouth to speak.

Anson politely held up his hand. "But I accept your apology and I decline your offer to help even though you brought me lunch today," he said. "Let's consider the matter squared away."

"Oh," she said, looking disappointed.

He was surprised by an urge to put a smile back on her face.

She convinced Carina to leave me.

Anson looked on as she slid her basket onto her arm and glanced around the kitchen as if to make sure everything was back in its place.

Carina left a long time ago, before she even ended the engagement. Before she even sought this woman out to match her with a new mate.

"I really would like to help, so I'll leave my number just in case, and please feel free to call me," she said, moving over to the pantry door where a chalkboard hung for recipes.

Anson smiled, not at all surprised that her handwriting contained plenty of curls and spirals and a happy face in place of the zeros. The daisy was a surprise but not shocking.

She hit you with a car. She hit you with a car. She hit you with a car.

"I can't promise I won't be back," Mona said.

"And I can't promise I won't call the police this time," he said, following her out of the kitchen and into the hall.

"I got you figured out, Anson Tyler, and you're all bark with no bite. So save it," she said dryly, looking up and around at the interior of the house. "You really need to let me find you a good woman to fill this house with love for you. Someone who sees past the bullshit too."

Anson frowned. "It's called being no-nonsense, not being a bullshitter."

"It's all walls to shield something so . . . tomato— toma*tah*."

Anson stiffened as Carina's words came back to him. *"You're cold. Distant. Unreachable."*

He had admitted that he didn't love her. Never really did, but still the thought of the tears that filled her eyes that day made his gut clench.

"There is a part of you that is closed off to me emotionally and I can feel it. There is a shield around your heart. And it made me feel less than. Lacking."

"Were you able to help her?" he asked as they neared the front door.

Mona stopped, her brows dimpled with confusion for a moment, but then her eyes lit with understanding that he spoke of Carina. She shook her head and looked away from him, but then softly said, "Yes, she's been on a few dates."

Anson nodded. "Good," he said with genuineness.

Mona looked surprised. "I'm the modern day cu-pid," she sang slightly off key, before doing a little tap dance and giving him jazz hands with a big toothy smile.

Anson chuckled.

"My number. More apologies. I may be back," she warned.

"I'm fine," he assured her.

With one last soft wave Mona left the house and walked down the stairs to climb into her car. Anson stood there until her car disappeared down the drive and her logo on the trunk was no longer visible.

Shaking his head at the turn of events, he stepped back and pressed his crutch to the door to ease it closed. "I'm the modern day cu-pid," he sang lightly just as it shut.

Chapter 5

Mona glanced at the time on her computer before looking back at one of her new clients, Ulysses Davies, with a smile that was meant to put him at ease. It was nearing four o'clock and that was hours since she'd taken Anson lunch. The thought of him hobbling around the kitchen trying to fix dinner concerned her, and she was hardly able to focus on her work even though she had enough tasks to fill the rest of the day.

"Miss Ballinger."

Mona drew her eyes away from her cell phone and gave the middle-aged gentleman another of her soft, engaging smiles. "Yes, Ulysses. I was just saying that based on this meeting, I have a good idea of just the type to match you with. I actually think someone with slightly different interests would be better for you because in the past you've always dated like-minded women. You need a yin to your yang and I have a few women in mind," she said, reaching over to clasp his hand reassuringly.

She closed her eyes for a few seconds and an

image played of him walking along the Savannah boardwalk with a middle-aged beauty whose body defied her silver hair.

I wish I could be the direct connection to his love. But I don't have her in my database.

She gave him a smile that he probably didn't see was slightly sad, and then she leaned in a little to him. "Mr. Davies, my wish for any man or woman who comes through that door is to match them up with their soul mate—the one person that perfectly fits them like a puzzle piece. Their one true love. During my years of business I have had some success with that, but I have to be honest and say I cannot promise that for you," Mona admitted. Even as she fully disclosed the limits to her ability, she knew that he truly had no clue how true her words were. "What I *can* promise you is finding a woman who will offer you companionship, friendship, someone to spend time with and someone to get to know better and maybe even love. Someone who, like you, wants to meet a good person and enjoy spending time with them."

She paused and widened her smile. She had this gift that she loved, cherished, and respected, but she could not in good faith take his or any other client's money knowing through that gift that the person she matched them with was not their true soul mate.

"I understand," he said, congenially, seeming to want to comfort her.

"I believe everything in life serves as a step toward the next goal, and although I may serve as a bridge to the next phase or phases in your life that will eventually lead you to find 'the one,' I doubt that a direction to her, whoever she may be, will be made through my services."

Ulysses patted her hand. "My wife, Louise, passed away five years ago and I have sat nearly every day still missing and wanting and loving her. I believe she was my one and only soul mate. What I'm looking for now is companionship. Someone to laugh with. Someone to fish with."

Mona sat up a bit straighter. "I bet you're carrying a picture of her, aren't you?" she asked, her curiosity about her vision rising.

"Sure am," he said, reaching in the back pocket of his slacks for his wallet.

She took the well-worn photo he handed to her with pride.

And there she is.

The silver-haired beauty Mona envisioned was indeed his wife.

Her heart fluttered and her hand trembled a bit. Just amazing. That's why she believed in her gift and the idea of true love.

Mona blinked back tears and rose to her feet as she handed him the photo he securely placed back in his billfold. "I'm going to go through my database and I should have two or three profiles to send to you by e-mail later this week," she promised him.

"I look forward to hearing from you," he said.

As soon as she walked him out, she locked the glass door of the office and leaned back against it, fighting the urge to kick off the neon green heels she wore with her linen suit and white blouse. Sliding her hands into the pockets of her slim-fitting pants, she walked across the hardwood floor to her desk. She picked up her phone. *No missed calls.*

She'd given Anson her number, but foolishly forgot to get his to check on him. He was a grown man and capable of taking care of himself, but she just felt so guilty. She was tempted to pop in again even though she wasn't certain how serious he was in his threats to call the police. Mona had been so tempted to tell him that she had gone to his house to warn him that he would be in an accident, but the fact that she was the one who had hurt him made the premonition seem all the more foolish.

And then for him to think I want him.

She bit her bottom lip as she thought of his strong shoulders and defined arms in the white sleeveless tee he wore. *He is a good-looking man. . . .*

"A good-looking mistaken man," she said, grasping the edge of the desk to pull her chair forward. She opened her folder of incoming online applications.

The love business was booming.

She focused on going through each application and ensuring she nor her clients were not getting catfished with phony identities and photos and that all applicants were of good standing, with no criminal history outside minor offenses. Mona prided herself on being diligent that everyone was aboveboard, including running SLED background checks and checking them against any Facebook, Twitter, or Instagram profiles. Even though she required them all to sign the appropriate waivers to protect her from liabilities, she still made it her business to deliver nothing but the best service in all aspects. She'd caught a few frauds during her years of business, but the disclaimers on her site let it be known that she checked backgrounds and most understood, respected, and appreciated that.

An hour later she ran her fingers through her hair and massaged her scalp as she pushed back a bit from her desk. She'd processed just half of the applications and still had to do the monthly billing, plus speak to her Web master to do some updates to the site.

Frustrated, she stopped massaging her scalp and freed her hands. Crossing her legs, she leaned forward to pick up the folder of résumés and applications the temp agency had sent over to her for the assistant position. Based on credentials, there were a couple in the stack she would hire on the spot, but she had no clue if she could trust them and that was most important to her. Their ability to respect confidentiality and a lack of sticky fingers beat out how many words they correctly typed per minute.

Her sister Reeba would be ideal, but Mona pushed that idea away. There was no way she was going through the headache of explaining herself or the good nature of her business again.

Her stomach grumbled and she thought of Castillo's Pizzeria down the street. She picked up the phone to order a lasagna to go. She thought of Anson and ordered another.

I'll just drop it off and keep it moving.

Anson hated being cooped up inside. He wasn't even twenty-four hours into his injuries and he felt like a caged bird. Even as a small boy in Walterboro in the small house his family rented, he was always outside playing in the dirt yard or exploring the city for mischief to get into it. Working with the Jamisons to build homes while he was in college had been ideal for him, and he thought nothing felt better than the sun on his bare back as he hammered away.

Releasing a heavy breath, he sat back in the chair before his drawing board and studied his initial sketches for a law office to be developed in Mount Pleasant. He wanted something that would stand out but not look out of place with the abundance of brick structures in the area. He hoped they loved the glass and wood structure as much as he did.

"I can't promise I won't be back."

But she hadn't been back. Not yet anyway.

Looking up through the lightly tinted windows of his office, he saw nothing but his landscaped front yard and only his vehicle parked in the drive. The quiet of the house seemed so . . . loud.

Her laughter—*their* laughter—had been nice. Not in a forever after way, but nice. Cool. Refreshing.

He was no more interested in anything with Mona Ballinger than she was in him.

I mean, she's fine. Don't get me wrong. She's just too flaky for me. Too spontaneous. Too quirky. Too different.

Besides, Anson wasn't interested in looking for a love match. The knowledge of Carina's betrayal and the final words she'd said to him had hit home and left him heavy with thoughts of needing—then wanting—to change the way he viewed love and relationships.

You're so cold and distant.

Grabbing his crutch from where it leaned against

the side of his drawing board, Anson raised up off the high chair and moved over to the leather love seat positioned in front of his fireplace. He dropped down on it, careful of his injured wrist and ankle, and elevated his foot onto one of the thick and lush throw pillows Carina insisted he purchase to break up the darkness of the room. He had a conference call at four, which wasn't for another couple of hours. He picked up the remote and used it to turn on the flat screen television on the wall over his fireplace.

This was the first business day he'd had off in years and he was clueless to what was on television during the day. He had just settled in to watch *Poetic Justice* on BET when his cell phone vibrated in his pocket. Leaning over, he retrieved it. "Anson Tyler Design," he said, wedging the phone between his ear and shoulder.

"Well, this is Devon Jamison of Jamison & Jamison Contractors, Inc., and welcome to the team, young boy."

Anson punched the air in victory. "Yes!" he exclaimed.

Securing the position as lead architect would mean plenty of business, money, and prestige for his own small firm. Another check on the list of plans for his life. "Thank you so much. I appreciate the opportunity and I will come through each and every time for you guys. I can promise you that," he said.

"Well, we believe in you, and we are so anxious to lock this deal in, so we called an emergency board meeting instead of waiting for next month," Devon said.

Anson looked at his foot in a cast and then the cast on his wrist. "There's just one thing," he began.

He filled Devon in on his injuries and vaguely told him how it all happened.

"I should be all mended in six weeks and neither break will affect my ability to design," he assured him.

"It's all good. We still have some other minor issues to clear up in forming this new venture; it will be a month or so before we really get the ball going. Okay?"

"Perfect."

"Take care, Anson."

This was a great opportunity for Anson Tyler Design. Anson was usually laid back and reserved. He held his emotions in check, but in that moment he was so excited he thought his heart would burst out of his chest.

Lying back with his head on the arm of the sofa, he allowed himself to think of the past only because he had just moved further away from it. Like the night he watched his mother and father physically fight each other over drugs as he stood in the doorway of his nearly empty bedroom. Neither his presence nor the tears streaming down the face of their seven-year-old son had stopped them.

"Go back in your room," his mother had screamed at him.

The memory of that day and many others was just a dull ache and not a sharp pain that radiated. He hadn't felt that for nearly a decade or more.

He smiled so broadly he was sure every white tooth in his mouth was on display.

He tilted his head back at the sound of a car door closing. Not expecting Malik, until the next day, Anson grabbed his crutch and made his way over to

lean past his drawing board and look out the window.
Mona stood by her obnoxious little car. She had
changed out of the casual clothing she'd had on
earlier that day. She carried a plastic bag obviously
filled with takeout containers.

His stomach grumbled at the thought of food.

Or did his stomach clench at the sight of her?

Anson frowned as he watched Mona come up
to his porch and then turn to head back to her car.
Two times.

Mona lifted her foot up onto the first step of
Anson's porch and then whirled around and turned
back to her car. She made it halfway to her vehicle
and then turned back, strode up the walk, and
stepped up onto the porch once more. Only to step
down again.

She knew she looked ridiculous and was glad the
road running by the house was a dead end so that no
one was witness to her foolishness.

"Mona."

She let out a little squeal and turned in surprise to
find Anson leaning in the now open doorway. "I
brought you some lasagna from my favorite pizzeria," she said, slowly climbing up the steps. "I just
wanted to drop it off and make sure you weren't
hopping around the kitchen trying to cook."

"Thanks," he said.

She looked up at him and smiled as she reached
into the bag and pulled out one of the round metal
containers. She handed it to him. "Okay, bye," Mona
said, turning to head back down the stairs.

"You're welcome to join me . . . if you want," he called behind her.

Mona paused and turned on the stair. "No idle threats of calling the police because you know you weren't gonna call them anyway?" she asked. "And no more questions about Carina . . . ?"

"Cool. Now you promise to stop offering to match me up," he said, stepping back as she climbed the stairs.

"Your loss," she said, cutting her eyes up at him as she eased past him to enter the house.

"Since your services aren't free, I believe it's *your* loss," Anson countered.

Mona paused long enough for him to lead her into the kitchen.

"So you only know how to act like a grown-up when you're dressed like one," he threw over his shoulder.

Mona eyed the back and forth motion of his hard buttocks in the pants he wore. "I was a little pushy this morning, but you were being so mean and bull-headed," she said, sitting the bag on the island. "Pushy and cute works for me."

"Yeah, you're pushy," he agreed, allowing her to come over and guide him to the same stool he used earlier for lunch.

"Not cute?" she asked, glancing up at him.

"You're a'ight."

"Hmph. The lies you tell."

"Conceited much?" he asked, grimacing a little as he took the seat.

"Foot up," she demanded softly, helping him lift it

onto another stool before moving around the kitchen to retrieve plates, utensils, and glasses.

She felt his eyes on her and she hated the nerves that made her so aware of that fact. "And I believe every woman is beautiful, should feel beautiful, and she should have the nerve to say she's beautiful. I don't care if she's crossed-eyed and buck-toothed; she's beautiful. That's called confidence, not conceit. Thankyouverymuch, Mr. Dark Skin Men Rule the World," she finished with mockery as she did air quotes with her fingers.

"And it's that confidence that gets these oh so beautiful women to pay top dollar for you to match them with men?" he asked, swiping a fine sheet of sweat across his brow.

"Are you okay?" she asked, moving closer beside him.

"Actually, could you go in my bedroom and get my pain pills off the nightstand?" Anson asked before clenching his teeth.

"Is it your wrist or ankle?" she asked.

"Both," he said before pressing his lips together.

Mona kicked off her shoes and dashed from the kitchen. In the long hall she checked every closed door including the glass one leading to a large circular pool room in the center of the house. Continuing on, she finally reached the master suite at the end of the house. "Well, my damn." She gasped, gazing at the rich wood and copper furnishing and architectural details with sleek, dark brown decor.

Forcing her gaped mouth closed, she rushed over to his nightstand and scooped up the two medicine bottles sitting beside a carafe of water and a glass on a bronze tray.

Before she left, she did pause to lightly stroke the fur throw across the foot of the bed. It felt too creepy not to be real and there was a matching throw in front of the fireplace.

With one last look over her shoulder at the room that could easily swamp the entire house she rented, Mona went dashing on her bare feet back to the kitchen. "Sexy room, Mr. Tyler," she joked as she continued past him to fill a glass with water.

"What would I do without your approval?" he said with sarcasm.

Mona handed him the glass. "Which one is the pain pill?" she asked, showing him both bottles.

He pointed to the one in her right hand and Mona rushed to open it and drop one into his waiting palm. "I was supposed to keep it elevated, but I was working at my drawing board since you left," he admitted before tossing the pill into his mouth and following it with a deep swig of water.

Mona fought the urge to wipe his sweaty brow with her fingertips. "Is this high enough?" she asked, looking down at his foot upon the stool.

He shook his head.

"Then why are you up? Why aren't you in bed?" she wailed, reaching for the crutch and tapping it against the floor. "Let's go. Back to bed, Anson. Don't shred my nerves. Please."

He opened his mouth to protest, but then he winced. "Okay," he acquiesced, rising to his feet and taking the crutch.

"Are you too proud to let me help you?" she asked, looking up at him.

He raised his left arm and she instantly moved to his side to lightly grasp his waist as he carefully settled his arm across her shoulders, being mindful of his injured left wrist.

Mona's head reached just at his shoulder and the spicy and warm scent of his cologne or deodorant was pleasant. Beneath his thin T-shirt she could feel the hard and defined contour of his waist. And she could feel his pain causing his pulse to race.

"You finally gonna get me in the bedroom, huh?" Anson joked.

"Really. Like . . . like really?" she asked, looking up at him.

He chuckled.

They made their way to the rear of the house and into his bedroom. He turned to sit on the edge of the bed before she helped him raise both legs. "Thanks," Anson said, leaning back against the pillows stacked high against the towering leather headboard.

Mona picked up some pillows strewn across the bed and propped them under his foot.

"You really jacked me up with that little bug, you know that?" Anson asked, his eyes following her as she moved around the bed to place some pillows under his wrist.

Mona looked pained. "I know. I'm sooo sorry," she said.

"How do I know this is not like that movie *Misery*?" he asked, already sounding sleepy from the medication.

"Misery?" she asked, carefully sitting down next to his legs.

He nodded. "This famous writer gets kidnapped and held hostage by one of his super fans. She's crazy and eventually whups his ass for the whole movie until he escapes."

Mona arched a brow. "And what reason would I have to be a *fan* of yours?"

"You copped a feel last night when you were getting my phone. So you tell me," he said, just before his eyes drifted closed and his mouth opened to release a low snore.

Mona felt her cheeks heat up with shame. "That was an accident. . . ."

She rose from the bed and searched for the door to his bathroom—which was equally stunning—to dampen a washcloth with cool water. Back by his bedside she lightly dabbed his brow.

He mumbled in his sleep and snored again. She lifted the cloth from his head and looked down at his features, relaxed in sleep. *He really is fine.*

His deep chocolate complexion with his jet black hair and bright white teeth and eyes were a sight to behold. *Especially when he smiles.*

Her eyes dipped down to his lips and she took note of the middle of his bottom lip, which had a small dip that was just the right groove for a woman's tongue. *My tongue?*

Startled by that thought, Mona stepped back from him and went to toss the cloth in his hamper—which was free of dirty clothes. She allowed herself a longer look around at the ivory and chocolate decor.

Every bit of the house she had laid eyes on was neat as a pin. Even his sink was free of the usual glob of toothpaste or the splatter against the mirror that most men cared nothing about.

She gave him one last look and then left the bedroom, leaving the door ajar. As much as she wanted to wander about and see more of the decor of his home—and the former of home of a celebrity like Chloe Bolton—Mona resisted the urge and respected his privacy. Instead she headed back to the kitchen and slid the take-out pans in the fridge before she padded barefoot out to her car to retrieve her iPad and the files she brought from the office.

Not wanting to leave him, she settled herself at the kitchen island and busied herself with work as she waited for him to rise.

Anson licked his lips as he stirred in his sleep. When he finally opened his eyes, the darkness surrounding him was a surprise to him, as was the light-weight throw across his body. He recalled how the small, nagging pain he had felt all day had suddenly escalated to what felt like sharp daggers being stabbed into his ankle. And Mona had helped him to bed. *But she didn't put a throw on me . . . not that I remember.*

Shrugging, he'd assumed by now she had gone home. He reached over with his right hand to turn on the bedside lamp. Carefully he rose and used his crutch to go to the bathroom to relieve himself. It wasn't easy, but he got the job done.

Anson brushed his teeth and washed his face while he was at it, before heading back to bed. He still felt a little loopy from the pain pill. Because of his parents' addictions, Anson had always been leery of any type of drug and alcohol. He'd learned in college that children of addictive parents were more prone to develop dependency themselves. The only time he had ever voluntarily taken a pain pill had been that day and only because the pain had become intolerable. If he had to stay in bed and elevate his foot to prevent another dose, then he would do just that.

"You're awake."

Anson looked over at the bedroom door to find Mona standing there with a tray in her hands. Her presence surprised and pleased him—which was a whole other wonder. "I thought you left," he said, moving back to the bed.

"I waited," she said, stepping into the room. "I wanted to make sure you were okay and that you ate something. I didn't know you would sleep so long."

"What time is it?" he asked.

"Almost ten," she said, sitting the tray on the wide ottoman at the foot of the bed as she again helped him prop his limbs up on pillows. "Did you want to get under the covers?"

He shook his head. "No need. I'm used to sleeping naked, so I'm already uncomfortable."

"Oh. Okay. That's a lot of info there, big boy," she teased as she moved away from him and retrieved the tray to sit it across his lap.

"I didn't mean it to be disrespectful," he said,

enjoying the myriad sides to her. She was complex. One minute she could be fiery and angry. The next cute and coy. Bold and brash. And then shy and innocent.

She was truly a free spirit who held nothing of herself from the world.

"No disrespect. I felt you up first, remember?" she reminded him with a twinkle in her eyes.

"Well, we've relaxed the normal rules of strangers," he said, using the side of the fork to cut the cheesy lasagna.

"You mean me being in your house?" Mona asked, reaching up to twist her hair into a loose topknot that exposed the tendrils of soft hair at her nape.

"No, in my bedroom."

Mona looked around. "Yes. You're right," she said, as if it never occurred to her that she was alone in the bedroom of a man she hardly knew.

Anson chuckled at the nervous look she cast him. "You have the upper hand, remember?" he said, lifting his chin toward his ankle and raising his sprained wrist.

"Well, you have a total stranger wandering around your home," she reminded him gently.

"If you were gonna kill me or rob me, you'd have done it already and hauled ass while I was sleeping," he said around a bite of food.

"True," she agreed.

They fell silent.

"Did you eat?" Anson asked.

"Definitely, Mr. Sleepy Head."

He eyed her and she met his stare for just a second

before looking away. She had removed her blazer and the white tank she wore hugged her and showed off that although she was slender, her breasts were full and plush. He felt like a perv for eyeing them and shifted his eyes up to her face. "Why did you come here last night?" he asked, needing to address the elephant in the room.

She smiled and moved around the bed to lean a knee against the ottoman. "I was stalking you, remember? *Misery* the movie, right?" she said lightly.

"No. The truth. What's up?" he insisted.

For a long time she bit her bottom lip and stared at him. Assessed him. Made him feel as if she wasn't sure if she could trust him with her truth. He remained silent, not wanting to rattle her.

"I'm telling you this so that you can once and for all erase this thought that I was stalking you, like some obsessed fool," Mona finally said.

Anson wiped excess sauce from his mouth with the napkin she had folded on the tray.

"Since the day you came to my office acting like an ass—"

"Hey! What happened to our unspoken truce?" Anson asked.

"Sorry. Sorry," she said, holding up her hands. "Since the day we met in such an incredibly warm and welcoming fashion"—she gave him a "yeah right" expression—"I've been having these premonitions that you would be hurt, so I felt like I should warn you to be careful, and that's why I came here."

Anson frowned. "So you came to warn me to be careful, and in the process *you* were the one to hurt me?" he asked. "If that ain't the definition of irony."

"I know," she admitted. "But that is what happened."

"And you're sure that's the story you want to run with?" he asked, feeling his chest fill with laughter. Moments later it filled the air and he couldn't fight it back.

Mona looked hurt. "That's the *truth*."

"So you're psychic?" he balked. "Okay. . . . Well, tell me what numbers to play to win the Powerball or the Mega Millions."

"That's not funny, Anson," Mona said with the utmost seriousness.

"What's next? You going to tell me you use your magic powers to make your love matches?"

Her face went blank.

Anson swallowed back his laughter. "Mona—"

She rose up off the ottoman and came over to pick up his tray. "Good night, Anson," she said, turning to leave the bedroom.

"Mona," he called out to her.

Not long after he heard the front door close solidly.

Chapter 6

Mona sat Indian style on the padded swing of her porch and looked up at the moon filling the sky as she swayed gently back and forth. She was constantly amazed that a southern night could still be peaceful even as the sounds of the wood's creature echoed in the air. She closed her eyes and took a sip of the white wine from the goblet she propped atop her knee.

The peace was very necessary.

Her stress about work. Her anxiety about hitting Anson with her car. Her disappointment about her love life. Her sadness about her parents' death at such young ages.

"Father God," she said in a soft whisper, calling on Him for strength, clarity, and clear vision.

And there were many times she leaned unto Him, especially when she had to let it settle within herself that as much as she wanted to be the champion for soul mates and the ultimate love connection via her business, that it was not meant to be. Her database did not include everyone in the world. And she always tried to be just as upfront with the rest of her clients as she had been with Mr. Davies. It was those very few and far between moments when Mona did connect two destined loves in her database that she cherished. She was a hopeless romantic who believed in true love and fate.

Bzzzzzz.

She opened her eyes and picked her iPhone up from the seat next to her. She didn't recognize the number, but knew from the exchange that it was someone who lived in Holtsville. Someone like Anson.

As the phone continued to vibrate in her hand, she ignored it and took another long, satisfying sip of wine and smacked her lips for good measure. She hadn't appreciated Anson's ridicule. Even though she understood he didn't even know he hit the nail on the head, it still irked her that he obviously didn't understand it and clearly didn't want to.

The vibrating finally stopped and she sat the phone back on the seat as she unfolded one of her legs and pressed her foot against the porch to send the swing gently swaying again.

But what if something is wrong?

She crossed her legs again and picked up the phone, going to her missed calls to dial the mystery number back. It rang just once.

"Mona?"

It was Anson indeed, and his voice was deeper and stronger with it filling her ear via the phone. "Yes, Anson," she said.

"Are you busy? I just called you a second ago."

"I know," she admitted, eyeing a stray cat walking

up the middle of the road with its tail high in the air, strutting like it was indeed on its own catwalk.

"Oh," he said.

He fell silent and she did too.

"Listen," he finally said. "You're not to blame for Carina and I ending."

Mona sat up straighter in surprise. *Say what now?*

"I've owed you an apology about that day I came to your office," he said.

Her eyes widened. "Ummm . . . I guess if you can forgive me for causing you bodily injury, then I can overlook a rocky introduction," she admitted.

"And whatever I said to hurt your feelings earlier this evening?"

"A two-for-one?" she countered, freeing her legs and leaning forward to set her goblet on the porch floor before pressing her elbows onto the top of her knees.

"Running into me with your car should balance out my two errors against your one," he said dryly.

Mona chuckled. "True," she said, nodding in agreement.

"So I really could use your help . . . if the offer still stands."

"Oh, the offer still stands . . . because you still cannot."

"Have you always been such a smart ass, Mona Ballinger?"

"Pretty much," she said, and then hung up on him. She laughed as she pushed off with her foot again and sent the swing back in motion.

* * *

In the morning Mona was surprised to find a sticky note on Anson's front door. Holding the stack of mail she'd retrieved from his mailbox at the end of the long driveway, she pulled the note off with her free hand. "The door's unlocked," she read.

She tried the knob and indeed it was. "Good thing this is Holtsville," she said dryly, knowing there were many cities with high crime rates where an injured man sitting in a house with his door unlocked would lead to a top news story on robbery, assault, or worse.

Closing the door, she headed for the kitchen and busied herself using the microwave to warm up the breakfast of grits, fried eggs, and bacon she'd purchased from Donnie's Diner. Setting the mail on the tray as well as a glass of apple juice, she headed back to his bedroom. Steadying the tray with one hand, she knocked even though the door was slightly ajar.

"Hold on," he hollered.

Through the sliver of opening she saw him hobble past the door with nothing but a thick towel wrapped around his waist. In just that quick moment she had seen the strong contours of his back and the definition of his square buttocks against the towel. She turned her back to the door so quickly that juice splashed over the rim of the glass and onto the tray.

"So it's casual Mona today?"

She turned and entered the room behind him just as he limped to the bed and positioned his body on top of the covers again. She stopped and posed in the off-white capri sweats she wore with a bright red tube top and gold wedge sneakers. "I'm working from home today," she told him, eyeing the black V-neck tee he wore with matching basketball shorts.

"Yeah, me too," Anson quipped.

"I actually called your doctor and he wants that foot elevated—"

Mona swallowed back the rest of her words at the stormy look that clouded Anson's face.

"I know you're making up for hitting me, but calling my doctor is taking some liberties, don't you think?" he asked, his voice hard.

Mona looked taken aback. "That stick must be mighty uncomfortable," she said, moving to the bed to set the tray across his lap.

"What stick?" Anson asked, looking around.

She gave him a pointed look.

His face filled with understanding and then tightened again in annoyance. "Ha-ha," he said with sarcasm.

"You know, on second thought I hereby withdraw my offer for the services of Modern Day Cupid indefinitely," she said, placing her hands on her hips. "You're beyond help and determined to grow old and gray right here in this big old house all by your lonesome."

"I wouldn't ask for your services anyway," he muttered under his breath. "If you're a big enough busybody to hunt down my doctor—"

Mona rolled her eyes and retorted, "Hunt down? What am I, Sherlock Holmes? Not when the info is on your medicine bottles."

"Still—"

"And I only busy this body with people who appreciate what I do—be it matchmaking or calling to make sure a person is following the care plan given to him by his physician," she said, turning to walk toward the door.

"A'ight. A'ight. I'm sorry."

She stopped and slowly turned to cross her arms over her chest. "You have to be tired of that same old sad song you're singing."

Anson stared at her.

Mona didn't dare to blink as she stared back.

"You're a tough little nut to crack, aren't you?" Anson asked, before stirring his grits with his good hand.

"Yup . . . I'm almost as hard as your head."

With that she turned and left his bedroom, securely closing the door behind her.

Anson was tired of his bedroom, his bed, his injuries, and his own company. It had been a couple of hours since Mona had brought his breakfast and left for work. "One week tops," he promised himself as he flipped through the channels. "I can only take one week of this and I'm going back to work broke foot, sprained wrist, injured pride and all."

Bored with the same old selection of daytime programming or movies nearly twenty years old, Anson turned off the television and tossed the remote aside before he grabbed his crutch and got out of bed.

"Man, bump this," he muttered under his breath. "I'm going outside."

And he continued to grumble as he made his way down the long, wide hall until he came upon the circular pool room that was the centerpiece of the one-level structure. The sound of water splashing stopped him.

"The hell?"

Pretty sure he looked like something out of a comedy movie, he turned around and walked over to the glass doors. First he spotted the pile of clothing with the familiar metallic gold sneakers on one of the teak pool chairs, then a brown figure swiftly moving underwater from one end of the pool to the other.

"Damn, she's just comfortable as hell," he muttered, using the crutch to lightly tap on the glass door as soon as her head came up from under the water.

Mona looked up at him as she raised her arms to wipe her wet hair from her face. She dipped down a little lower below water at the sight of him.

"Who just hops their ass in someone's pool?" Anson wondered aloud as he motioned with the crutch for her to get out.

She shook her head no.

Anson felt his ire rise like lava about to spill over the top of a live volcano. He motioned again, not caring that his face was once more lined with annoyance.

"I can't," she called to him with another shake of her head.

Carefully Anson opened the door and pushed it wider with his body before he hobbled inside the pool room. Her hair was slicked down and her lashes seemed to drip water from the tips. She was nervously biting her bottom lip, and the combo of her damp face and bare shoulders made him pause for a second. *She's beautiful.*

"I hope you don't mind, but this pool was calling

my name and I said to myself, 'Mona, he won't be able to use this pool for another month and a half or so. So why not take a dip?' So I did."

Anson stopped just short of the tiled edge, fearful he would slip. "And you always follow your first thought?" he asked.

She nodded. "You ought to try. Life is amazing that way," she assured him.

"Yes, but as the owner of the home—and thus the pool—your whimsy comes second to my wants," he reminded her.

"If it was my house I wouldn't mind you swimming in it . . . unless you're a pee in the pool kinda guy," she added, before lowering herself under the water and rising up again until just her head showed above the edge.

Anson watched as she swiped her hair back again.

"And if I could get out of the pool right this second, I would. But I can't . . . so I won't."

Shaking himself free of staring at her, Anson asked, "Why can't you?"

Mona smiled and lifted her chin toward her pile of clothing. "I'm very Eve-like right now," she said, with a twinkle in her eyes.

Anson glanced at the clothes and then to her before he forced himself to look away as he clearly visualized her naked body in the midst of the heated water. "And naked pool day in someone else's home is okay for you?"

"It's fun for me, Anson."

He turned his head to look as she dipped beneath the water and took another lap. He started to pull his eyes away, but then posted up on the top of his crutch and watched her, wishing the water didn't blur the visual of her nakedness. If she wanted to swim naked . . . in his pool . . . in front of him . . . then why should he be the conservative one by looking away?

She was midway down the length of the pool when he glanced at her clothes and wondered just where she drew the line of her spontaneity and fun. Whistling, he made his way over to the teak lounge chairs lined up around the pool and leaned next to the one where Mona had "spontaneously" shed her clothing . . . including a delicate black lace thong.

Nice.

Anson pulled his iPhone from his pocket and read some e-mails, including a brief one from Carina—saying she'd heard about his accident. He deleted that one.

"Do you use your pool much, Anson?"

He looked up at her and turned off his phone before sliding it back inside the pocket of his shorts. "Not really," he said with patience.

"Not at all, I bet," she countered, raising up just enough to push her elbow atop the edge and then place her chin on her hand. "Learn to live a little, Anson."

He nodded and licked his bottom lip to keep from revealing a smile. "Maybe you're right," he said.

"I bet you plan when you poop on your calendar."

He waved his fingers at her. "Keep them coming," he urged smugly.

"Probably sex too."

He stiffened because that one hit too close to home. *I'm busy as hell. What's wrong with "date nights"?*

"It's okay to just say 'fuck it,' you know?"

"Really?" he drawled.

"Yup."

He nodded.

"You know what, Anson Tyler, I'm going to teach you how to have fun," she said with a wink.

"You are?" he asked.

"Down with the stick. Down with the stick," she chanted, as she lightly pounded her fist.

"Down with the stick . . ." He joined in with her with a smile that was fake.

"Yes!" Mona said enthusiastically. "Now . . . if you'll excuse me," she said, waving her slender fingers at him.

And here we go . . .

"You know I think you might be on to something with this whole spontaneity thing," he said, turning to press his back against the wall as he crossed his strong arms over his chest. "You go ahead and enjoy the pool."

"I'm ready to get out, though."

"Okay," he said, not moving one inch.

Mona gripped the edge of the pool. "I'm naked," she reminded him.

"Yeah, I know. You were being spontaneous, right?"

Mona's eyes shifted to her clothes, then up to the seemingly innocent expression on Anson's face, and then back down to her clothes. She chewed the corner of her bottom lip as she squinted her eyes in thought.

"It must be amazing to live life without rules—no

worries, no concerns, no cares," he said, his tone slightly mocking. "No inhibitions."

Mona tilted her head to the side and arched one brow.

He arched his brow as well.

Mona released a heavy breath. "Anson—"

"Yesss," he responded, loving her discomfort.

"Anson," she repeated sharply.

"Not feeling very spontaneous, are you?" he asked, pushing up off the wall to leave her alone. "Judge not, Mona. Judge—"

She lifted her eyes up out of the water with her eyes locked on his as his slowly widened in complete shock. He looked up at the glass ceiling over the pool, but it didn't matter. The sight of her naked body dripping with water was imprinted on his brain.

Her soft laughter mocked him.

He knew from every hair on his body standing on end that she was within inches of him, but he could only imagine what she was doing because he kept his eyes looking to the sky above the ceiling.

He jumped when her soft hand lightly patted his cheek. "Judge not, Anson. Judge not," she said with smugness.

The hand slid away.

The hairs on his body relaxed.

His heart continued to pound.

Anson looked over his shoulder. He could just make out the sight of the small of her back, her smooth brown buttocks and endless legs as she raced down the hall with her clothes balled up in her hands. He chuckled as he limped out of the pool room and wisely decided to give her space by heading back to his bedroom.

Mona tapped her fuchsia stylus against her chin and looked out the window of the breakfast nook at the stretch of emerald grass and towering trees surrounding Anson's house. She couldn't believe she had climbed from that pool in front of him naked as the day she was born. She loved that he had challenged her and hadn't been expecting her to do it. *Hmph, don't dare me . . .*

She wasn't a nudist by any means, but she wasn't a prude about the naked body either. Still . . . she had just flashed a man who technically could still be considered a stranger. *Thank God it's all right and tight . . . and clean shaven.*

Bzzzzzz . . .

She picked up her iPhone. "I'm outside," she read, before setting the phone down and making her way out of the kitchen and down the hall to the front door.

Mona had just stepped out onto the porch as her sister pulled a large Tupperware bowl from the rear seat of her car. "Thanks, kiddo," she said as she watched Reeba climb the stairs.

"This house is freaking amazing," she said, pushing the Tupperware into Mona's hands as she breezed past her inside.

"Reeba," Mona said harshly, motioning with her head for her to leave.

"What?" she asked, tossing her bone-straight hair over her shoulder. She wore a black strapless maxidress and patent leather flip-flops. "Do you know how long I have waited to get a look inside Chloe freaking Bolton's house?"

"It's not her house anymore, and he said he re-decorated, so it probably doesn't look a lot like it did before he moved in," Mona said, briefly wondering if she'd been this annoying to Anson that first day she pushed her way into his house.

"Chloe freaking Bolton," Reeba repeated, excit-edly jumping up and down in one spot.

"Okay, you *gots* to go," Mona stressed, using her hip to push the front door open wide.

Reeba rolled her eyes. "I feel so used," she said, eyeing the Tupperware of oxtail stew Mona held.

"Not used. Loved and appreciated. *Very* loved and appreciated," Mona said as she nudged her sister toward the door.

"Okay, okay," Reeba said, stepping out onto the porch. "But if this situation goes left—as it may—then you keep this near you."

Mona hung her head as Reeba pulled a container of pepper spray from inside her bra.

"To unlock it, flip the little red switch to the right and have at it, Mo. Have. At. It." Reeba punctuated each command with a snap of her fingers.

"Thanks, sis," Mona said, looking on as she sat it atop the Tupperware container.

"So, is he fine?" Reeba asked, raising up on her toes to look over Mona's shoulder. "What have you two being doing all day? When are you going home?"

"Text me," Mona said, again using her hip to push the door closed.

Mona was picking up on Anson's need for privacy; one Ballinger sister bombarding his life was enough.

Heading to the kitchen, she washed her hands and set about warming the stew on low in a large copper pot. She reclaimed her seat and pushed her glasses up higher on her nose as she continued her search through her database for dates for Mr. Davies.

She was finding it hard to focus though, and in a few minutes she pushed her glasses up atop her head and tapped her stylus against the top of the island. *Is he sleeping? Awake? Hiding? Annoyed? Embarrassed?*

Just what did Anson think of her stunt? She meant it to be cute and funny. Did the uptight Mr. Tyler agree? He had looked away as if the sight of her naked body would burn his eyes.

She stood up and posed as she took a selfie with her phone. "Hmph, who wouldn't want to see all of this?" she said, doing a snakelike move as she studied her photo. "No shame in my game."

"If that is a part of your work, I have an office you could be using."

Mona closed her eyes at the sound of Anson's voice behind her. *Okay, a little shame.*

Holding her chin high, she turned to face him. "Umm, you also have a bed you could be using," she reminded him, reclaiming her seat at the island and knocking her glasses back down onto her nose.

"I will literally become a bedbug if I don't get the hell *out of* that bed," Anson said, hobbling over to sit down at the island.

Mona fought the urge to cover her breasts with her arms as she pointed her thumb over her shoulder toward a pot simmering on his Viking stove. "There's oxtail soup," she said.

Anson looked skeptical.

"My sister Reeba is the cook in the family and she made it," she told him. "Your tummy is safe."

"No, I didn't mean . . ." He could see Mona's skeptical expression, and the rest of his words trailed off. "Okay, yes I did," he admitted. "I'm not hungry yet though."

"You really should put your foot up," she reminded him. "And maybe up on the island so it's higher than your heart."

Anson nodded. "Doctor's order, huh?"

"Yes," she said, turning her attention back to her iPad.

"What are you working on?" he asked.

Mona arched a brow as she paused the stylus above the screen and cut her eyes up to look at him. She forced a smile. "I am going through my database of beautiful, professional women to see which one is the best match for a new client."

"And they will go on dates . . . because you say so?" he asked.

"Yes, that's the basis of you know . . . matchmaking. You know, the very essence of my business. Modern. Day. Cupid," she said with emphasis.

"Right," he said, and then looked away dismissively.

Mona pierced the back of his head with her eyes. She closed out the screen she was in and opened the one with her female clients. Humming lightly, she waved her stylus around the screen.

"Maybe I should get some work done," Anson

said, beating a rhythm against the top of the island with his good hand. "I'm going stir crazy."

Mona continued to hum as she swiped through each photo. She paused on one. Turning the iPad around, she pushed it toward him. "What do you think?" she asked, setting her chin in her hands as she eyed him.

Anson looked over at her and then down at the iPad. "She's pretty," he said, picking it up with one hand to study closely. "Why?"

"She's a banker from Savannah, Georgia, who I think could be someone you could have a lot of fun with," she said, using one finger to pull the iPad back across the table.

"How can you say that when you don't even know what I like in a woman?" he balked.

"Her profile, build, and background are similar to Carina's," she said simply, with a one shoulder shrug.

"Well, I was mistaken in thinking Carina was the perfect woman for me."

Mona continued to swipe through profiles.

"Just as mistaken as you are in thinking you can—"

"Can what? Have an over seventy percent success rate? Have a large majority go on to wed and to have children?" she said proudly. "Are we judging again, Anson?"

She looked up at him.

He looked over at her.

A few seconds ticked by between them before they both looked away.

Mona licked her lips and brushed a curl from her cheek. "Have you ever been in love, Anson?" she asked, even as her heart continued to flutter in her chest with some feeling she wasn't ready to acknowledge.

"No," he admitted. "I haven't. Have you?"

She smiled softly and shook her head. "I've loved . . . but I've never been *in* love. The difference between us, I think, is I want to know what that feels like. I want to lay up in it and cherish it and enjoy it and become fulfilled by it. I can't *wait* to fall in love."

"I'm good," he said, again dismissive.

"I know," she said with a touch of sadness in her softly spoken words. She reached over to lightly grasp his hand and squeeze it. She closed her eyes. She waited. Too many seconds passed. Nothing came to her. Nothing showed behind her lids but darkness.

That was a first. Was he so against love that he had no soul mate?

Drawing her hand away, she sat up straighter as she eyed him.

"What?" he asked, studying her.

Mona shook her head and forced a smile. "Nothing," she lied.

Her brain couldn't reconcile that touching him drew nothing at all. She blinked away tears filled with the sadness she felt for him.

Anson squinted his eyes. "What's wrong?" he repeated.

"I . . . I can see a vision of a person's soul mate when I touch them. Always . . . always I can see that vision. Always. Except right then when I touched you," she said, rising to run from the room.

Chapter 7

Anson felt a throbbing in his foot that was increasing in intensity, but he grabbed his crutch and went in search of Mona. He was confused as hell by the little bomb she'd dropped before running from the room. *Visions? Soul mates? The hell?*

He turned his head to the right at the sound of the front door softly closing. He headed that way, hoping she hadn't left.

Anson opened the front door. She looked up from her seat on the padded bench as he stepped out onto the porch. He stopped himself from frowning at her wiping tears from her cheeks. He sat beside her on the bench.

"You should lie down and put your foot up," she said, still sniffing.

It is throbbing like crazy.

"Put your foot in my lap and then lay flat," she offered, patting her thighs.

And he did because there were no pillows to stack beneath it.

"Thanks," Anson said, as she crossed her legs to lift his foot even higher, above his heart.

They fell silent.

"We have the weirdest friendship ever," he said.

"So we're friends now?" she asked, her hand lightly resting on his shin.

"Well, I have my legs in your lap . . . and you're hanging out here crying about my soul or something," he said lightly.

"And you've seen me naked," Mona added with humor in her voice.

Anson nodded. "Yeah, yeah. There's that," he said, thinking of how the design of his pool with its intricate emerald, turquoise, and cobalt mosaic tile on the floor was beautiful. Stunningly so. But topping it easily was the sight of Mona Ballinger's naked body coming up out of that pool with tan lines from a string bikini that emphasized the sweet spots. No comparison.

Lawd have mercy.

He shook his head and wiped his mouth with his good hand.

"I shouldn't have told you that," she said.

Anson bent his arm and settled his head on top of it so that he could see her clearly. "Because it's not true?" he asked.

Mona made a move to rise and he pressed his leg down against her lap to stop her. "Broken foot," he reminded her.

She relaxed. "Do you really not care about falling in love?" she asked, glancing over at him.

"Do you really believe you have premonitions about soul mates?" Anson countered.

"Yes," Mona admitted, meeting his stare with her own.

So that's why she stormed out last night.

Anson remembered his words clearly.

"What's next? You going to tell me you use your magic powers to make your love matches?"

Moments later she was gone.

"All of the women in my family on my father's side—going back many, many generations—have like a sixth sense about love," she said.

His skepticism must have shown on his face.

"It's true," she insisted, looking at him.

"So what happened in the kitchen just now?" he asked, to steer away from revealing that he was a complete skeptic.

"Nothing. That's what happened, and I don't know what it means," she said. "Is my gift broken or are you?"

Another tear fell.

Anson's heart ached and he maneuvered to sit up and catch the tear with his thumb. "Let's have some wine," he said, wanting to steer her away from the whole foolish conversation. He refused to even waste precious moments on witches and visions and soul mates. *Oh my.*

"You can't take wine with your pain pills," she reminded him.

"I'm not taking the pain pills," he said.

Mona eyed him in exasperation. "I swear you have got to be the most bullheaded man I have ever met," she said. "Hands down. No question."

"I don't want to be a junkie like my parents," he said, surprising even himself.

Mona opened her mouth.

Anson held up his hand. "I don't want to talk about it."

"Okay," she said, holding up her hands.

He sat up and grabbed his crutch to rise. "I need that wine," he said.

"Me too," she agreed, rising as well.

She placed a soft hand to his back as he limped into the house. It felt comfortable and familiar.

"What a day it's been," he said as they entered the kitchen.

She retrieved wine goblets from his glass front cabinets and Anson moved over to a large wine rack on the counter to select a bottle. "Yes, it has," she agreed.

He didn't miss that her eyes rested on him for a few moments before she looked away. He wondered about her thoughts as he opened the bottle and poured them each half a glass. "Did I get over you hitting me with a car too quick?" he asked, glancing up at her.

"Probably . . . but I appreciate it," she said, smiling broadly.

Anson eyed her deep dimples.

"Here's to forgiveness and healing," she said, raising the wine to him.

Anson noticed the tattoo on her inner wrist. "Believe," he read aloud. "Believe in what?"

"Love," she answered without equivocation, touching her glass to his with a light *ding*. "Maybe you need a tattoo too, so that you can believe in it."

"I believe in love," he said.

"True love? Made for each other love? Destined love?" she asked, looking up at him.

Anson felt uneasy. He set his wineglass down on the island and moved over to wash his hands at the sink. Talk of visions. Soul mates. Destiny. It wasn't his cup of tea.

"This stew smells delicious," he said, after raising the glass lid.

"The worst part of having this gift is not being able to use it on myself or anyone in my family, for that matter," she said from behind him.

"I'm starving," he said, choosing to ignore her.

What's next? She's going to tell me she see can see dead people? Or she's like the little blonde off Long Island Medium—*the Holtsville edition?*

"Don't you think that's a curse and a blessing?" she asked, coming to stand beside him at the stove. "To be able to help others, but you can't help your-self?"

Anson released a heavy breath as he turned to face her. "Listen, I'm trying not to say something to make you angry again or to hurt your feelings. So can we just talk about something else?" he asked, looking down into her bright eyes.

"Yes, if you want," she said, reaching over to lightly touch his hand.

When she closed her eyes and her brows drew in like she was concentrating, he jerked his hand away. "Mona," he snapped.

"Sorry," she said. "Just trying again to get a read."

"You really believe all of that?" he asked, his skepticism obvious.

"Yes," Mona stressed. "My aunts in Baton Rouge

are the best at it. I promise you. Maybe they could get a premonition on you."

Anson's eyes widened. "No," he said at the sight of her face becoming reflective. He didn't doubt that Miss Spontaneity wouldn't call in the aunts.

She held up her wrist to him and tapped her tattoo with the index finger of her opposite hand.

"I only believe what I can see, taste, hear, and touch," he said.

"And feel," she added.

"I *said* touch," he defended himself.

She shook her head and reached up to press her palm against his heart.

Anson stiffened from her touch just as his heart beat wildly and every hair on his body stood on end. Like it did earlier when she was so close to him in the pool house.

"Feel in here," she stressed, patting her hand against his chest.

Anson felt his nipple harden. He walked away from her. "In there is a weakness," he said. "You don't know me and you know nothing about what I've been through. So please leave this whole subject off, Mona. Please."

"But—"

He grabbed his crutch and jerked it under his arm before taking a step. His eyes widened as he felt himself slip and lose his footing. "Shit," he swore as he stumbled and then fell backward.

Mona hollered out in alarm.

Anson winced and closed his eyes as pain radiated across his back and buttocks. He felt Mona place one hand to his chest and the other to the side of his face.

"Are you okay?" she asked.

The touch of her hand. The coolness of her breath against his face. The sweetness of her perfume. All of it was a lot to take in, and when he opened his eyes they looked directly up into hers while his heart pounded loudly and quickly. Her beauty struck him. Her lips teased him. *What the hell . . . ?*

"Anson . . . Anson. Say something. Are you okay? Should I call an ambulance?" she asked, bending in closer to him.

"Kiss me," he said.

Mona's look surprised him as her eyes searched his. "Is this you being spontaneous?" she said softly in the small space between their faces.

Anson reached up with his good hand and lightly cupped the back of her head to close the gap between their mouths.

The first touch of their lips was awkward. A little too wet. A lot too hard.

"Oh my," Mona sighed.

Anson frowned. "That's a first," he said, sounding surprised. "The worst first."

They looked at each other and burst out laughing.

Anson sat up and pressed his back against the wall of the kitchen. "I'm gonna need your help getting up," he admitted.

Instead of doing that, she moved to straddle his thighs. "Failure is for fools," Mona said.

"I'm no fool," he said, bringing his hands up to lightly grip her hips as she leaned in slowly.

Mona lightly touched her lips to his as they stared at each other. With less than an inch between their mouths, Anson tilted his chin up to do the same as his entire body felt alive. "Not bad," he whispered.

"Not at all," she admitted with a hot lick of her lips.

Anson traced her bottom lip with his tongue.

Mona captured it in her mouth and sucked it deeply as she pressed her hands against his shoulders and lightly gripped his shirt.

Anson massaged her hips and brought his hand down to lightly jerk her body closer to his until her breasts were pushed against the hardness of his chest. He moaned as their kiss deepened. His pulse raced. His heart pounded and his head got hard . . . down below.

"Shit," Mona swore as they broke the kiss to deeply breathe in air.

Anson pressed kisses to her jawline.

SLAM.

The sound of the front door being solidly closed echoed.

Mona climbed off his lap and sat on the floor, her fingers lightly pressed to her open mouth as she panted like she was in heat. With her eyes glazed over she looked sexy as hell.

"Guess who, big brother?"

Anson had never been regretful of the appearance of his brother . . . until that moment. "In here, Hunter," he called out, thankful their kiss hadn't brought his dick to a full hard-on.

"Your brother?" Mona said, rising to stand by the doorway.

"You must be the curly-haired she-devil."

Anson winced at his brother's forthrightness.

"Oh really?" he heard Mona ask. "Is that what he called me?"

"Hunter," Anson called out as he avoided Mona's stare.

His brother poked his head in around the doorway, searching the room with his eyes.

"Down here," Anson said dryly.

Hunter looked down. "Damn, I didn't even see you, bro," he said, stepping into the kitchen and extending his hand.

Anson accepted it, and his younger brother, who was twenty pounds lighter and a foot taller, pulled him up to his feet with ease. Mona jumped in with the crutch and Anson felt like all was "upright" with the world.

He looked on as his brother turned back to Mona. "I'm Hunter Tyler, and your name?" he asked, smooth as fine brandy.

"Mona Ballinger," she said, crossing her arms over her chest.

"And I'm Kyra Nollings."

Anson swiveled his head in surprise as his college sweetheart stepped into the kitchen. She was still thick, still curvy, and still beautiful, with her red hair and shortbread complexion. "Kyra?" he said, surprised to see her again after nearly seven years.

"I thought you would need some help recuperating and I swooped by and picked Kyra up," Hunter said, moving over to the stove to look inside the pot.

"Surprise," Kyra said, moving in to press a kiss to Anson's cheek and give him a hug that was tight enough to blend them into one human form.

* * *

"I guess I'll leave you to your guest."

Mona rushed over to the island and gathered her items, quickly sliding them into her briefcase.

"No, no, don't go," Hunter said, coming to tower over her. "With you here I won't feel like a third wheel."

Mona winced. Anson was standing there hugging a woman with the taste of her still on his mouth. *That's enough sharing for me with this crew.* "Actually I have to go. And now that the cavalry is here I can head out."

She breezed past Anson, whose ex was still holding him close and rubbing his back. *Well damn, let him breathe. . . .*

"Yes, you go on with your business. *Kyra's* here now," the woman said.

"Nice to meet you, Carina . . . I mean Kyra," Mona said with a fake smile.

"There's only one Kyra," the woman said, giving Mona a slow once-over.

Mona did the same. "Yes, I can see you have invested quite a bit into an individual look," she said, before she left the kitchen without sparing Anson another glance.

"Well, Anson, I see she is quite a little spitfire with about four bundles of fourteen-inch deep wave weave."

Mona stopped at the woman's voice carrying from the kitchen. She gave herself a ten count. *Weave? Bundles? I should go in there and give her a Porsha Stewart level dragging and see if her tracks can stand it like Kenya Moore's.*

"Meow, Kyra. Put the claws away," Hunter teased.

Mona waved her hand to dismiss them all and left the house with a solid closing of the door. There was a black Jeep Wrangler parked next to her vehicle, but Mona hardly paid it any mind as she started her car.

She briefly thought about stopping to chat with Reeba on the way, but headed straight home instead. Once she took a hot shower and pulled on a pair of her favorite brightly colored pajamas, Mona lay across her bed on her back with her head dangling over the side.

The last couple weeks of her life had been a rollercoaster ride ending with her in Anson's lap kissing him until they both were breathless. The first kiss? Not so much. But the second time around? *Lawdy.*

Regardless, a kiss was all it was. Anson Tyler had no belief or respect for true love and Mona considered that the very core of her being. To love and be loved. To help others love and be loved. She could never consider herself getting involved with someone who felt different.

But that kiss.

And he was fine.

And that kiss.

She raised her hands and touched her plump lips. "Guess he's kissing on Kyra now," she muttered, lifting both legs high in the air for no reason at all.

Mona turned up her nose as she thought of the curvy cutie with the "see me, notice me" red hair. "He sure likes 'em with meat on the bones," she said, rolling off the bed and standing before the mirror over her dresser to pull her nightclothes tight against her body. She turned this way and that.

Both Kyra's and Carina's lush size-twelve forms made her size-six body look boyish. "I do have *some* curves," she said. *Just not as much as them.*

Screwing up her face, Mona left her bedroom and walked into the kitchen to pour herself a large glass of white wine. "I wonder what they're doing," she mumbled into her glass, walking around her living room.

She paused by the sofa table holding all of her favorite family photos. She picked up the one of her aunts, Millicent and Winifred. They were identical twins who had never lived separately. Even now they shared the family home in Baton Rouge.

Clutching the photo of them with identical smiles to her chest, she sipped from her wine and made her way over to the fireplace mantel to pick up her cordless landline phone. "Lord help me," she mumbled as she used her thumb to hit the buttons.

It seemed to ring endlessly. It *always* seemed to ring endlessly.

"Millie and Winnie."

Mona was overcome with love and missing them and she allowed herself a quick moment to wallow in that as she closed her eyes and swayed back and forth.

"Mona?"

Her eyes popped open in surprise. *Good Lord, were they psychic now too?*

"How'd you know it was me?" Mona asked, moving to sit down on the bright pink leather ottoman she used as a coffee table.

"Millie finally got rid of that old phone we was renting from the phone company for the last thirty years, and this one has caller ID," Winnie said with pride.

To live in a world where caller ID was a major technological advance? *God bless their seventy-year-old hearts.*

"I actually need to ask both of you something. Is Aunt Millie there?" she asked, looking down at their photo and stroking either Millie or Winnie's cheek with her thumb.

"Where else my shadow gon' be?" Aunt Winnie said, her Louisiana accent as thick and southern as their famous gumbo.

Mona smiled as she heard the rustling of another phone in their house being picked up.

"Hey there, Mona," Aunt Millie said, although there wasn't an iota of difference in their voice.

"Hey there, Aunt Millie."

"How's you matchmaking business going?" one of them asked.

Mona stiffened, preparing herself for the speech. "Real good . . . although Reeba and you both don't agree," she said. *Might as well get to it.*

"Well, we still support you," Aunt Winnie said.

"And we know it's a different time," Aunt Millie added.

Mona could now tell them apart because one of the phones had a little echo. "Tell Reeba that. Please," she added, to make sure she didn't come off disrespectful.

"That's y'all's fight."

"Yes, ma'am," she agreed, looking up to the ceiling.

"Okay so come on with it."

Mona smiled a little. "I tried to get a read on a man today and nothing happened. I mean nothing at all. Has that ever happened to anyone and what do you think it's all about?"

"Nothing at all?" they asked in unison.

"Not a thing," Mona assured them.

"Never happened to me. You, Winnie?"

"Nah. Not me either."

"But with every generation there's always something new thrown in the mix."

"Sure is."

"He doesn't believe in any of it. Not our gift. Not true love. Nothing. You think he doesn't have a soul mate?" Mona asked, rising to sit their photo back in its spot.

"Everyone has one, or everything about what we believe and we're blessed with is not true, and I rebuke that in the name of sweet Jesus," Aunt Millie said with fire.

"Bring it, sis," Aunt Winnie cheered her on.

"I agree," Mona said softly, moving into the bathroom to stand at the sink.

"What's his name?"

Mona fought the urge to ask them why it mattered. "Anson. Anson Tyler," she said, tucking the phone between her shoulder and ear to reach up and loosen her hair from the topknot she'd put it in to shower.

"Anson Tyler?" one repeated.

"White man?" the other asked.

Mona dropped her head and smiled. "No, ma'am."

"Oh," they said in unison.

"Well, if you can't help him, you just can't help him. Everything is for a reason and he just gon' have to go it alone."

But I don't want him to.

Her eyes widened in the reflection and her heart pounded real fast and real hard. *Me and Anson Tyler?*

She squinted her eyes and arched a brow. *No way. Right?*

Mona's eyes got soft as she remembered the kiss. Her lips opened a little and she tilted her head to the side, letting her eyes drift closed as she remembered the feel of his mouth. She smiled delicately and bit her bottom lip hotly.

"So when you coming home to visit?"

She jerked her eyes open and the memory of the kiss cooled in an instant.

"Maybe when Shara gets in town the three of us will come for one of the holidays . . . if you promise me some gumbo," she said, turning out the light as she left the bathroom.

"I'll promise you anything if you girls would come see us while we here to be seen."

Guilt swamped her. "I promise. We're coming," she said with honesty.

"We'll see," they said in unison.

Knock-knock.

"I gotta go," she said, already moving to the door.

"Bye there," they said in unison.

The sound of the *click* of one phone and the *beep* of the other echoed in her ear as she pulled back the curtain to look out. Mona was surprised to see the Jeep in the drive behind her car and Hunter standing on the porch.

Mona was still clutching the phone as she opened the door. "Hello again, Hunter," she said, standing in the doorway.

He smiled at her and it spread as slow as honey on a hot biscuit. "Is there anything you don't look beautiful in?" he asked.

Mona kept her eyes wide like a doll baby to keep from blinking or rolling them. "Is that my Tupperware bowl?" she asked, pointing to it in his hands.

"Yeah. When Anson said it was yours I thought I should get it right to you," Hunter said, his eyes lingering on all points south on her body.

He was as handsome as Anson but far, far too eager. Too complimenting. Too leering. Too *everything*.

"Thanks," she said, taking it from his hand. "It's actually my sister's, but I'll get it back to her."

Hunter reached out and grabbed her hand as she stepped back. "Wait a sec," he said.

Mona blinked, and in that instant she saw an image of herself in a wedding gown dancing with . . . Hunter in the center of a crowd of people. She gasped dramatically and snatched her hand away as she backed up and reached blindly for her front door. "Thanks, I have to go. Thanks. Bye," she said, securely closing it.

She turned and slumped back against the solid wood. Hunter was her soul mate? *No way in hell. No way.*

Mona turned again and opened the door. Hunter was just turning to leave. He turned back and smiled broadly.

She had the utmost respect for her gift—her legacy. Her lips moved but words would not form.

"Are you okay?" he asked, staring at her.

He has Anson's eyes.

"Yeah. Yeah. I'm . . . I'm fine," she said, knowing that in that moment of discovering that the man standing before her was her soul mate that she shouldn't be thinking of his brother. Wishing he was his brother.

Mona released a breath filled with her regret and her confusion.

Hunter slid his hands into the pocket of his slacks as he took a step closer to her. "I really brought the bowl back because I wanted to ask you—"

"Hunter," she said, purposefully interrupting what she knew was a date invite. "I really need to get back to work. Thanks for the bowl. Maybe we can chat tomorrow?" she asked, forcing her voice to sound hopeful.

He nodded. "We can—"

Mona nodded. "Tomorrow. Please. Okay?" she said gently, reaching for his arm to turn him back towards the steps.

"Tomorrow. Definitely tomorrow," Hunter said with a roguish wink before going down the stairs and over to his Jeep.

Mona waved at him as he started his vehicle and reversed out of the yard. That smile faded as soon as the Jeep pulled off down the road.

She needed time to think and to process. One day would not stop destiny.

What is meant to be will be?

Right?

Chapter 8

One week later

"Miss Ballinger?"

Mona turned away from the storefront window of her office. She had been staring down the street at the man-made waterfall that served as a memorial for war veterans from Colleton County. Her gaze had been so intense that she had clearly missed the young man walk through the door just two feet away from her. Going over to him, she extended her hand. "Yes, I'm Mona Ballinger. How may I help you?" she asked. The short and stout man's boyish face wouldn't reveal if he was in his late teens or early thirties. A Pharrell "I'll never age" Williams kind of face.

Shaking her hand, he smiled and lost another five years. "Actually I'm here to assist you. I'm Malik Freedman, Mr. Tyler's office manager," he said. "He sent me over to help you this week in any way that I can—including vetting out a new employee."

Mona's gloss-covered plump lips opened in surprise. "Did he?" she asked softly, still taken aback.

Over the last week Mona had made it her business to stay clear of Anson and his houseguest, Kyra. She was more than relieved to find Hunter had already made his way back to Atlanta to resume his residency. That "tomorrow" they discussed on her porch that night never materialized and Mona was okay with that. Mona was not ready to deal with him and the future. Not yet.

Not when she had to deal with the fact that it was Anson who claimed her thoughts at random moments of the day. It was the memory of Anson's kiss that made her smile. It was Anson that she desired.

But she was fighting it, reconciling herself that it was Hunter that she would love and desire. One day.

She called a few times to quickly check on Anson and let him know the offer to pay his medical bills still stood, but that was all. It was up to Kyra to make sure Anson stayed off his feet and was well fed.

What was odd was that this past week she had spent more time away from Anson than she had with him and she found that she missed him.

And now this.

"I could use the help," she admitted, turning to look around the office for a spot to set him up. "I guess you'll have to use my desk while you're here."

"Mr. Tyler asked me to pass this on to you as well."

Mona looked down at the envelope before taking it. She figured it was his hospital bills and stuck it inside the top drawer of her desk once she reached it. "Thank you."

She spent the rest of the morning walking Malik through every area in which she needed assistance. Then she dropped down on the sofa in the lounge/

waiting area at the front of the room to finally pull her cell from the front pocket of the linen motorcycle jacket she wore with wide leg jeans. She was just about to call Anson and thank him when the front door opened and Hunter strolled in, rather handsome in a bright green Polo and khaki shorts.

She allowed herself a moment for her pulse to race or her heart to skip at the sight of him. Instead she felt nothing but overwhelmed by his sudden reappearance. *Mrs. Hunter Tyler. Mona Tyler.*

Standing, she walked over to meet him. "Look who is back in town," she said with a smile that was more forced than not. *Why is he here?*

"I thought I might take you out to lunch," Hunter said.

Her lips formed to decline, but she hesitated. He was just as fine as Anson, maybe a little cockier, and he was going to be a surgeon, definitely making him an eligible bachelor. Was he her soul mate and was she not giving him a chance because it was Anson she felt attracted to?

"Let me get my clutch," she said, walking over to her desk.

Malik rolled to the side in his chair to allow her to retrieve her clutch from the bottom drawer of her desk. "I shouldn't be more than an hour," she said to him.

"Enjoy," he said.

Hunter held the door as she exited and then walked a few steps ahead to open the door to Anson's BMW. "I thought this was better than my Jeep," he said, holding the passenger door.

She smiled at him before entering the car. Once

inside she lightly touched the gear shift, but only because Anson's hand had once gripped it the way he had cupped her ass as they kissed. She felt her cheeks warm and her pulse race at the memory. "Does Anson know you're taking me to lunch?" she asked, once Hunter was in the driver's seat.

"Yeah," he said, checking the side-view mirrors before pulling away from the curb.

Oh. Her disappointment hurt to the quick and she looked out the window, not really seeing anything at all.

"He actually went back to work at the office today," he said, glancing over at her.

"His doctor wanted him to wait two weeks before going back," she said, her eyes filling with concern.

"I know, but my brother is stubborn."

Yes, he is.

"I'm sure Kyra has the . . . know-how to convince him," she said.

Hunter laughed. "She knows him well. Kyra's definitely the one who got away, and now she's back," he said simply.

"Not Carina?" she asked.

"I think he loved Kyra more," Hunter said, reaching over to take her hand. "Hopefully they can get their shit together this time."

Mona actually was glad he took her hand, and she sandwiched his in between both of hers and closed her eyes. The same vision flashed. *Shit.*

She held on to his hand, but this time she was waiting for some type of thrill. Any type of thrill. Sparks. Chemistry. Desire.

Whomp-whomp.

Releasing him, she pretended to look for something in her clutch. "So you're going to be a surgeon?" Mona asked.

"Cardiologist," he said proudly.

"Matters of the heart," she said. "I guess we have something in common."

He frowned. "Kinda, but not really," he said.

"Oh, Lord. Don't tell me you don't believe in love and soul mates either," she said.

Hunter shrugged as he pulled into a parking lot outside Fat Jack's restaurant. "I believe in soul mates, but if Anson doesn't . . . you just have to understand he's been through a lot. So it makes sense that he views things differently from me."

Mona waited for him to come around and open her door.

"I don't want to be a junkie like my parents."

She knew it had cost Anson a lot to reveal even that much of his life to her.

As they entered the restaurant and were seated at one of the booths lining the walls, Mona's heart tugged for Anson. If years later he still was so deeply affected that he didn't want to speak on his past and his own brother said things had been tough, she hated to think what he went through.

"What's on your mind?" Hunter asked, setting his plastic-covered menu down to eye her from across the table.

"Nothing," she lied.

The waitress took their drink and food orders. Mona handed her the menus with a smile.

Hunter reached for her hand before she could pull it out of his reach. "I really want to get to know you, Mona. I like your style. Your looks. That body. Plus you're smart and run your own business. You're something like fly, right?"

She smiled. "If you say so."

"And I do."

"I'm just not looking to get involved with anyone right now," she said. "My life is kind of hectic."

"I'm a surgical resident, so time is tight for me too, but when I come back to Holtsville to visit, I just want to know you'll spend some time with me," he said. "Get to know me."

"I can't promise you that," she said, her thoughts filled with Anson. "Plus, I wouldn't doubt you have enough ladies lined up in Atlanta to sate you before a brief trip back home."

"And you're going to regret one of them locking down a doctor," he boasted.

Mona was completely taken aback. He not only copped to a lineup of women, but also assumed that throwing them in her face would urge her competitive nature to go for him? *What in the hell?*

She was glad when their food arrived. She plowed through her cheeseburger so fast she got indigestion and the hiccups. She just wanted the lunch to be over. "Thanks so much," she said, sitting her napkin on her nearly empty plate.

Hunter eyed her plate as he continued to chew on his own fried shrimp platter. "Hungry much?" he asked, swiping his mouth with his napkin.

"I just need to get back to my office," she said.

Hunter continued to eat his food. "Why'd you become a matchmaker?" he asked.

Mona swallowed back her irritation. "It just

seemed a natural gift I could combine with my knowledge of business models to make a successful venture for myself. I get paid to do what I love," she said.

Is he stalling?

"And why are you a doctor?" she asked, as he continued to enjoy his food.

"I owe my brother everything and it was his wish for me to be a doctor or lawyer," Hunter said.

"You must really love him," she said.

Hunter nodded. "We were wards of the state. He aged out first and worked like a dog to get himself set up to take me in," he said. "I watched him every day work two jobs and go to school full-time to give us both a better life. Most eighteen-year-olds would have been caught up in themselves, but my brother wanted nothing but the best for me and never once did he make me feel like I owed him anything— other than to be the very best I could be."

Mona believed that she had just witnessed the man be the most sincere he ever was. *I guess Anson must bring that out in him.* "Your story is inspiring. Both of you are," she said.

Hunter nodded and finally dropped his napkin atop the few fries he didn't demolish along with the shrimp. "Yes, I know."

And he's back.

As he paid the check and tipped the waitress, Mona stood at the glass door of the small restaurant and looked out at Anson's BMW. The car, the house, the clothes, the plan for his life. All of it was testament to the man trying his very best not to be the boy he was. There were holes in the story of his past that were easy to fill in. She could see how a little boy so focused on not failing could have no time for or belief in love.

Her heart tugged with sadness at that. Understanding but still sadness.

"Ready?" Hunter asked, holding the door open for her.

"Yes," she said.

"When can I see you again?" he asked as they walked to the car.

"I don't know," she said, choosing her words carefully. "I really don't know if I'm interested in anything."

"You'll change your mind," he said with confidence.

Mona let him help her into the car. They rode in silence most of the way, and she was anxious for some space. The vision and her lack of chemistry with Hunter were waging a war in her that was bringing on a headache.

"Thanks for lunch," she said, her hand already on the door handle as he pulled to a stop. "No need to get out. You get back to Atlanta safely."

She opened the door and climbed out before he could. "Bye, Hunter," she said, waving.

She stood on the sidewalk and watched him wave and pull off. She hated to be rude or standoffish, but she'd kissed one brother and then had a vision of marrying the other. The whole thing was awkward and confusing.

Knock-knock.

Mona turned and eyed Malik in the window

pointing to a bouquet of long-stemmed roses in his hand. Her eyes widened in surprise. "For me?" she mouthed, pointing to herself.

He gave her a thumbs-up.

She walked into the office. "Oh my God, they are gor-geous," she sighed, taking them from him.

"They just came," Malik said, before walking back to the desk.

She plucked the small red envelope from the roses and pulled out the card. Her smile faltered a bit. Her first thought had been that they were from Anson. Not Hunter.

"Think of me when you smell these," she read, and then eyed his number scrawled across the bottom.

Great.

Dropping down onto the red leather sofa, she set the roses on the small, low slung, white table before it. She felt Malik's eyes on her, but was thankful when he asked no questions. Sinking against the sofa, she let her head rest on the back of it and closed her eyes before rubbing them with her fingertips. *This is a mess.*

"Anson . . . Anson . . . An-son!"

He broke his gaze outside the window of his office to look over his shoulder at his receptionist peeking her head inside the door. "What's up, Greta?" he asked, adjusting his leg on the desktop.

"Two quick things. The blueprints for the gym-nasium just arrived. You want them in here or the conference room?" she asked. "And what are your lunch plans?"

"Conference room, and spinach pie from Dimitrio's," he said, dropping the pencil he uselessly held and stretching his muscled arms high above his head in the hand-tailored shirt he wore.

"How are you feeling?" she asked.

Jealous as hell.

"I'm good," Anson said aloud, smoothing his hand over the waves of his low cut ebony hair.

At that very moment his brother, whom he loved above anyone else in the world, was borrowing his car to take Mona to lunch and Anson didn't like it one damn bit. Not one damn bit at all.

Picking up the pencil, he stroked the length of it with his thumb, hating that he visualized his little brother kissing Mona. They shared many things, but women wasn't one of them. He frowned deeply and looked down at the two halves of the pencil, not even realizing he had snapped the thin wood in half.

Ever since Mona Ballinger had entered his normal, sedate life, his days had become roller coasters of emotions. He had run the gamut from anger to excitement and everything in between . . . including desire. He had never had a woman so easily influence his feelings.

And when he was honest with himself he knew that she'd lit a spark in him that first day they'd argued in her office. In the midst of their harsh encounter he had been thrown by a desire to rush across the room, pick her up, and press her body against the wall as he kissed away any more words being hurled at him.

In those days before she reappeared in his life and drove into him, she had crossed his mind many times. He'd pretended it was annoyance, but it was much more, and it pissed him off that he could desire someone who was causing such havoc in his life.

But that kiss they shared was a whole other type of beautiful chaos.

"Failure is for fools. . . ."

Anson licked his lip at the memory of the feel of her lips. They were softer and plusher than they looked. Sweet. Hot. Good.

Hunter had picked the absolute worst moment to come home, ruining what might have been the best kiss ever. And now they were at lunch. He absolutely hated it.

Shit. Shit. Shit.

"I should have told him we kissed," he muttered, viciously tossing the broken pencil in the black wastepaper basket by his desk. "And that I've seen her naked."

Would Hunter see the same gloriously sexy spontaneity in her?

He assumed she had accepted Hunter's invitation to lunch since his brother had yet to return to swap back the BMW for his Jeep. *Why did she go?*

That kiss had to mean something. That lazy and soft look in her eyes when they broke the kiss didn't have anything to do with fatigue.

But he knew the answer. It was clear why she accepted Hunter's invitation.

Kyra.

He could choke the hell out of Hunter for that as well. She had reappeared in his life and within minutes Mona was gone, never to brighten his doorstep again. It would take a fool not to guess at the reason why.

Bzzzzzzzzz . . .

He reached for his cell phone and flipped it over. Kyra. He instantly felt like an ass for being disappointed that it wasn't Mona. Kyra had been at his home cooking meals and assisting him all week. Wiping his mouth, he answered the call and put it on speakerphone. "Hello."

"Anson, I was thinking I would make that chicken piccata dish you love so much," she said. "And maybe we can talk about some things."

He leaned back in his chair and pinched the bridge of his nose. Kyra was making it clear that she wanted them to try again. They hadn't ended on bad terms years ago; they had just drifted apart with her move to Atlanta for her career. He knew she and Hunter spoke occasionally, but he honestly had moved on without even considering picking up where they'd left off. And it was clear she was open to it.

She was beautiful, intelligent, and goal oriented— everything he'd liked in Carina even though he never proclaimed to be in love with her. And he had to admit Kyra had been the one woman he'd cared for the most.

So why the hesitation?

"Actually I'm swamped here at work and I'm not sure what time I'm getting in," he said. "I'd hate for all your hard work to go to waste."

"Oh," she said, sounding disappointed. "I only have another week off work and I just thought . . ."

His mind didn't absorb the rest of her words because he was too busy watching his BMW being parked in his reserved spot outside his window. "I agree," he said.

"Well, no matter what time you get in, I got a little something sexy planned for you. Check your messages," she said before hanging up.

He was confused when Hunter just hopped out of the BMW and then hopped in his Jeep before he reversed out of the parking spot. "Where's he going now?" he asked aloud.

Anson swiped across his phone with his thumb and a nude selfie of Kyra filled the screen. Closing that with an agitated mumble, he dialed Mona's number. It rang twice.

"Hello."

His heart double-pumped. "How's Malik working out?" he asked.

"I really appreciate it and he's great," she said. "I was going to call and thank you."

"I remembered you mentioning you were swamped at work and he's really good at getting things in order. . . . Just don't let him flirt with you," he said, his shoulders relaxing.

"He's been a perfect gentleman—plus, I'm too old for him," she said.

They fell silent. He didn't want the small connection to her to end.

We're as different as night and day and now my brother is chasing behind her skirts. What am I doing?

"I got the bill. I'll drop a check off by your house tonight," she said.

"Bill?" he asked. "Oh, you mean the envelope I sent by Malik. That's not a bill. I'm insured."

"There must be a co-pay—"

"Mona? Stop it."

"I just think—"

"Mona," he said again.

"So what's in the envelope?" she asked.

"A surprise."

"I love surprises. . . . You sure Kyra won't mind?"

"It has nothing to do with her," he said, his suspicion confirmed.

"Does she know that?" Mona countered.

"How was lunch?" he shot back smoothly.

"Certainly not as interesting as the last five nights at your house, I'm sure."

"Never assume anything."

"I could tell you the same."

' A standoff.

Mona let out a soft gasp.

"What's wrong?" he asked, his body tensing.

"I . . . uh . . . wow . . . I opened the envelope," she said.

A broad smile spread across his face. "You like it?" he asked.

"Yes."

"Good."

He wished he could see the expression on her face as she looked at the sketches of her he had drawn from memory.

"And you did these?" she asked.

"I'm a man of many talents," he boasted playfully.

"Good Lord, I thought Hunter was the cocky one," she said.

Anson laughed because he knew better than anyone just how self-assured and self-loving his little brother was. "Life will humble him down a bit. Life . . . or a good woman," he added.

"True," was all that she said.

They fell silent again.

"As a matter of fact," she began, "I had a vision that Hunter's my soul mate."

There was silence on Anson's end.

"When he touched my hand that's what I saw, Anson," she said. "I know you don't believe in it all . . . but I do."

Anson licked his lips and leaned back in his chair to look up at the tray ceiling. He honestly didn't know what to say. Or how to feel.

"Anson, my next client just walked in," she said.

"Okay."

"Thanks again for the sketches and take care of yourself."

Anson nodded and moved the iPhone from his ear to end the call.

He'd had no intention of pursuing anything with Mona and the kiss . . . the kiss had been a fun moment of her beloved spontaneity. Still, it had felt like there was much more to be said, but neither ventured toward it.

Mona sat on the foot of her bed going through the four sketches Anson made when there was a knock at her door. She checked the time on the digital cable box. It was a little past nine.

Still carrying the sketches, she padded barefoot to the front door. She peeked out the window.

Anson?

Looking down at her fuzzy bunny slippers and bright orange pajamas with green aliens on them, she turned her lips downward before taking a deep breath and opening the door. "Well, hey there, Anson," she said, and then grimaced because she sounded like her elderly aunts.

He stepped past her inside her house and Mona was left to shut the door and turn to find him limping back and forth in front of her fireplace. He paused, looked at her, opened his mouth as if to say something, and then started pacing again.

"Anson," she said sharply, before licking her lips. "What do you want?"

He stopped. His eyes took her in from head to toe and then up and down again. He locked his gaze on the sketches she still held gently in her hand. "I sketched those from memory. When I close my eyes I see you so clearly," he admitted, his conflict evident on his handsome features. "I could create just as detailed a picture of your naked body coming out of my pool that day. I can't forget it."

She met his look and a warm shiver raced over her body. "Anson—"

"I can't get you off my mind."

She released a long breath, hoping to ease the hard pacing of her heart.

He limped over to her and gripped the sides of her face with his hands. She felt breathless and weak at the knees as he looked down at her with an intensity that shook her to the core.

"I want you, Mona. That's what I want. You," he whispered against her face before capturing her mouth with his own and kissing her with a moan that seemed torn from his soul.

Chapter 9

The sketches gently fell to the floor as Mona brought her hands up to clutch the back of Anson's head as he deepened the kiss and traced her tongue with his own. She offered no protest when he wrapped his good arm around her waist and picked her body up against his. His lips moved from her lips to press hot kisses against her jaw. She tilted her head back as he kissed the length of her neck and hoisted her up just a bit higher to taste her collarbone.

"Yes, yes, yes," she sighed heatedly. "Yessss!"

It was everything. The chemistry that pulsed in the air. The passion that flowed between them. The desire they both craved.

He lowered her again and she kissed his face before finding his lips and opening her eyes to look at him. He pulled back from her just enough for their panting breaths to mingle in the air between them. Their chests heaved. Their hearts pounded like crazy. Their eyes stayed locked.

"I can't get enough of you," he admitted, swallowing over a lump in his throat. "I can't stop."

She kissed each corner of his open mouth. "Then don't," she said in a heated whisper.

Anson's eyes glazed over as she released him and leaned back in his embrace to pull her pajama top open. She cupped her breasts with her brown hard nipples showing between her splayed fingers.

"Damn, Mona. Damn," he said, his eyes feasting on her.

He dipped his head to lick one taut nipple with the tip of his tongue.

She flung her head back and gasped.

He licked the other nipple.

She shivered and called out his name, clutching his shirt at his shoulders with her fists.

Anson hobbled them over to the couch and sat down with Mona straddling his hips. He buried his face in the sweet and warm valley between her breasts, inhaling deeply of the scent of her skin covered with a sweet mist. Jerking her top down, he held the material tightly, locking her arms to her sides as he sucked one brown nipple slowly, as if relishing ambrosia, and then dipped his head again to pleasure the other.

Mona shook her upper body, causing her topknot to work free and her breasts to sway back and forth across his face. He jerked her body up close to his and she smiled before she licked his bottom lip and then dipped her head to suckle at his neck. She inhaled deeply of his scent as she did. She allowed herself to get lost in him. Completely.

Nothing else mattered at all. How could it?

Anson shivered from her kisses and continued to bless her with his own as he worked the shirt down her arms to fall to the floor. She moved to stand between his legs, looking down at him as she removed the pajama bottoms to puddle at her feet.

Anson shook his head in wonder at her nakedness. He reached to lightly trace the tattoo of a colorful butterfly on her right hip before he slid his hand around to grip one fleshy buttock and jerk her body close to press the side of his face against her belly and her soft mound.

"Say hello to Miss Kitty," she taunted him sexily as she lifted one leg to sit her thigh on his shoulder.

He turned his face to kiss her inner thigh and inhale deeply of her womanly scent. It was fresh and sweet and calling to him. "Come and get it."

"Here kitty kitty," he said, looking up at her as he opened her plump lips from behind and stroked her clit.

Mona hissed in pleasure and locked the knee of the one leg still on the floor as she felt it give way from under her.

"Why must I chase the cat . . . nothing but the dog in me," he sang softly and playfully as he reached down to unzip his pants and free his hard dick.

Mona eyed his thickness. His darkness. His length. "Bow-wow-wow-yippie-yo-yippie-yeah," she said, enjoying their banter.

She kicked the leg on his shoulder high and over his head to turn and sit down on his lap, rolling her hips and enjoying the feel of his dick against her buttocks.

Anson brought one hand around to cup her breast and the other down between her open thighs to stroke her swollen clit with his thumb. "She's wet," he moaned against her back, in between heated kisses up her spine.

"He's hard," she moaned, backing up against the length of him.

Mona spread her legs wide as he slid one and then another of his thick fingers inside her. Her back arched as she cried out and grasped wildly at the edges of the couch, gyrating her hips against his hands.

"She's tight."

Mona purred before she rose from his lap and bent over to wrap her hands around her ankles.

Anson sat back and massaged the length of his hardness as he watched her work the inner muscles of her core before him. Feeling hungry for her, he shifted up to the edge and licked her before sucking her clit between his lips. He felt her thighs and buttocks shiver against his face. He sucked harder. Her knees buckled and he reached up to support her thighs with his hands.

Her moans and mumblings egged him on.

"Whoa," she said, sounding breathless as she rose and took two steps forward from the unrelenting pleasure of his tongue. She jumped up and down as she eyed him like he challenged her, and she wasn't having it.

Mona came back to him and dropped to her knees between his thighs, moving her hand to his dick to grasp his hardness. He thrust his hips upward, sending his dick up through her grasp. With a wicked little smile, she lowered her head and took the smooth and thick brown tip into her mouth.

At the first feel of her tongue circling him he

arched his hips high off the couch and flung his head against the back of the couch. *Shit.*

She sucked him deeply and Anson literally bit his bottom lip to refrain from releasing a howl that would scare a pack a wolves.

She cut her eyes up at him as she continued to work him with her tongue. "Nothing to say?" she whispered against his moist flesh. "I should be the one tongue-tied."

I love her.

Anson dug his fingers in her hair and gripped it from the roots, rolling his hips to send a little more of his dick into her mouth as he bit his own tongue lightly and tilted his head to the side to watch her work.

Knock-knock-knock.

Mona paused with her mouth still wrapped around him to look over at the door.

"Oh, hell naw," Anson complained. "Let them go away."

Mona smiled and gave him another suckle and a lick.

Knock-knock-knock.

Freeing her mouth, she rose and quickly grabbed her pajama top to pull on and wrap around her. She headed over to the window and pulled the curtain back. She quickly closed it at the sight of Hunter.

The reality of her actions sank in. Her beliefs in her gift and everything it stood for meant Hunter was her soul mate, but there she stood with the taste of his brother still on her tongue. "No, no, no, no, no," she wailed, lightly pounding her own forehead with her tiny fist.

Knock-knock-knock.

"What's wrong?" Anson asked.

"It's Hunter," she whispered harshly.

Anson calmly stood, his erection still standing off from his body through the open zipper. "Let him in. I should have told him about us from the jump anyway," he said.

Mona looked at him as if he was crazy.

Knock-knock-knock.

"You expect me to hide from my brother?" he asked.

Mona came over to rush into her pajama pants, her top hanging open and exposing her breasts swaying against her body as she moved. "What do you suggest?" she asked. "You want to stroll to the door, open it wide, and poke him in the stomach with your dick?"

Anson worked his now semihard inches back inside his pants as Mona rushed to button her top. "Let him in," he said when they were done. "Or I will."

"Anson," she said by way of pleading.

"So you were what—going to have sex with me and then marry him because of some stupid vision you think you had?" he asked, his face incredulous.

"I'd rather be with you. And this is all confusing for me because I am not feeling Hunter like a soul mate, and all I know is what the visions mean. . . . So don't be an asshole and act like my visions aren't real just because you don't think so, Anson Tyler," she finished with ferocity, her eyes blazing from the anger stoked by his insulting words.

"I can hear y'all."

They both jumped in surprise and looked to the

door at the sound of Hunter's voice through the wood. Mona walked over to the door, pausing to pick up her sketches before she opened it.

Hunter strolled in and gave them both a leisurely look before shaking his head. "You know, you two could have told me you were messing around," he said, moving around Mona's living room looking at or picking up this item or that without a care in the world.

"It wasn't like that," Anson said.

"It's pretty clear what it's like, but I just left the house and I'm dying to hear what Kyra thinks with all those candles and rose petals everywhere," he said, reaching behind him to pick up one of her frames from the sofa table.

Mona's head snapped up to glare at Anson. "But you know what you want, right? First me, then her. You really had all your spinach, huh?"

"Y'all triplets?" Hunter asked, showing her a photo of her and her sisters.

Anson threw up his hands. "It's pretty clear where I was planning on laying my head tonight . . . until this knucklehead"—he jerked his thumb at his brother—"interrupted."

"Whatever, Anson."

"Whatever?" he repeated with attitude.

"What's this about visions? And I'm your soul mate?" Hunter asked, sounding as doubtful as his brother as he plopped down onto the couch.

"Get out, Anson," she said, storming to the door and opening it wide. "Get your one leg Hopalong ass outta here."

He walked over to stand beside her.

"So it's his turn now," Anson said snidely, low in his throat, his eyes brilliant with his anger. "Because the silly vision said so, right?"

For a moment, Mona allowed the pain of his words to permeate before she stiffened her back and her jaw.

"I wouldn't do that. Man, bros before—"

"Say what now?" Mona snapped, cutting Hunter off.

"Hunter!" Anson roared, his glare now for his brother.

Hunter looked alarmed. "I didn't mean it like that. I meant I would never let a woman come between my brother and me."

"Then you should have said *that*," Anson said in a hard voice.

"You know what? I want you both to get the hell out."

"My apologies, Mona," Hunter said, moving past both Anson and Mona to step out onto the porch. "Is the sister who made that stew in that picture? If my brother is blocking me and you're supposed to be my soul mate, then you could at least hook me up with one of—"

Mona slammed the door in his face.

Anson chuckled.

She glared at him with her arms crossed over her chest.

Anson grasped her elbows with his hands. "I'm sorry," he said.

She twisted lightly to free herself of his hands and move away from him. "You're just happy because your brother's not mad at you," she said, disgruntled.

"How Hunter feels doesn't change what I know. What I saw. What I believe. Period."

"And your vision doesn't change what just happened between us either."

"You don't understand," she said.

"So you want to marry Hunter?" he asked, his eyes locked on her.

"No," she said, turning up her lip.

Anson looked offended.

Mona shrugged. "He's a lot to swallow," she said dryly.

Her eyes widened at what could have been a double entendre after the interlude Hunter had interrupted. "Don't you dare," she said at the amused expression on his handsome face.

Anson just held up both his good hand and the one in the cast as he shook his head.

She began pacing in front of the unlit fireplace. "It just doesn't make sense, and before you . . . before you everything made sense," she stressed, lightly tapping the fist of one hand against the palm of the other.

He limped over to her.

Mona held up her hands as tears filled her eyes. "You don't understand how serious this is to me, Anson. I believe what I believe and now I'm so caught up in you . . . in us . . . that I will forever know that I gave the brother of my future husband a blow—"

"I get the picture," he said, meaning to interrupt her.

She just ran her fingers through her hair.

"So you would marry my brother?" he asked.

She looked over at him, her fingers still entwined in her curls. "Why? Are you asking me first?"

Anson looked alarmed. "I didn't say all that."

Mona fought the childish urge to flip him the bird. "I'm not saying all that either, Anson."

"What are you saying?"

"That I don't know it all. I don't know how Hunter and I get from this point to the next, being in love. I don't know. But in time we all will get past this—maybe you with the help of the chick at your house with the roses and candles." Mona plopped down onto the sofa and crossed her legs Indian style. "I don't know."

Anson came over to sit down on the couch beside her. He pulled her body close to his side, settling her head against his chest as he massaged her arm.

"You're not getting any," she mumbled against his chest.

Soon his chest shook with laughter as he pressed a kiss to the top of her head.

Anson was disappointed his brother's Jeep wasn't parked in front of the house when he got home an hour later. It was nothing for Hunter to hop on the road and head back to Atlanta at a moment's whim. Sometimes Anson didn't even know his brother had left the state until he got a call from him telling him he was back in Atlanta.

The lights were off, but there was a definite glow in the windows that let him know candles—and plenty of them—were lit. Anson may not have believed in love being as deep and profound and lasting as Mona did, but there was one thing about relationships he knew for sure. There was no way he could marry a woman, live under the same roof and have a sexual relationship with her, while his desire was for another.

He would never cheat on any woman he married—that was all about his character. But to lust after another—that was all about a serious breakdown in the relationship. *Before it even begins . . . again.*

Knuckling up his will for a confrontation, he shut the car off and reached for his crutch, leaning against the passenger seat, before slowly making his way across the drive and up the stairs to unlock his front door. "Well damn," he muttered. The multitude of filled glass votive candles on the floor was enough to heat the foyer. The layers of red roses making a trail down the hall was so thick that he couldn't see the floor beneath it.

His first instinct was to ignore the red rose road and go hide out in his office. He noticed the roses led to his bedroom door and not the guest room where Kyra had been stationed all week.

Knuckle up, Anson. Knuckle the hell up.

Carefully he limped his way down the hall and, surely enough as he reached the pool room and continued past it to his bedroom, the roses and candles awaited his every step. Before he could reach for the door, it opened. Kyra filled the doorway in nothing but a few strategically placed petal bunches.

"Welcome home," she said with a beguiling smile.

He knew from the soft glow emanating within the room and the sweet scent of roses that more of the same was to be found inside. "Umm, Kyra.

I thought we would get a chance to talk first," he began.

She had been reaching over to stroke his cheek, but her hand paused. She tilted her head to the side. "Talk? You want to *talk?*" she asked, waving her hand up and down the length of her body and then turning to jiggle her buttocks before swiveling back to face him.

"I just want to apologize for sending you the wrong signals about us," he said.

Kyra leaned back so far to stare at him that he thought she was squaring up to hit him.

"I really appreciate you coming to help me out this last—"

WHAP!

He was looking dead at her the whole time and still didn't see the slap coming. "I'm sorry," he said, his words morphed as he worked his jaw to erase the sting of her hand.

Kyra pushed past him and flew down the hall so quickly that when he looked over his shoulder he saw nothing but errant rose petals floating in the air in her wake.

WHAM.

He stepped inside and quietly closed his bedroom door—a direct opposite of the slam heard around the world. He moved about the room blowing out the candles and retrieved the wastepaper basket to scoop the petals into it.

WHAM.

He didn't even wince at the slam that time.

He was stretched across his bed counting the random slams here and there—twenty so far—when his door opened. Lifting his head, he was relieved to see his brother. "Thank God," he said with plenty of emphasis.

"You had to ruin my night because I ruined yours," Hunter said.

"What's the plan?" Anson asked, reaching for a pillow to shove under his head as yet another slam echoed through the house.

"Angry rejected ex. Hysterical phone call to horny brother. One ride to Atlanta at ten at night. Thanks," he said, coming over to sit on the edge of the bed.

Anson didn't dare to show his brother his relief that Kyra was on a one-way ride back to the ATL.

"Listen, I didn't know you had your sights on Mona," Hunter said. "I figured Kyra was your focus."

"You didn't know and I should have told you. Not that it's anything serious . . . but it's not anything casual either. It's complicated. I don't know what it is. I just like her a lot. She makes me look at life differently sometimes," Anson said, looking up at the ceiling.

"But *I'm* her soul mate?"

As another slam resonated through the house, Anson gave his brother the abbreviated version of Mona, her "gift," and the premonition she had of her marrying him.

"Crazy, right?" Anson asked, looking at the odd expression on his face.

"Maybe."

Anson reached for a pillow and swung it at his brother's head. "You believe all that?" he asked in disbelief.

"I don't know," Hunter said.

"I've heard that a lot tonight," he said before covering his face with his pillow.

"I'm not ready to settle down no matter how fine Mona is—that I do know," Hunter said.

"I'm ready, Hunter," Kyra called out to him.

Anson didn't bother to remove the pillow from his head as he silently counted down. *Three . . . two . . . one . . .*

WHAM!

"It's going to be a long-ass ride. Bye, bro."

Anson removed the pillow. "Hey, Doc, on your way out, please blow out all those damn candles."

"You want a kidney too or you good?" Hunter asked.

"Drive careful," he said, before covering his face again.

Anson awakened with a start. He checked the time on the cable box. Two hours had passed in what seemed the blink of an eye. Hunter and Kyra were halfway to Atlanta—if not farther, depending on how much Kyra's anger motivated his brother.

Anson yawned. He was exhausted still, but he reached for his cell phone and dialed Mona.

"Hello," Mona said, her voice husky and low.

"You asleep?" he asked.

"Yeah, I finally dozed off a little while ago," she said. "I just got a lot on my mind."

"I started to drive back to your place just to check on you, but I fell asleep," he admitted, picking up the remote to tap lightly against the top of the bed.

"Anson," she said, her tone chiding him.

"Not on that level. Just to hold you and tell you everything will be okay," he said.

She didn't say anything.

"I hated to leave you earlier, but I had to come home and handle some things."

"I bet you did."

Anson stopped his tapping. "Oh man, come on. Not like that."

"I believe you," she said, the sound of a smile in her voice. "But it's handled?"

Anson smiled. "She and Hunter are two hours outside Atlanta by now."

"Awwwww," Mona sighed, obviously sarcastic.

He chuckled. "I should have handled it sooner to avoid hurting her feelings," he disclosed.

They fell silent. It was comfortable.

"Do you really think you could sleep by me and do nothing?" Mona asked.

"Wouldn't be easy, but yes . . . yes, I could."

"I don't believe you."

"Could you?" he asked.

"It would be hard."

"As hard as you had *it* earlier?" he asked, allowing himself to replay the wonders of her mouth against his and down below.

She laughed softly. "See? Sex on the brain."

"Okay, what's the last book you read?" Anson asked.

"Aesop Fables."

"Really?" he asked, sounding doubtful.

"Yes. I was cleaning out a box from my childhood, flipped through some pages reminiscing, messed around, and got caught up."

Anson climbed off the bed and limped to the bathroom to relieve himself.

"Your bathroom echoes," she said.

"What do you hear?"

"Lots and lots of pee."

He laughed as he quickly flushed and then washed his hands.

"Don't wash them just because I'm on the phone."

"You might be right," he said, removing his clothing and limping back into the bedroom completely nude.

He wanted a shower, but he wasn't willing to get off the phone with Mona to do it. Flinging back the covers, he lay down on his bed and positioned his pillows to elevate his wrist and foot. "I'll be glad when these casts come off," he said, enjoying the feel of the cool and crisp cotton sheets against his brown skin. "You really do owe me big time, Miss Ballinger."

"You turned down my offer to pay your medical bills and to match you up with someone."

"Does the offer for a match still stand?" he asked, baiting her.

"Uh . . . no," Mona stressed.

He turned off the bedside lamp. "Why not? You and Hunter are getting hitched," he said, lying there with just the light of the moon streaming through the windows.

"Not funny, Anson."

He chuckled. "I kid. I kid."

"I know you're new to frivolity and humor, but your funny bone needs some strength."

He just laughed.

They fell silent again.

Anson glanced at the clock, surprised that they had been on the phone for nearly twenty minutes. The time had slipped by with such ease.

"Does the offer for a sexless sleepover still stand?"

Anson looked over to the doorway at the sound of Mona's voice. She stood there with the doorknob in one hand and her phone still pressed to her ear. He hadn't even heard the bedroom door open.

He thought the vision he saw—light streaming in from one of the sconces of the hallway framing her in the bulky pajamas and fluffy slippers—was one of the most delectable sights ever. "Of course," he finally said, sitting his phone on the bedside table and then patting the bed beside him.

Mona kicked off the slippers and came around the length of the king-sized bed to climb up onto it on her knees. "I shouldn't be here, Anson," she whispered down to him.

Even with just a portion of her features peeking through the shadows, he could see the conflict on her face. He reached up and stroked her jawline with his thumb.

"I couldn't stay away," she confessed, pressing her face against his warm hand.

He pulled her down beside him, loving the feel of her face against his chest. He hated that she lay above the covers and he was beneath them, but with her obvious reservations and his nudity, he knew it was for the best.

He pressed a kiss to the top of her head, feeling her long lashes brush against his chest as she closed her eyes. Soon her body rose and fell with the deep breathing of slumber.

Anson could hardly believe that even though he'd known her such a short time, her lying there in his bed—in his life—seemed so comfortable. So reasonable. So necessary.

Chapter 10

Mona looked out the window of the taxicab at the landscape of Baton Rouge, Louisiana. It wasn't New Orleans, where her parents had settled, but years ago her family had traveled the eighty miles to Baton Rouge almost weekly to visit with her father's sisters, so it felt just as much like home. "Thanks for coming with me," she said, not taking her eyes off the changing scenery.

A hand very similar to her own grasped hers tightly. Comfortingly. "We'll get this all figured out, Mo. I promise," Reeba said.

Mona smiled and let her head rest on the back of the seat. "If the twins can't figure it out, no one can."

"O-kay? Hey there, bye there," Reeba said, lightly teasing their aunts' odd salutations.

"I wish Shara could come."

"Me too."

They both fell silent and looked out the windows at the familiar landscapes of the city. But Mona's mind was on Anson . . . and Hunter. She was in

Louisiana looking for a resolution to feeling connected to one brother while believing she was destined to be with the other.

Early that morning as Anson snored in his sleep, she lay there with his arms still around her body, her head on his chest, not wanting to get up. And she waited for the moment that laying there next to his body didn't feel so necessary. But the longer she relished being near him, the more she felt conflicted by it all.

So she forced herself to leave his warmth, wrote him a note, and quietly left his home. Two hours later she and Reeba were boarding an airplane at the Charleston International Airport headed to Baton Rouge.

"What did the aunts say when you told them we were coming?" Reeba asked.

Mona twisted one of her curls around her pinky. "I didn't," she said.

Reeba shook her head. "No one loves surprises but you and Mama. You know the aunts hate that."

"Yes, *but* . . . they love us, so it will all be fine as wine. Right?" Mona asked as an afterthought.

"Chile, please. I'm laying that at your door—keep me out of it."

They had long since left behind the bustling downtown area of Baton Rouge for the more sedate surroundings outside the city limits. Mona sat up as they reached the Iberville Parish, just south of Baton Rouge. Here there were plantations that once housed slaves. Some were in ruins. Others now served as historical landmarks open for tours or were converted to inns.

That was not the case for the Toussaint-Guilliame House.

With just two floors, it was small in comparison to the more noted neighboring plantations, but it was just as grand in its Greek Revival architecture. Slaves had once dwelled and even helped to build the small mansion for its owner. Those slaves' descendants had taken ownership of the property years ago when the original family fell to ruins and couldn't afford to pay the property taxes. The story of the role reversal of her great-great grandparents, Tomas Toussaint and his wife, Aimee Guilliame-Toussaint, was a point of pride in their family and a story they would continue to pass on to future generations.

"You forget how beautiful it is," Mona said, as they pulled up the long drive lined with oak trees.

Most of the land surrounding the home had been sold to pay off bad debts long before her great-great grandfather had purchased it, but it didn't matter. It was the owning of the home his ancestors had built that was the feather in his cap.

The cab pulled to a stop on the stone-paved drive. Mona quickly paid and tipped the driver before she climbed out of the car behind her sister. Even as she waited for the driver to pull their luggage from the trunk and sit it on the ground, Mona's eyes kept going to the house. She was surprised by how good it felt to be there.

Pulling their luggage behind them, Mona and Reeba climbed the stairs. The doors opened before they could reach the top step. Both their aunts filled the doorway. Reeba rushed ahead to be embraced by them. Mona hung back, struck by how much they resembled her father. She released a breath, hoping to ease the pain of missing him.

"Hey there, Miss Modern Day Cupid," one of them said with a toothy smile, her accent as thick as molasses.

They were tall and thin and regal even in the "Welcome to Louisiana" T-shirts they wore with black leggings and brightly colored sneakers. Their soft silver hair surrounded their heads like halos. Seventy never looked so good.

Mona stepped up and hugged each one, burying her face in their neck and enjoying the scent of whatever they were brewing in the kitchen—be it food or a home remedy. "Didn't know I missed you two so much," she admitted, blinking away tears.

One of them swatted her hip. "Shouldn't take no man trouble to get you home, but you're here, so come on and get this gumbo we promised you."

Mona stiffened. As the twins turned to enter the foyer, she stopped her sister from entering the house. "Did you tell them about Anson?" she whispered.

"Tell them what? I didn't know anything until today, remember?" Reeba said, looking slightly offended.

They shared a long look and, as they pulled their suitcases into the house, Mona saw her aunts share a long look as well. Her forehead was still creased with curiosity as they made their way to the same bedrooms on the second floor that they'd slept in during their overnight stays with their parents. The windows were wide open and the bed made.

Mona set her carry-on bag on the leather luggage rack by the door and picked up the sprig of leaves on the pillow. She didn't need to smell them to know they were from the lemon groves. Sitting on the bench at the foot of the four-poster bed was a small sweetgrass basket filled with all the citrusy home-made products her aunts knew she loved, and even a box filled with her favorite lemon tea.

"What the hell is up?"

Mona turned to find Reeba strolling into her room holding a sprig of lavender—her favorite scent. "I know," she said, drawing it out as she widened her eyes and held up her own pillow treat.

"Are they running a bed and bath and we don't know about it?" Reeba asked, poking in Mona's basket.

Mona swatted her hand away.

"Girls, come down," one of the aunts called up.

Mona took a deep inhalation of the scent of the leaves before setting them in the basket. "I'ma tell ya, I'm a little freaked out," she admitted as they strolled from the room and moved down the long hall to the steps. "Are they psychic now?"

Reeba shrugged and pressed her face into her lavender. "I don't know, but I needed those soaps and creams, so either way I'm *so* good."

"Me too. Their last care package of stuff just ran out," Mona said as they crossed the foyer with its black and white tiled floors. They followed the long hall to the kitchen at the rear of the house.

"Could you two hurry? I'm starving."

"Ooooooooh shit," Mona and Reeba exclaimed in unison at the sight of their baby sister, Shara, lean-ing in the entryway to the kitchen.

All three rushed toward each other and hugged as they jumped up and down excitedly.

"When did you get here?"

"How long are you staying?"

"How was Dubai?"

"Did you get you some while you were traveling?"

Shara ran her hands over her short cropped hair before holding them up at her sisters. "No more questions. My head is about to burst and you're firing them at me like crazy."

"You're right," Mona said, her eyes bright and excited as she soaked in her little sister, whom she hadn't laid eyes on in months.

"It's so good to see you, Ra-ra," Reeba added.

"I feel tears . . . y'all know what that means," Mona said, bouncing her shoulders and snapping her fingers.

"Boogie break," Reeba and Shara said in unison.

The three sisters danced around the hall with one another as they did the same steps they did when they were just little girls.

"Hey there, ladies."

All three paused midsnake motion and looked over to find one of their aunts motioning for them.

Laughing, they headed into the kitchen.

Mona paused when Shara sat down at the round wooden table in front of a place setting with a small net of dried apple slices beside it. She didn't doubt something similar had been on her pillow when she arrived.

"I'm just glad I listened to the aunts and came for a last-minute visit this week, because otherwise I would have missed you guys," Shara said. "I didn't even know y'all were coming too. No wonder they asked me not to tell y'all."

"Oh they did, did they?" Mona said, giving both her aunts a look filled with suspicion as they all took their seat at the table.

"What?" they both said innocently, before sharing another look.

They all held hands and Shara said grace before Reeba opened the Crock-Pot lid to the gumbo and began filling everyone's bowl once they were passed to her.

Both Mona's body and her heart were happy and felt blessed to be in the company of her sisters and her aunts, but her mind was elsewhere. On someone else.

I wonder what he thought of my letter. . . .

"'Dear Anson. Thank you so much for being the shoulder—or is it the chest?—for me to lie on,'" Anson read aloud for the tenth time that day. "'I'm heading back to Louisiana to visit my aunts. Hopefully they will guide me through this, because I can't do it on my own. It's funny how it's barely been two weeks since you've been in my life and I will miss the hell out of you.'"

Ditto.

Waking up to find she was gone had been such a surprising letdown for him.

"Hey, boss man. You busy?"

Anson swiveled in his drafting chair to find Malik standing in the doorway of his office.

"I went by Modern Day Cupid, but it was closed, so I just came back here."

Anson nodded. "Yeah, I should have called you about that. Mona's out of town indefinitely," he said, still holding the folded note in his hand.

"I hope everything's okay," Malik said, his face concerned.

Me too.

"Yeah, I'm sure it is," he said, turning back around to look down at the letter.

"Let me get to work."

Anson dropped the letter and turned again, careful of his foot. "Hey, Malik," he called. The office manager stepped back into the doorway. "What do you think of all that matchmaking business?"

"As a business model or personally?" Malik asked, leaning back against the door.

"Both."

"To respect her privacy—as I assume you understand—she really has a good thing going. Very profitable. And I have to admit I like the way she goes about doing the matches. Very detailed. Very thoughtful," he said. "Thinking about signing up myself."

Anson was stunned and it showed.

Malik laughed with a shrug before he saluted Anson and headed to his own office.

Anson reached for the note and used his index finger to unfold it.

"'I hope you will understand and respect my wishes not to call. I need the distance and the time to clear my head. Not running from you—just trying to deal with my innate desire to run to you. Mona,'" he finished, tracing his thumb over the ink of her words and feeling connected to her.

Closing the letter, he tapped it against his chin as he stared out the window at a light rain falling down. It was perfect lie-in-bed weather. Whether cuddling or making love—he preferred the latter. And he could imagine how steam would rise from their bodies if he was to make love to Mona outside in the rain.

The image of her holding her breasts with her nipples poking through her fingers might have been just as hot as seeing her coming out of the pool naked. *Maybe. Close. No. Nah. No way.*

Buzzzzzz.

He picked up the remote for his intercom system and pointed it over his shoulder before he hit the button. "Yes, Greta," he said, calling over to the machine on the corner of his desk.

"You asked me to remind you of your appointment with your accountant."

Anson glanced at his gold watch. "Thanks, Greta," he said, rising to his feet.

Anson was a suit and tie man, but in the wake of his broken foot he had to settle for a shirt and pants. He was okay with splitting the seam on a few pairs so that they would fit over his cast. He cranked his car with the automatic start button on the remote and picked up his briefcase before leaving the office. During the short drive, he fingered his phone, fighting the urge to call Mona. He really just wanted to hear her voice.

"Not running from you—just trying to deal with my innate desire to run to you."

Parking his car in front of the renovated brick house, he made his way up the stairs and hobbled through the door, a smile spreading across his face to see the wife of his accountant. "Another receptionist bit the dust, Jade?" he asked as the chocolate beauty with brown hair rolled back her seat and stood up.

"You know it," she said, her hand pressed to the swell of her belly.

He bent to kiss her cheek. "You're pregnant! Congratulations."

"Finally," she said, her eyes beaming. "I told Kaeden that if we had to go through one more round of in vitro fertilization, we'd have to go get one of those beautiful African babies like all the white Hollywood celebrities."

"How far along?" he asked.

"Just four months."

Anson turned to see Kaeden Strong walk through the door of his private office. He came to stand behind his wife, pressing a kiss to her neck as he palmed her belly.

"I think it's gonna be another big old strapping Strong boy to grow up into a big old strapping hard-headed man," she said.

Anson pursed his lips and laughed as he thought of each of the Strong brothers, all broad shouldered, solid, and well over six feet too—at least. They were built for the farmwork they did. And even Kaeden, who he knew hated the outdoors, had the same build.

"Hardheaded?" Kaeden balked.

"I didn't mean it," Jade said, looking up at him with love as she leaned against him in the way a woman does when she knows her man has her back.

Anson watched them. There was no denying the love between the two. Their marriage was more than companionship and breeding offspring. It was all of those things under the umbrella of love.

He and Carina had never shared that type of intensity . . . and never would. Their bond had been forced. A charade that imploded.

"You ready to get these taxes done?" Kaeden asked.

Anson nodded. "Yeah. Let's do it," he said, giving Jade one last smile before following her husband into his office.

Kaeden took his seat in front of the bay window overlooking the front yard and street outside. "I really just need your receipts to go through," he said.

"Got them all ready," Anson said, handing him a folder.

"You or Greta?" Kaeden asked, slightly loosening the paisley tie he wore with a pale gray shirt.

"Well, I pay Greta . . . so same difference."

"Right, right."

Knock-knock.

Both men looked at the door. Jade's head was peeking in.

"Yeah, baby," Kaeden said.

"Before you guys get started I wanted to make sure Anson and Carina got their invite to Kaitlyn and Quint's wedding," she said.

Anson shifted uncomfortably. "I got it, but Carina and I are no longer engaged," he said.

Kaeden looked up from the receipts he was flipping through. "Man, I didn't know that."

Jade looked pained. "Are you okay?" she asked.

He nodded. "It was for the best."

Jade stepped into the room belly first. "Well, if you want my opinion—"

"Jade." Kaeden's voice was filled with censure.

Anson glanced from one to the other. "What?" he asked, looking at her.

He and Jade both ignored Kaeden, who was clearing his throat behind Anson.

"You two didn't seem that happy," Jade said, walking up to Anson with one hand on her hip. "Anytime I saw you together you looked as miserable as Kanye and Kim."

"Jade . . ." Kaeden began.

"I never saw any passion between you two," she said. "You know?"

Anson actually chuckled. "I need someone to bring out the lighter side of me. To take the proverbial stick out of my ass."

Jade held up her hands. "*Well*, if you want to be honest . . ."

"Baby, the phone is ringing," Kaeden said, obviously lying.

Anson laughed. "You're the second person to tell me," he said to Jade, thinking of Mona.

"Well, my mother-in-law always says 'the truth don't hurt and lies don't work,'" Jade said.

"I agree."

"So you'll be at the wedding?" she asked, turning to head back to her office.

"And miss seeing Kaitlyn Strong tied down? Never. But don't tell her I said that," he added.

"Love can change people," Jade said, then blew a kiss to Kaeden over her shoulder.

Real love can.
He surprised himself with that thought.

Sitting on the swing under the large oak tree, Mona could clearly remember the day her parents and her aunts had sat her and her sisters down to tell them about their gift. She had been pushing her mother and sisters in the swing when their father walked out to the yard to retrieve them.

Nothing about that talk could have prepared her for the quandary she was in. Nothing they said had prepared her for this possibility.

"Hey, there. You ready to talk?" Aunt Millie called from the porch.

Mona only knew them apart because one wore small diamond hoop earrings and the other wore studs.

"Yes, ma'am," she said, picking up her iPad case as she rose to her feet to cross the large yard.

She entered the house through the rear door leading right into the kitchen, the center of the old servants' quarters. Walking through the empty kitchen, she followed the voices into the sitting room off the foyer. They all looked up when she entered the room. She laughed a little to see a bevy of snacks on the table, including homemade lemon bars.

Kicking off her shoes, she tossed her iPad on the sofa beside Reeba as she sat on the floor directly in front of the loaded coffee table. "So y'all know it's serious then, right?" she said dryly before picking up two lemon bars—one for each hand.

"So what you want to know?" Aunt Millie asked.

"You sure you two don't already know?" she asked, thinking they did.

With her mouth full, and not caring, Mona told them of everything from her first encounter with Anson up until the night she slept in his bed. She only left out the X-rated parts. *A woman's got to have some business of her own not to share.*

"Anything ever happen to you like that, Shara?" Mona asked once she was done with her story and the lemon bars. "You ever run up on someone you just couldn't get a vision on?"

Shara shook her head as she loudly bit down on a mouthful of Doritos.

"Hunter, as nice-looking a man and future successful doctor that he is, does absolutely nothing for me, while his brother—his arrogant, bullheaded, reserved, slightly uptight brother—is just . . ."

She closed her eyes and shook her head as she licked her lips with a little moan in the back of her throat.

"Damn. Is it like that, sis?" Shara asked.

Mona opened her eyes just as Reeba passed Shara her phone. "What's that?" she asked.

"A picture of Anson I got off his Facebook account," Reeba said.

"Really, Reeba? Really?" Mona said, exasperated.

Shara held the phone close. "Oh. Okay. I get it. Oh, I *get* it," she said with a vigorous nodding of her head. "Yup."

"I was curious what he looked like," Reeba said, handing the phone to Aunt Winnie.

Mona eyed the phone. "I wanna see the picture,"

she said, as the aunts' heads came together to peer down onto the screen.

"Oh, we get it too," Aunt Millie said.

"Ladies, can we focus?" Mona said, rising up on her knees to reach across the table and pluck the phone out of her aunts' clutches. She sat back as she enlarged the photo of Anson smiling in a tailored three-piece suit that fit his strong physique.

Mona smiled and stroked his photo with her thumb. *I wonder what he's doing. . . .*

"You're in love," one of the aunts said.

Mona looked up to find four sets of eyes on her. She shook her head. "No, not love, not yet. But I like him. I like him a lot," she admitted, reaching for the iPad in its sleeve and pulling out her sketches. "He sketched these of me from memory. He hadn't seen me in a like a week and he drew this like I was in his mind the whole time. So yeah, I like him a lot."

Reeba reached for the four sketches on four squares of what looked to be parchment paper. "Wow," she said, obviously impressed.

The Ballinger women all passed the sketches. The aunts held on to them.

"Stories have been passed down through the generations of our family," Aunt Millie said, glancing over at her sister, who sat next to her on a love seat.

"Stories to make you laugh, make you cry, and make you wonder," Aunt Winnie added. "And stories to make you realize that this gift we all have been blessed with is ever changing."

Mona sat the phone on the table as she and her sisters paid attention.

"We've always believed and been taught to believe

that the reason we can't see our own love or that of our family members is because too much knowledge can be . . . confusing."

"And in our seventy years we have learned that what happens to us was meant to be, and sometimes you just have to take the highs and lows to get where God wants you to be."

The three sisters all nodded.

"So we have a new story," Aunt Millie said, leaning over slightly to touch her shoulder to her sister's.

"Of a young, beautiful girl who is completely ignoring all the signs that she has met her soul mate," Aunt Winnie added.

"Hunter?" Mona asked, her eyes troubled.

The aunts rolled their eyes. "You can't see the forest for the trees, baby girl," Aunt Millie said.

The aunts tsked at her. "When life is giving you all this newness, why would you continue to think of things the same way?" Aunt Winnie asked.

"Right," Aunt Winnie chimed in.

"First she gets a vision to go help Anson—something that has never happened before," Reeba said, sitting up straight as her face filled with the light of clarity.

"Hey there," the aunts said by way of agreement.

"Then she can't get a read on Anson—another first," Shara added, looking to the aunts for their approval.

"Right," they said.

All eyes turned to Mona.

Mona's eyes searched all of theirs. "Then I have a vision about myself when I touched Hunter and that means I'm his soul mate. So . . ."

"Change the way you think of things."

"God is trying to tell you something," Reeba sang under her breath.

"O-*kay*," Shara added.

They reached across the table and softly high-fived.

"You ever think that you're dancing with the brother of the groom . . . and not the groom?" Aunt Winnie asked.

Mona's heart raced, but her brain reigned. "But that doesn't make sense, because why wouldn't I see whomever Hunter's soul mate is if it's not me but I'm in the vision."

Shara and Reeba shared a look before looking at the aunts. "She's got a point, aunties," Reeba said.

Aunt Millie picked up her glass of lemonade and sipped. "Neither did you having premonitions of Anson getting hurt make sense, or that you were the one to hurt him."

"Besides, maybe you were so focused on you that you missed his soul mate in the vision, because maybe it's not your story to tell," Aunt Winnie said.

Mona thought of the brief vision. There had been people surrounding Hunter—plenty of women—but she couldn't recall specific faces in the short space of time . . . except her sisters standing there in their bridesmaid's gowns.

"Ooooh," she said in sudden understanding, looking from Reeba to Shara.

"So the vision wasn't about me," she said.

"Right," the aunts agreed.

Hunter was the soul mate of one of her sisters, but she held on to that revelation. It was not her story to tell. But the fact that Anson was her soul mate and future husband was.

"Anson," she gasped, her chest filling with happiness.

"Anson, Anson, Anson," her sisters teased her.

Aunt Winnie smiled. "Spirit has a way of giving just enough . . ."

"But not too much," Aunt Millie finished.

Mona picked up Reeba's phone and swiped the screen to look at the man she was meant to spend the rest of her life with.

Chapter 11

"Well, lookey-lookey," Reeba said, mimicking Sheneneh from the still popular nineties sitcom *Martin*.

Mona's heart raced. "Take my car," she said, her eyes locked on Anson sitting on her porch as her sister parked behind his BMW in her drive.

Reeba had driven from the airport where they had left Mona's car parked while they were away. She pulled to a stop on the road at the end of the driveway. "I'll meet my future brother-in-law another time," she said. "Don't want to ruin the reunion."

"Good girl," Mona said, climbing out of the car with her tote and not even bothering with her luggage still in the trunk.

Anson rose to his feet and smiled at her as Mona came down the drive. She had barely made it around his car before he took long strides to pick her up.

She wrapped her legs and arms around him as he captured her mouth with a kiss. At first soft and sweet. Then deep and passionate.

"Hey, stranger," Anson said after one last taste of her mouth.

"Hey," Mona said, resting her forehead lightly on his.

"Awwwww."

Mona looked over her shoulder, whipping Anson in the face with her hair, to see her sister still sitting there with the passenger window down, all in their business.

"That's my sister," Mona said, motioning with her head for Reeba to leave.

"Hello," Anson said from beneath the cover of her hair.

"Have fun, y'all," Reeba said, before pulling away with a small *toot* of the horn.

Mona shook her head.

Anson laughed and sat her down on her feet. "I'm glad you're back finally," he stressed, reaching over to tug at the hem of the white shirt she wore with flare-legged jeans and red flats. "Did you work everything out? What was the result?"

Mona reached up to touch his cheek. "It was . . . revealing," she said lightly.

Anson turned and caught her hand. "Mona, you've been gone for over a week. You said don't call. I didn't. You text to say you'll be home tonight and you'll call when you get here. Well, I'm here. I'm waiting. I want to know what's going on."

What a mighty fine husband he will be.

She shifted past him and jogged up the few steps to unlock the door.

"Mona, do you want me to go? Are we gonna talk

about this? Is it over before it began? What's going on?" he said behind her.

Pushing the door open, she leaned against it and beckoned him with a bend of her finger. "Come make love to me, Anson Tyler," she said softly, before she began to unbutton her shirt as she entered the house. She turned on the lights in the house as she moved through it.

Mona barely made it a few steps into her bedroom before she felt the air of the door being closed and then Anson's arms around her, pulling her body back against his. She gasped and raised her arms to massage his shoulders and neck as he planted hot kisses along the side of her face. Then he pressed his hands against her belly and drew them up to cup her breasts in the red lace brassiere she wore.

"Mona," he said deeply.

She arched her back as his fingers lightly stroked her nipples. She lowered the demicups. "Yes, Anson," she sighed, as she floated on the waves he created.

He lifted her up from behind and lowered one hand to undo the button of her jeans before working them down her hips and thighs to fall to the floor.

She bent her legs, locking each foot behind his thighs as he dragged his fingers across the red lace of her low-slung bikini before pulling it to the side to massage her plump mound. His middle finger stroked her throbbing clit. The combination of his touches on her nipple and her clit made Mona shiver and cry out as she lay her head back on his shoulder.

"Look, Mona. In the mirror," he whispered against her neck.

She raised her head as he turned so that they faced

the wide, full-length mirror braced against the wall next to her closet door. "Looks good," she admitted in a soft voice.

In her face she could clearly see the desire he stoked in her. Her eyes were half closed with her curly hair gone wild and surrounding their faces. She looked on as he continued to touch her. Stroke her. Tease her. Never had she felt so sexy than she did in that moment. And knowing their future, believing in what was meant to be, she felt a heightened sense of their passion. The love to come.

She blinked away emotional tears and lowered her hands to cover each of his, gripping them as he pleasured her.

He added the deep sucking of her neck right where her pulse pounded and she felt dizzy with desire for him, arching her hips in tiny moves against his ingenious fingers. "Damn," he swore.

With her eyes locked on them in the mirror, Mona gently broke his hold on her and slid to the floor to move around him. She brought her hands from behind him to pull his sleeveless T-shirt over his head, exposing the sexy contours of his body. Tracing the grooves of his abs to reach the rims of the red basketball shorts and black boxers he wore, she hitched one side down to expose first one hip. Then the other. Then the first soft tendrils of jet black hair. Then the bush surrounding the thick base of his dick.

Looking around him at his reflection, she moaned in the back of her throat and licked her lips as one last jerk brought the shorts down, momentarily caught on his erection, before falling to his thighs. She wrapped both hands around his hardness and smiled wickedly as he dropped his head back and released a deep groan from well within him.

She felt his buttocks clench and release as he thrust his hips forward, sending his dick sliding inside the sheath she created with her hands. It was sexy as shit and she was mesmerized as she watched his reflection and enjoyed the feel of her taut nipples lightly touching his strong back.

Mona brought her hands down to massage the smooth and shiny tip with her thumb as she pulled downward on him. Milking him.

He bit his bottom lip and grimaced in sweet pleasure. "You gonna make me nut," he admitted thickly.

"I don't want that," she said huskily, reluctantly freeing him. "Not yet."

She came back around him.

They looked at each other intently. An unseen energy floated around them. Pulsed between them. Left them breathless.

Slowly they reached for each other and at the points where fingers met flesh there were tiny shocks like static. They both moaned as they held each other close and enjoyed the feel of their warm bodies pressed together. Her softness to his hardness.

"Kiss me," he demanded softly.

Mona rose up on her toes and offered him her mouth as her eyes drifted closed.

The uniting of their lips and tongues was passion and fire and the perfect expression of everything they both felt in that moment. Slow and sensual. It was profound. It was deep. It was more than the physical. It seemed even beyond the spiritual. It was everything. All things.

Anson's heart pounded in his chest and his body was tingling with so much awareness that he was dizzy. But he didn't want it to stop. Never would he want it to stop.

Slowly massaging the sides of her plush breasts and then her hips, he brought his hand around to knead her soft buttocks with his fingertips as she sucked the tip of his tongue. His dick hardened against where it was sandwiched between their bellies. He was consumed with a need to be inside her. Deeply.

He backed up until he felt the bed against the back of his thighs. Turning, he lowered her onto the bed under the weight of his body as she stroked his back and buttocks while she spread her legs wide. He shifted down to suck one nipple into his mouth as he stroked her thigh and eased one leg up on the crook of his bent arm. Using his hips he guided his dick to her core, sliding it across her slickly wet clit as he looked down into her face, enjoying the way she freely displayed her passion. "I want you, Mona," he said thickly, seconds before he reclaimed her mouth and plunged his dick inside her with one swift thrust of his hips.

They both broke their kiss and gasped in the intimate space between their open mouths. They looked at each other before they kissed again, just as Anson began to stroke deep within her, loving the feel of her walls tightly grasping him as he tried to ease every inch of himself within her until the soft hairs surrounding his shaft touched her clean-shaven mound.

He worshipped her body with his thrusts and his words as he dug his hands into her hair and gripped the curls tightly to tilt her head back and expose the length of her smooth neck to his bites, his licks, and his kisses.

Mona dug her fingers into his buttocks and worked her hips in perfect unison with him as she cried out from the feel of his tongue against her tongue. It pounded wildly, echoing the beat of her heart. "Anson," she cried out with each thrust that united them until she couldn't know where he began and she ended.

It was perfection. Complete and total perfection.

She reached for his face and held it tightly in her grasp as she lifted her head to hotly lick at his lips like a cat to milk. "You surprised me," she said in the heat between them. "I wanted to come to you."

Anson's eyes glazed over as he looked down at her intently. "Just come for me," he said thickly.

Mona gasped and nodded as his thrusts deepened and he sped up just enough to make her do just that. She cried out and arched her back as she came for him endlessly. She knew when his body stiffened as he fought to stroke through his own release that she was not falling through the bliss alone.

Neither had felt so much chemistry and passion in their lives. Never. And in that moment they both knew that what they'd experienced was a fusion created by just them. Their synergy. Never to be replicated or duplicated with anyone.

Mona lay on her belly on the bed as Anson sat and drew soft circles across her buttocks and back. She turned her head to press a kiss to the side of his buttocks before closing her eyes again with a smile. In the hour that had passed they said nothing. Nothing was needed. The silence and the afterglow of what they just shared was enough. They were pleased. They were sated. They were together.

That was all. And it was enough.

Mona bit Anson's bottom lip as she rode his dick slowly and with purpose as they swung on her front porch naked as the day they were born. It was three in the morning and while they both hoped no car happened by on the secluded road, neither cared in that moment. Not one damn bit.

Anson lay there with Mona's body atop his as she slept. He stroked her hair and pulled the sheet up higher on her body. She lightly snored in her sleep and that made him chuckle. And in the moment just before he joined her in sleep, he placed a kiss to her forehead and slid his good hand on her lower back in that deep curve just before her bottom flourished into the soft mounds that were pure perfection to him.

The shower spray beat against his head and strong back from his spot kneeling with plastic sleeves protecting his injuries. He held Mona's lips open and licked at her clit with the tip of his tongue with her leg up on his shoulder exposing her sweet pleasure to him. He sucked it deeply between his lips and loved the jerk of her hips against his mouth. He didn't let up and soon she was quivering and giving his tongue and lips its own shower.

Mona eyed Anson as she sat across from him in her kitchen in nothing but a T-shirt and her fluffy slippers with her hair still damply curled from their shower. She playfully licked her tongue out at him as he took a sip of coffee with his eyes locked on her above the rim. She used her foot to kick and loosen the knot holding the towel around his waist. It opened and exposed his now limp tool lying across his thigh looking as exhausted as it should after the night they shared.

He caught her foot and lifted it high to sit on his shoulder as he kissed her calf.

Mona pressed her free foot onto the edge of the chair and spread her leg, exposing her core to him with a slow arch of her eyebrow. Never breaking their stare, she reached down and dragged her middle finger up the length of her core and then sucked it.

Anson swiped her foot from his shoulder and stood up, bringing his now erect dick to her eye level.

Bringing her buttocks to the edge of the chair with her eyebrow still arched, she opened her mouth wide and covered the tip of him with her lips.

Mona looked over at Anson sitting on the other end of her sofa and smiled at his head tilted back with his mouth wide open as he slept. They both had decided to get dressed and get some work done, but the papers in his slackening grip were about to hit the floor and his iPad was teetering as well.

Pushing her bright pink spectacles up atop her hair, she eased up off the couch and plucked his papers and iPad from him and put them on the ottoman beside his briefcase. She sat back down and lifted his injured foot up onto the couch beside her. He shifted in his sleep with a soft smack of his lips.

With a shake of her head, she knocked her specs down on her nose with her index finger and went back to work.

Bzzzzz.

Mona and Anson both reached for their iPhones from where they sat at the island, now in his kitchen, dining on the grilled lamb chops and salad he made for their dinner.

They paused and eyed each other.

Bzzzzzz.

They both drew their hand away and continued with their dinner, completely lost in their own little world.

The images from *Love and Basketball* on the hundred-foot screen of Anson's media room illuminated their naked bodies as he and Mona paid the movie no mind. Anson sat on the floor with his legs open wide as Mona sat astride him backward with her legs atop his. Her upper body bent to the floor in the space between his legs. As she circled her hips in a slow motion he gripped her hair, pulling her head back.

The movie ended, casting them in darkness, but they had only just begun.

"Back to the real world," Anson said as he stroked the tendrils at Mona's nape before pressing a kiss to her forehead.

Mona tugged on his blazer where she held it with her arms wrapped around him. "I'll see you at five, Anson," she said. They had ridden to Walterboro together.

Someone cleared his throat.

They both looked over at Malik walking up to them. He waited by the locked door to the offices of Modern Day Cupid trying not to look surprised to see them together.

"Welcome back, Miss Ballinger," he said. "Morning, boss man."

They both smiled and shared one last kiss that deepened with ease.

Mona reached out her arm and let the keys dangle from her fingers.

Malik wordlessly took them.

The smoke alarms wailed as Mona sat the pan of what was supposed to be seared fish on the butcher block of her kitchen counter. The smoke was thick and pungent and the fish was as black as midnight with no moon. She fanned it with her oven mitt and rushed to open the back door and the window over the sink.

The alarm was unrelenting.

Anson limped into the kitchen and reached up to remove the cover of the alarm and pull the battery free before he turned to walk back out. "Pizza will be here in a few," he said over his shoulder.

"In a few? But I just burned this," she said to his back.

"I called time of death on that fish ten minutes ago, babe."

She tossed the oven mitt at the back of his head and punched the air in victory when it hit him squarely.

"See, isn't it fun being naked for no reason at all?" Mona asked as she strolled from the bar with her glass of wine in one hand and his snifter of brandy in the other.

Anson eyed her from his spot in his favorite leather recliner. "I can make it even more fun in less than a five count. Please believe me," he said with bravado.

She gave him his drink with a jiggle of her boob and then turned to give him a wiggle of her buttocks before reclaiming her seat on the sofa to watch the evening news.

"Big bro, I'm home," Hunter called out.

"Oh, shit," Anson and Mona swore in unison.

"Don't you believe in throws?" Mona asked, frantically looking around the room as she covered her breasts with one arm and the V between her thighs with the other.

Anson limped over to shield her with his body. He didn't make it there fast enough.

"Where you at, bro?" Hunter called just before he stood in the doorway.

His eyes widened and he turned around. "So . . . *that* just happened," he said dryly. "Let's . . . uh . . . let's not let it happen again."

They remained frozen in place as Hunter left them alone.

"Umm, Mona, you and your sisters . . . do you look alike everywhere?" he called back into the room.

"Hunter," Anson snapped.

"Sorry, bro. But that *was* a compliment," he called.

Mona giggled and Anson glared at her.

She knew Naked Day was suspended indefinitely.

Mona sighed and sank down deeper beneath the depth of the scented bath water until her chin was covered in bubbles. "This last week with you has been amazing," she sighed as he massaged her feet where they sat in his lap on the other side of the claw-foot whirlpool tub as he draped his cast-covered foot over the side.

"I agree," he said, tilting his head to the side to eye a small tattoo of a heart on her inner ankle. "How many tattoos do you have?"

"Just three," she said, wiggling her foot for him to continue his spoiling. "Why?"

"I just discovered the last one I haven't seen," he said.

They fell silent.

"Is this gonna last?" she asked suddenly, opening her eyes to gaze across the short span at him. "I mean, is it always going to be nice and fuzzy and cozy?"

"As long as we want it to," he said, meeting her stare.

"Promise me we will work to keep it like this," she said.

"I promise."

She eased her foot from his grasp and lifted her legs high in the air before opening them to bend each one over the edge of the tub. Gripping the sides, she slid forward between his legs. She gasped as he sought and found her sweet center beneath the bubbles. Letting her head drift back, her grip on the tub tightened as he slid his middle finger inside her and twisted his hand to stroke her sides with it. "One more," she gasped hotly, spreading her legs wider as he slid another finger inside her and stroked her G-spot.

She freed one hand from the tub to grip the back of his neck as she leaned forward to suck his bottom lip. "That shit feels so good," she swore in a hot whisper.

"You like it?" he asked.

She nodded and licked her bottom lip.

"You love it?"

"Yes," she gasped, closing her eyes.

Anson grabbed both her legs and put them on his shoulders before he lifted her by her ass and slid her down onto his dick to surround him tightly. He smiled before he took a breath and slid down under the water, straightening his body and causing the final few inches of his dick to rise into her.

Mona gasped and gripped the tub as she rode him like he was her lifeline. Back and forth with a steady one-two thrust that was hot. Back and forth. Back and forth. Faster and faster as she felt her nut rising. Beneath the water he sucked at her nipples and grabbed her buttocks with his good hand to slam her down against him, sending water carelessly splashing over the sides. She lost it completely.

Hoarsely crying out, she pounded the tub with her fist as she came with a thunderous force that made her fear she wouldn't make it through it alive.

He emerged from the water, sending it over the sides, as he rested his head back against the edge of the tub and cried out with his own release.

Spent and exhausted, Mona fought through her sex fatigue and repositioned herself to ride him until he was soft inside her.

"Just like this?" she asked, referring to her earlier question.

"I promise," he swore, barely able to speak.

"Good. Damn good. Whew."

Chapter 12

Four weeks later

Anson pulled to a stop at the gas station on the main road in Holtsville, parking in front of the small store. "You want something?" he asked Mona, who was still deep into her work on her iPad even though it was Saturday and they were headed to a wedding.

"Lord, do I miss Malik," she said, glancing over at Anson from the passenger seat.

"I thought you liked the young lady you hired to assist you," Anson said.

"She's no Malik," she said, picking up her cell phone.

Anson chuckled as he climbed from the car and entered the store. "Afternoon, Cyrus," he called to the grizzly old man behind the counter on a stool in front of the register.

"Afternoon," he called back.

Anson grabbed a bottle of orange juice and a banana nut muffin as he usually did every morning on his way to work. Their shower that morning had quickly switched from a hygienic necessity to a freak fest and they were running too far behind to eat before they left his house. He was almost to the counter when he backtracked and picked up the same for Mona. She had a bad habit of denying his offer to get her something but then asking for some of his.

"You're not going to Kaitlyn Strong's wedding, Cy?" Anson asked as he set his items on the counter.

"Nope," he said. "I figured there would be some extra traffic in little old Holtsville, so I decided to stay open and offer my services to the attendees if need be."

"A businessman," Anson said.

"That's all for you, Anson?" Cyrus asked, leaning forward to use one arthritic finger to hit the keys on the outdated cash register.

Anson nodded, waiting patiently out of respect for his elder and because Cyrus Dobbs was an institution in Holtsville. He was as much a part of the fabric of the small southern town as the man who originally settled it back in the early 1800s. For as long as Anson could remember, Cyrus had worked at the little store. First as the gas attendant and in time he became the owner. It was through his hard work that he sent his lone son to college. He had plenty to be proud of, and Anson respected the old man and his homespun wisdom immensely.

He would never forget when he was eighteen and his little hunk of junk truck overheated as he passed through the small town from neighboring Summerville, where he had been looking for a second job. Out of frustration he had filled the old man in on that day's woes. Cyrus helped him fix his truck and guided him to the Jamison brothers to look for work.

"Glad to see your foot done healed," Cyrus said, accepting Anson's cash and handing him his change.

"I'm a brand-new man," Anson said.

"I don't know about all that," Cyrus said, his teeth far too bright and big to be real.

Anson chuckled.

"Give this to that pretty girl of yours," the old man said, rising from the stool to pick up one of a dozen different carved wooden figures sitting in the window.

Anson accepted the winged cupid, amazed that the carving was so detailed even with Cyrus's hands suffering from arthritis.

"Don't get jealous," Cyrus said with a laugh.

"You think you can steal my girl, old man?" Anson asked as he picked up the plastic bag holding his items.

Cyrus shrugged one shoulder and winked.

Leaving the store, Anson walked over to the passenger side.

Mona held the cell phone from her face and lowered the window.

"Got something for you," he said, glancing back at Cyrus looking at them through the window with a mischievous twinkle in his ebony eyes.

"Oh, I'm not hungry," she said, eyeing the bag he held.

Anson extended his hand and opened it to reveal the wooden cupid.

"Let me call you back, Reeba," she said, before

ending her call and reaching to pluck the figure from his hand.

"Compliments of Cyrus," Anson said.

"Awwwww," she said, opening the car door and nearly hitting Anson with it as she climbed out.

He followed her back inside the store.

Cyrus's smile was already big, and toothy, and smug as hell.

"Thank you so much, Mr. Cyrus," she said, going behind the counter to kiss his cheek and then hug him close.

Anson just shook his head as the old man winked at him. "You are *so* welcome," Cyrus said.

Mona continued to study it as she gave Cyrus one last kiss to his cheek and made her way out of the store. "Isn't Mr. Cyrus just the cutest thing?" she asked Anson before she left the store.

Cyrus held up two gnarled fingers. "Two kisses *and* a hug from *your* woman," he bragged, chuckling.

"One of these days the men around here are going to get tired of you trying to steal our women with that big smile and those figurines," Anson joked, pushing the door open.

"If that's all it takes, then y'all got other"—he cleared his throat—"*things* to worry about."

With one last wave and a laugh, Anson left the store.

"It's a beautiful day for a wedding," Mona said as they walked inside the elaborately decorated sanctuary of Holtsville Baptist Church.

"Yeah, it's a nice day out," Anson said as they took a seat on a middle pew.

"You'd think you would be in a better mood with the cast off," she said to him as she smiled and waved at people she knew.

He crossed his leg and motioned down at his foot, showing her how well it was working by circling it in his handmade leather shoes.

Mona pretended to applaud before looking around at the elaborate floral arrangements transforming the church. She loved how although it was mid-May, the colors were not soft and light colors, but deep and rich plums that matched the stained glass windows, wooden pews and floors, and the carpet runner down the aisle. "They really went all out with the decorations," she said, eyeing the altar covered in fresh flowers and the small round arrangement of flowers dangling from the end of each pew with a thick satin ribbon.

"I wouldn't expect anything less for the Strong family's only daughter," he said. "*Especially* Kaitlyn."

Mona nodded. Since her move back to Holtsville she was kind of in her own bubble, but her sister Reeba had filled her in on the family of wealthy ranchers. She was now well-equipped with plenty of backstory. *Well, as much as Reeba knew from the outside peering in.*

She just needed to put faces to the names. A fun little game of match-up to keep her mind occupied while watching the wedding of people she didn't know from a can of paint.

She spotted four men whose hair was flecked with silver and who all shared rugged good looks and she knew these were the Strong brothers. They all sat in one row, each of the four with a beautiful woman by his side. *Well, Reeba was right—they are fine.*

She just couldn't tell which was which. Not that it mattered. The juiciest thing Reeba gave up about each one was how much they loved their wives. No drama. No scandals. No breakups. No whispers of affairs or thirsty side chicks.

Mona continued to look around the church.

"I wonder if this many people will come to our wedding," she said almost to herself as the music began to play.

"Say what?" Anson asked, leaning over to hear her more clearly as the pianist began to play.

The aunts had forewarned Mona to keep her mouth shut and not to tell Anson about how she was interpreting her visions. She bit her lip and shifted her eyes left and right. "I meant, you know, *if* we work out and if . . . you know, *if* we . . . *if* we get married," she stumbled.

The double doors at the back of the church opened and they turned in their pew as the members of the wedding party began to enter. Throughout the ceremony, Mona found herself looking at Anson's handsome profile. The couple's words of devotion, trust, commitment, and most importantly love touched upon everything she'd ever wanted for herself. And now that she knew with whom she wanted to share her future, she wanted them all the more.

She reached for Anson's hand and clasped it within her own as the groom raised the veil and kissed his bride.

* * *

Anson chuckled into his glass of champagne as he watched Mona continue to stare at Chloe across the room as if she was one of the seven wonders of the world. He leaned over to her. "Close your mouth, baby," he whispered into her ear before returning to his own conversation with Devon and Deshawn about their ideas for the design of their new corporate headquarters to be stationed in Charleston.

"Oh, shit," he heard her swear beside him.

He looked to see Chloe and Anika making their way over to their husbands. When he saw Mona digging her iPhone out of her bag, he lightly touched her wrist and subtly shook his head.

He knew one of the things the former supermodel loved about her return to her mother's hometown was that once the townspeople got over such a huge celebrity moving to their small city, they gave her privacy and let her blend in without hounding her for photos and autographs.

The Chloe Bolton she was today was known around Holtsville as someone who could cook her ass off and always won the most prizes at the annual fair. They respected Chloe Bolton the celebrity, but they had come to love Chloe Jamison the down-home girl. And that's just what she wanted after her semi-retirement nearly fifteen years ago.

"Excuse me, folks," Anson said, turning to their wives. "I want to introduce you both to my date, Mona Ballinger. Mona, this is Chloe and Anika."

"Nice to meet you," they both said with warm smiles, extending their hands.

He swallowed back his annoyance when Mona accepted each woman's hand, closing her eyes as she did. It was just for a second or two and not long enough for anyone to notice, but he *knew* she just did her little love vision thingy.

"I hope you don't mind, but we came to get our husbands to hit the dance floor," Anika said.

"Enjoy yourselves," Mona said, no longer starstruck. "The band is really good."

They watched as the couples began to slow dance to the band's rendition of "Be without You" by Mary J. Blige.

"Question," he said as soon as they were alone.

"Sure," Mona said, swaying to the music and snapping her fingers.

"Let's just say I actually believed this whole premonition thing. Isn't it a little intrusive to doublecheck if married folks are with their soul mates?" he asked, doing the air quotes.

She squinted her eyes as she looked at him. "Really with the air quotes?" she asked, arching a brow. "Is it the return of the infamous stick?"

She moved around him to lift the hem of his blazer.

Anson brushed her hands away.

"If you don't believe it how can you be annoyed about it, Mr. Contradiction?" Mona asked.

She had a point.

"Not feeling so nice and fuzzy and cozy," she said with a pout. She wrapped her arms around his waist and pressed the same pouting lips to his jawline to kiss him there.

Anson stiffened his body as he felt his annoyance with her fading fast.

She lifted up on her toes. "Maybe I need to get you back in the tub and help you remember your promise while you scuba dive again," she whispered in his ear before softly biting the lobe.

Mona leaned back and winked at him as she fought not to smile.

"Next time *you* go underwater," he said, his stance softening as he brought his hands up to grasp her waist.

"Oh, my," she said saucily as she backed him onto the dance floor as "Drunk in Love," by Beyoncé, started up.

"Surfboard . . . surfboard," they sang together, laughing as he twirled her on the dance floor.

"Is that Anson Tyler *dancing?*" Chloe said to Anika.

Anika instantly found him on the floor with her eyes, and her mouth gaped. "Lawd, quit," she said softly in surprise as they watched him raise his hand and twirl his date.

"Ladies," Devon said. He and Deshawn were looking at their wives, both men ready to go back out on the dance floor.

"So he found the right one, huh?" Chloe said, happy for the teenaged boy who once worked for their husbands, who grew into an educated, well-groomed, successful man who now worked *with* them.

Devon and Deshawn shared a look as their wives continued to speculate on Anson's love life.

"Be right back," Devon said.

"I don't know her. Do you?" Anika asked.

"No," Chloe said.

"Pretty as all get-out though," Chloe said.

"Reminds me of myself . . . a few years ago," Anika said.

"Just a few?" Chloe asked.

They grabbed each other's hands and laughed.

The band began to play "Dance with My Father" and Kael Strong led his daughter onto the dance floor for their dance.

Chloe glanced over her shoulder and did a double take. "Awww, look, Nik," she sighed.

Across the room Devon and Deshawn both bowed at the waist. The ladies looked on as Devon and Chloe's fifteen-year-old daughter, Nia, and Deshawn and Anika's ten-year-old daughter, Lillian, sweetly curtsied before they took their father's offered hands and began dancing as well.

"Nia is such a daddy's girl," Chloe said softly. "I really love that she has the type of loving and concerned father that I always wanted for myself growing up."

Anika hugged her friend to her side, knowing she needed it in that moment. "And look at my little lady. Deshawn got hell on his hands with that feisty little thing."

"Hmph. She got it honest," Chloe said, with a playful side-eye.

Anika just laughed, unable to disagree.

"Wanna dance, Ma?"

Anika looked up to find her fourteen-year-old son, Tyson, standing beside her. "Yes," she said, taking his hand and gliding out onto the dance floor.

"Aunt Chloe?" Tyree, Tyson's identical twin, asked with a big grin.

She let him lead her onto the dance floor, thinking the sight of all of them was just the type of scenario Devon's deceased grandmother, their beloved Nana Lil, would love to be around.

Chloe could swear she detected the scent of Nana Lil's favorite lilac perfume, and she knew she was there with them in spirit.

Mona walked over to where Anson sat as she waved the bridal bouquet that she'd caught among all the single ladies. He smiled at her, having learned over their time together that she was competitive. He was just thankful no one caught an elbow because she blocked them out like they were balling.

"Congrats, baby," he said, as she sat down beside him and lifted the bouquet to her face to inhale its sweet fragrance.

"And my God, that smells so good," she said, placing the flowers near his face.

"Whatever that scent is on your skin smells better," he said after a quick sniff.

"It's citrus. My aunts make each of us our bath and body products in our favorite scent, and mine is citrus," she said.

"Remind me to thank them," he said, leaning over to nuzzle his face against her neck.

She smiled and leaned into his affection as she

settled her hand on his thigh. "They look so happy," she said as she watched the bride and groom slow dancing to "Lately" by Tyrese.

With a final kiss to her neck, Anson lifted his head and looked at the couple in the center of the dance floor. "Yeah, they do," he said. "I'm really happy for Kaitlyn."

"*And* they're soul mates," she added.

Anson stiffened and shifted away from their bodies touching, reached for his glass of champagne and took a healthy sip. What Mona failed to understand in her need to stick to the concept of "real love" were the seeds she planted in him on her sincerity in their relationship.

"You about ready to go?" he said, rising to his feet.

Most of the wedding attendees had begun to leave with just the close family left behind to enjoy the last of the good times.

She looked surprised, but she rose to her feet as well. "I'm ready if you're ready," she said, reaching out to squeeze his hand.

He looked down at the move and clenched his teeth before he freed his hand to walk away.

He felt Mona grab his elbow and stopped.

"What's the matter?" she asked, her eyes filled with concern.

"Nothing," he lied, capturing her hand in his and gently tugging her to follow him out of the tent.

"Anson, you didn't even say good-bye or thank them for the invite," she said, almost running to catch up with his long stride.

"I was raised by addicts, not wolves," he said. "I don't need etiquette lessons, Mona."

She jerked her hand free.

Anson turned by the passenger door of his car.

"What crawled up your ass just that quick?" she snapped.

"Besides the stick you mean," he said, turning back to reach for the door handle.

Mona rushed ahead and brushed away his hand to open the door for herself. Her face was tight as she slid in the passenger seat and closed the door.

Anson grimaced as he came around the car to climb behind the wheel.

Mona's arms were crossed over her chest and she looked out the window as if he didn't exist. Her stance was angry, but she couldn't hide the hurt she felt from brimming in her eyes.

He started the car and they left the Strong family ranch and headed across Holtsville. His eyes kept falling on her even as he drove, and she remained like stone, not even fully sitting back against the seat, as if just being in the car was an offense to her.

Mona completely lived in the moment and flourished in whatever emotion reigned, Anson reflected. When she was happy, she was really happy. When she was mad, she was extremely mad. *And when she's sexy, she's phenomenally sexy.*

"Dinner was a few hours ago," he said, reaching to clasp her hand. "You want to stop at Donnie's and pick up something to eat?"

Mona jerked her hand away and turned her head

to eye him hard before she purposefully looked away and focused her stare back out the window.

Anson stopped in the middle of the main street running through the center of Holtsville. Cars blew their horns before speeding to drive around him.

Mona was still a virtual statue.

He put the car in park and left it to stride around the front. He jerked the passenger door open and squatted down beside her. "I'm sorry," he said, even though the seeds planted were growing, flourishing, and making him feel some kind of way.

She remained stone faced even as she twisted her cocktail ring around her index finger.

"Get out," he said, rising to his feet.

Mona eyed him. "If you think I'm walking home—"

Anson reached in for her hand. "Get out," he repeated, tugging gently.

"You better take me home where you got me from," she said with a sister girl movement of the head.

Anson stooped and scooped her out of the car and set her on her feet.

"Oh, no the hell—"

He pressed her body against the side of the car and captured her lips and the rest of her angry words with his mouth.

She jerked her head back and eyed him as several cars driving past them slowed down to check out the sidewalk PDA. Small southern towns were infamously nosey. "*What* are you doing?"

"Being spontaneous," he said, trying to bring levity.

She shook her head. "After just being an asshole for no reason?" she asked.

"Kiss me," he said, wanting to wipe away the doubts that had been growing in his mind.

She shook her head again. "Not your lips *or* your ass," she said.

Anson lightly gripped her face and planted kisses along her jawline, chin, and mouth until he felt the stiffness leave her body. "Kiss me," he whispered against her mouth.

Mona captured his mouth with her own this time as she brought her hands up to clutch his lapels.

He moaned as she slowly sucked his tongue between her lips and teased the tip with her own.

"Get a room," someone yelled from the window of a car passing by.

"You in a better mood now?" she asked, after jerking back her head to break the kiss.

He loved that her eyes were glassy with desire and her lips were extra plump from the pressure of his mouth. He could feel the pounding of her heart echoing his own. He knew without a doubt that Mona Ballinger desired him. He knew that.

It wasn't their sex that worried him.

"If you believe in this notion of 'the one,' soul mates, a love that is meant to be, and you don't see a vision of that for me . . . then why are you with me?" he asked, giving voice to his doubts.

As Mona reached up to stroke his face Anson stepped back from her. "What are we doing? What is *this?* If you believe so deeply in your gift—and you prove that day in and day out with your words—then why are you with me? Hell, you were touching on every damn body at the reception like a love investigator or some shit. But I thought you decided to be with me because your belief had changed and all that mattered was that you wanted to be with me. But if you still believe all of that, if you still can have these premonitions or whatever the hell they are, then what is *this?*" he asked, as he motioned back and forth in the space between them.

Mona looked away from him and he could see conflict in her eyes. He just didn't know the base of her struggle. "Anson," she said.

No other words came.

"Are you still believing you're really meant to be with my brother?" he asked.

"No, but—"

"But?" he repeated.

Mona bit her bottom lip. "You, Anson Tyler, are my soul mate. You are the person who was created just to love me like I was created to love you. You are the man I have the greatest love for. You are 'the one' for me," she said with conviction.

Anson looked exasperated instead of pleased.

"I couldn't see a vision of the woman who is your soul mate because *I'm* the woman. *I'm* her. *I'm* the one. *I'm* the love of your life. I will be your wife. I will have your babies. And I will love you even beyond the day one of us dies. Me. *I'm* it for you."

The surety in her words and in her face literally shook him to the core. It would be hard not to be affected by such impassioned words. But these thoughts, these doubts were new or foreign to him. "And do you believe that in your heart or in your brain?"

She looked confused.

"Do you believe all of that because it's what you want or because you believe it's what you're supposed to want?" he asked, his eyes pinned on her, searching her face, looking for the truth he sought.

Mona covered her face with her hands. "Anson, why are you making this *so* complicated when it is truly the easiest thing ever?" she asked, her voice rising.

He looked down at the ground as he gathered his thoughts. "And if your trip to your aunts had revealed that Hunter was the man for you . . . what then? Would you feel the same right now in *this* moment?"

Mona winced and shook her head. "You're jumbling things. That's why I shouldn't have told you," she said, bending her body to sit sideways on the passenger seat of the car as she hung her head.

"I'm not jumbling a damn thing, Mona, and you know it," Anson said, his voice low. "See, I'm in this because I want to be."

"And you think I don't?" she asked, raising her head to look up at him.

"If your aunts said Hunter was 'the one,' then you would have left me alone, right?" he asked.

Mona's eyes filled with tears. "Why are you doing this? Why are you taking something so good and pissing on it, Anson?" she asked. "Everything in life is not a hustle, it's not a battle, and it's not all bad.

Some things are just easy. And you have to get over your past. The struggle is over, and not just because you have money and a big house and a fancy car."

Anson felt a sting of pain from her words. Her judgment.

"Stop living life waiting for the other shoe to drop," she said.

"You don't know about my past," he said, his voice cold and hard and as unrelenting as he felt.

He checked the street for oncoming traffic and walked back around the car to climb in the driver's seat. It was his turn for his face to be like stone as he waited for her to turn her body forward on the passenger seat and close the door. He accelerated forward, quickly checking the rearview mirror before he made the right turn that would lead them to the section of Holtsville where they lived.

She attempted to talk to him as he drove, but Anson had completely shut down on her and had nothing to say. Not yet. He needed time.

He turned onto her driveway and sat there with the car running.

"You're not coming in?" she asked.

"I need to think about my past and you need to think about shaping your life based on visions of the future," he said.

"Anson—"

"When you asked me to give you space while you were in Louisiana I respected that," he said, avoiding looking at her.

"Okay," she said, her voice calm. "We'll get through this."

He snorted in derision. "Why, because we want to, or because you had a vision?" he snapped.

Mona climbed out from the car and closed the door.

He waited for her to unlock her door and enter her house before he reversed his vehicle onto the road and sped off.

Chapter 13

One week later

"Hey, sis."

Mona looked up from the monthly billings report to find Reeba walking through the door. She removed her glasses and dropped her ink pen. "Reeba Ballinger in all her wonderful glory is actually inside the office of Modern Day Cupid," Mona said teasingly as she came from around the desk to hug her sister with one arm.

Reeba pushed her long straight hair behind her ears, revealing diamond hoops as she looked around the space. "I guess I should check everything out since hell froze and I am in here," she joked.

Mona laughed, sliding her hands down the length of the fuchsia pencil skirt she wore with a crisp white shirt and a turquoise statement necklace. "What do you think?" she asked.

"I think Cyrus should be selling these carvings," Reeba said, picking up the wooden cupid sitting on Mona's desk.

"And?" Mona urged, honestly wanting her sister's feedback.

"Honestly?" Reeba asked, looking pretty in a fitted white tee and wide legged peach linen pants that showed she had a little more hips and buttocks than her older sister. "I love this red and white decor against the wood floors. It's really well laid out, and although I still have my opinions on it, I'm happy and proud of you."

Mona threw her hands in the air like she was in worship service. "Lord Jesus, hell has frozen over," she said.

Reeba walked over to the lounge area and sat on the red leather sofa. "So, how are you?" she asked.

Mona looked taken aback at Reeba's obvious concern. "I'm good. Why? What's wrong?" she asked, sitting next to her.

Reeba leaned back a little and eyed her sister. "Did you not call me last Saturday crying and whining about you and Anson having a big fight?" she asked.

Mona crossed her legs and smoothed her hands over her knees. "Okay, first of all I wasn't whining," she began.

Reeba nodded. "No, you were crying *and* whining," she insisted.

Mona puckered her brows. "An-y-way," she said pointedly, "I was in the moment. I was in my feelings, *Braxton Family Values* style, and I wasn't clearly thinking. I needed to vent so I called my little sister," she explained.

"And now?" Reeba asked.

"I just had to remind myself that Anson and I are

in the cards. We are a definite thing. We are soul mates. He just needs time to adjust and that will happen. You and I both know that," Mona said.

"You may very well be the case study for why it's not best to know the bigger plan," Reeba said. "And why did you tell him? Was I not sitting there when the aunts told you to stop with the oversharing?"

"Because he was questioning my intentions after my struggle with the vision about his brother, Hunter," Mona explained.

"Which you also overshared and kicked this whole I Need to Tell Anson Everything tour off," Reeba reminded her.

"True," Mona agreed begrudgingly. "But it is what it is, and what it is is—"

"Girl, huh?" Reeba asked with a pained expression and an eye roll.

"I am in the middle of a real romance novel right now," Mona said, her eyes bright with happiness.

"Say what now?" Reeba asked.

"Have you ever read a romance novel where there wasn't a happily-ever-after?" Mona asked. "The readers know going in that the hero will win that heroine and they are just along for the ups and downs of the ride. That's me. This is our romance novel with all the ups and downs of the ride to our *guaranteed* happily-ever-after."

"Why does that make sense to me?" Reeba wailed before she pinched the bridge of her nose.

Mona shrugged and smiled. In the words of Lil Wayne: "I ain't got *no* worries."

* * *

Anson removed his construction hat and climbed behind the wheel of the pickup truck he used to visit work sites. He tossed it onto the passenger seat as he pulled away from the construction of a new restaurant in Walterboro. He couldn't stifle the yawn that rose. He was exhausted.

Between the standard constant churn of work, the new ventures with the Jamison twins, and his lack of sleep at night because his thoughts were filled with Mona—missing her, annoyed with her, wanting her, wanting to avoid her—he had never stared at a ceiling so much in his life.

He knew they had to talk eventually, and although she had abided by his request and had refrained from contacting him, he knew there was no way Mona was going to let the lack of communication go for much longer.

He just wanted her to understand his point of view and not diminish it by deflecting on parts of his life she knew nothing about. As much as she felt her gift and her beliefs on love mattered, he was standing strong in his point of view having importance as well.

Instead of heading back to the office, Anson decided to go home. He planned to take a swim, warm up some leftovers, and veg out on the couch to let his mind and body relax.

His issues with Mona would just have to wait one more day.

Bzzzzzz. Bzzzzzz. Bzzzzzz.

Anson picked up his cell phone from the dash. Looking at the screen, he was surprised to see

Carina's number displayed. "What the hell?" he muttered, his thumb floating over the button to answer the call. *What does she want?*

"Hello," he said, turning on the speakerphone.

"Hello, stranger," she said. "Are you home? I wanted to ask you about something."

He frowned. "No, I'm not. Just ask me."

"I'd prefer in person."

"That's not feasible," he said, checking the rear-view mirror to switch lanes as he passed a car making a turn into the parking lot of a Dollar General.

"Our last talk didn't end well and we both said some things—"

"Aren't you seeing someone?" he inserted, not in the mood for the games most women played. The games he knew Carina played.

Not Mona.

"Oh, aren't you?" she asked.

"Carina—"

"Listen, I'm having regrets. Okay? There, I said it. Things just are not panning out like I thought and I'm having regrets," she admitted.

"I'm sorry to hear that and even sorrier to tell you the best thing you did for the both of us was end it, Carina," he said without any doubts.

"You're not missing this good-good?" she asked in a soft voice, referring to the nickname he gave their sex.

"No, I'm not," he said as gently as he could.

"Damn, she's *that* good?"

Yes.

And he missed it. He missed her, bad.

"Don't be crass, Carina," he said, making the left onto Highway 17A, which led directly into Holtsville.

"No, crass is advising a woman to leave her man so she can scoop him up," she said with a bit of a bite to her tone. "*That's* crass."

And there's the truth of her motivation for this call.

"So you know?"

"Damn right I know, and I *don't* like it."

"So your plan was to get back with me just to get back at her?" he asked, with a shake of his head. *Nothing but games. Sick, childish, petty-ass games.*

And to think he argued with Mona and blamed her for losing Carina. *Shit, she did me a favor.*

"And what?" Carina asked.

"And I'm not up for being used no matter what you're offering as bait to catch me," he said, insulted at her ploy. "Have a good life, Carina."

Beep.

Anson pulled onto the side of the road out of the way of traffic and blocked her number to cease any further phone calls or text messages from her. "Just crazy," he muttered, tossing the phone on the dash before checking the side mirror to safely pull back onto the road.

He was glad when he finally pulled the truck to a stop in front of his house. He left the vehicle and jogged up the stairs, kicking off his construction boots and leaving them by the door as he undressed. He left his clothes in a trail behind him as he made a beeline for the pool. Without breaking stride he got to the edge and dived in, enjoying the feel of the cool water against his nudity.

He forced his mind blank as his strong arms sliced the water with each stroke, traversing the pool from one end to the other. The silence beneath the water was calming and the swim therapeutic.

Pressing his feet against the bottom of the pool, he lunged upward to break through the surface and take a deep gulp of air, before falling back with his arms splayed wide. He floated with his eyes closed, just enjoying the gentle sway of the water carrying his body.

"My, my, my."

Anson shifted his body upward in the water. He looked at Mona standing on the edge of the pool just as naked as he. And she looked good.

His dick stirred to life in the water.

"A week has just made you finer, Mr. Tyler," she said, before she rose up on her toes and dived into the water beside him.

She rose up from the depths to wrap her arms around his neck and press her breasts against his strong back. "Miss me?" she asked, before kissing his neck.

"Mona," he said as she floated around his body and pushed him back against the wall.

"I really missed you, Anson," she admitted as she looked at him.

He rested one hand against her hip.

"But if you want me to go, I will go," she said. "I guess I misunderstood."

She made a move to turn from him.

Anson placed his hand on her other hip to stop

her. "What am I going to do with you?" he asked, because he truly could not bring himself to let her leave even though he fought so hard all week not to go to her.

"Right now you can just make love to me," she said softly, using one hand to cup his nape and the other to sink beneath the depths of the water to wrap around his dick.

The wrong head was in control as Anson felt himself harden in her hand. "Mona, I—"

"Shhhh," she silenced him, pulling his head to meet hers so that she could capture his mouth in a kiss. She blessed him with a few before sucking his bottom lip and then kissing him again.

"You're starting something—"

"And I'm gonna finish it," she promised him against his mouth. She rose up slightly in the water and pressed her knees back against the wall as she thrust her buttocks forward, aligning her core with his hardness.

Anson looked down as she flexed and released her core, calling for him. Wanting him. Missing him. *Shit.*

Gripping the sides of the pool's edge on either side of her, Anson used his hips to guide his hardness inside her inch by deliciously thick inch. He pursed his lips at the feel of her as her eyes glazed over and she arched her back, sending her brown nipples pointed toward the glass ceiling.

With thrusts that took power to fight against the sway of the water, Anson enjoyed filling her time and time again. He felt himself lost to time and place as they both grunted with their explosive release, fueled by seven days of wanting each other.

He stiffened and bit his bottom lip as she used her sugary walls to draw all of his seed from his dick. His tip was ultrasensitive and he knew he could hit a high note to shatter glass if he didn't keep a grip on himself.

"Now I have to drain the pool," he mused, his head resting in the sweet valley of her breasts as she held him close.

She laughed and it caused her walls to push his dick from inside her.

He swam around her and then climbed from the pool. He reached his arm down to her and when she gripped it, he helped her out of the pool with ease. "Mona, I thought I asked for some time," he said.

"And I thought you asked for the same time I did, which was a week, and that week is over today," she said.

"You hungry?" he asked, deciding they needed to be dressed for any type of serious conversation. "I'm going to warm up some leftovers."

Mona eyed him skeptically before she quickly moved past him to walk around the pool and pick up her clothes. "Do you need more time?" she asked, turning to look at him.

Anson looked up at the ceiling and then back at her. "No, because everything I felt and believed that night I still feel and still believe," he said.

She eyed him.

He could see her annoyance. He could see the words forming in her head to spill off her lips.

"Okay," she said simply. Too simply.

He eyed her. Assessed her. Tried to figure out where she was coming from.

"Carina knows about us," he said to her as she walked toward the door to the pool room.

She looked at him over her shoulder. "It wasn't a secret. Was it?" she asked, her voice unworried.

"Actually, she was pissed and wanted to steal me from you," he said, baiting her.

Mona's eyes instantly flashed, but then she forced a smile. "Really?" she said. "Well, I'm not worried about her or anybody, to be honest."

"Why?" he asked.

Mona began getting dressed. "I'm not having this same debate with you again, Anson," she said.

He walked over to the teak shelves against the wall in the middle of the rows of matching chairs. He grabbed one plush navy blue towel and covered his nakedness. His skepticism was with her confidence on the matter and how she refused to fight for her position.

"I can't believe that you don't get the fact that if your vision was interpreted by your aunts differently, then you wouldn't even want to be with me," he said. "How can you not see how that makes me feel?"

"And how can you not be thrilled with the idea that you are one of the lucky ones to connect and be with your soul mate?" she asked, now dressed in her tank and oversized denim overalls that she wore cuffed at the ankles. "How in the world could you think something bad about that?"

"You didn't answer my question," he said. "And here's another one for you. If your aunts said Hunter was 'the one,' then you would have left me alone, right?" he asked.

"Yes," she admitted.

One word spoken from her lips and he felt a pain as sharp as a knife's blade.

"And if there's another vision or the mirror ball shows you something else or someone's knee hurts or some other superstitious bullshit—then what? Then you leave me? You chuck deuces and haul ass because—oops—it wasn't meant to be?"

"That won't happen, Anson," Mona insisted.

"Just like this sudden ability to foresee your own future although you told me *that* had never happened before," he shot back at her.

"Anson—"

"I can't do this," he said, the truth of his feelings hitting him as he spoke them. "I just think we should go our separate ways."

"Okay, Anson," she said simply. Again.

He felt like she mocked him even though he knew it wasn't her intent. "Because I will get over this and we will be together because it's meant to be," he said mockingly, disturbed that she was unbothered by the breakup.

She smiled at him and nodded as she went to stand in front of him. "That's right. Listen, I'm sorry my big mouth got us into this. I really am. But you take all the time you need to let your brain wrap around it all, if that's what it takes," she said. "I'll give you all the time you want because we have the rest of our lives. Believe it or not, Anson, we *will* be together, and soon I will say 'I told you so.'"

He honestly didn't know what to feel outside of

frustrated. Part of him wanted to escort her to the porch and close the door on her and her foolish notions and another part of him wanted to kiss her.

She lifted up on her toes and leaned in to taste his mouth. She leaned back from him just before it landed. "I guess I'm not supposed to do this until we get back together?" she asked, truly doubtful. She shrugged.

"Now, during this time I will have to think about feminizing the decor around here for when I move in, because this is a bachelor pad. A big, beautiful bachelor pad made for a king . . . but not a queen. This queen. *Your* queen."

Anson was speechless.

"Which room would be good for a nursery?" she asked. "Maybe I can design that during our little break."

"Are you crazy?" Anson asked.

"Do you think I am?"

"I'm not sure," he admitted.

Mona reached for his towel and snatched it away. She slowly perused his body from head to toe. "And I do not want the dick returned to me with *any* extra miles on it," she said with the utmost seriousness.

"Maybe you should just go, Mona," he said, taking his towel from her and wrapping it around his waist again.

"I guess you're right," she said, walking out of the pool room and holding the door open for him to follow.

"You drive careful," he said, not really knowing what to say. It ranked pretty high as one of the most bizarre breakups he'd ever experienced.

On the porch she stopped to look back at him. "Just consider changing the way you think about it and the whole idea of all of this will give you goose bumps," she said.

"I'll miss you," she added, before she jogged down the stairs and climbed into the car.

She sent him one last sad smile before she drove out of his life just the way he wanted.

Then why do I miss her already?

Mona barely found the strength to knock twice on her sister's front door. As soon as the door opened, Reeba took one look at her reddened eyes and her heaving chest and spread her arms wide.

"What happened to 'I ain't got no worries'?" Reeba asked as she guided her to the sofa.

Mona flopped down and buried her head in her sister's lap. "He broke up with me," she said in between tears that fell freely. "It didn't really hit me until I was driving away, and then I realized he doesn't believe we will be together like I do. He was ready to walk away from me forever."

Reeba had a pained expression. "But you two will come through this even better and stronger on the other end," she reminded her.

"It doesn't make the road going through it any easier to handle, ReeRee," she said, closing her eyes as her sister stroked her hair and her back.

"Your life is already mapped out before you're even born, and whether you know your future or not, you have to go through every step of it to get where you're supposed to be," Reeba said. "Some of it will be blissfully good and some will be hellishly bad. You have to go through it, Mo."

"I hear you," she said, sitting up as she wiped her face with her hands.

Reeba rose and walked into the bathroom right off the living room. She came back with a box of tissues. "Feel a little better?" she asked.

Mona looked over at her. "I was . . . until it hit me that it might take thirty years for our time to come. Anson's six-pack will be a barrel and he'll probably be balding with false teeth and a broke hip."

Reeba side-eyed her. "Girl, that is so shady," she said. "Because you would still want his barrel belly, balding head, fake-teeth-wearing, broke hip self."

Mona smiled. "I sure would," she said without hesitation.

"You love him, don't you?" Reeba asked.

"With all my heart," she admitted. "Every last bit of it."

Chapter 14

One month later

"Thanks so much for coming," Mona said, shaking the hands of one of the many couples she'd invited out to a group dinner at California Dreaming in Charleston to celebrate their union.

The levels of the couples' relationships ranged from first dates up to those who had been married for several years. She was proud of each and every connection and she felt it was important to celebrate their love and her success. They went hand in hand.

"Mona, we're here."

From her spot at the top of the long stairs, she looked down at another familiar couple as they came up the steps to hug her before moving inside. At last count she was looking for two more couples, and she was determined to be the proper hostess and greet everyone outside before staff escorted them inside.

She looked up at the darkening skies and then glanced down at her diamond watch. It was a little after seven and she was starving. She turned and looked through the glass to make sure her guests were being seated. The other restaurant patrons not in her party had to be seated too, and a short line had formed outside the dining room.

"They have the best she-crab soup."

She smiled and turned at the sound of a woman's voice, but the smile faded at the sight of Anson—her Anson—and a woman who was obviously his date coming up the stairs.

He looked up and spotted her standing there watching them. His face filled with surprise and he halted his climb up the stairs as he stared up at her.

"Everything okay?" his date asked, turning to look back at him. "Did you forget something in the car?"

Mona shook her head and looked up as she released a heavy breath. *I really, really didn't need this right now.*

The last month had not been easy.

And this moment, standing there while the man she believed would one day be her husband arrived with a date, wasn't easy either. *Will he speak? Pass me by? Pretend not to know me? Give me a dap? What?*

He jogged up the steps beside his date—a sexy petite number in a bright red dress.

"Hello, Mona," he said, barely able to meet her eyes.

"Anson," she said softly, not even sure if he could hear her.

Her heart was pounding from being near him again. Seeing him again. Smelling his warm and spicy cologne again. And loving him still. Always.

This is one of the lows on the roller coaster ride to happy, Mona, she tried to tell herself.

Seeing him with another woman was not easy at all, and if she had known in advance there was a chance of this, she would have opted to miss the show.

Anson held the door open for his date. "Will you excuse me for just a moment?" he asked her.

Mona turned her head and closed her eyes as the beat of her heart kicked up another notch. In the last month her love for him had deepened while he was clearly moving on, and even though she believed it would all work out in the end, it was hard to swallow that fact.

"I'm sorry, Mona," he said as soon as they were alone.

She stiffened her spine and turned to face him. "For being on a date? For dating? Or for me seeing you?" she asked.

He hung his head. "It's not like that, Mona," he said, his eyes locked with hers.

"Oh, it's business? She's a contractor or something? That's one hell of a business dress," she said.

"No, it's not business," Anson admitted.

"Enjoy your she-crab soup and your *she-crab*, Anson," Mona said, turning away from him with an arched brow that was condemning.

When she turned back he was gone.

For a second she had the urge to run down the stairs, climb in her car, and speed away from it all, but she didn't. She pushed through. She would get through it.

Her last guests arrived and she smiled as she

greeted them and followed them inside the restaurant. "That should be everyone," she told the head wait-ress.

As Mona followed her to the rear of the restaurant where her party was seated, she spotted a flash of red and just knew it was Anson and his date at their table. She refused to look in their direction. She absolutely refused.

Anson's eyes followed Mona in the deep purple dress she wore, which clung to her body like a second skin, and he couldn't look away. He hungered not just for her body but also for the fun she had created with him. Her spontaneity. The spice.

The last month had been hell without her and although he had convinced himself that he was fine, seeing her again had brought it home that he was not. Not by a long shot.

"Is that your ex or your next?"

Anson tore his eyes away from Mona's retreating back and shifted in his chair before focusing his attention on his date, Diana Hawkins. "My ex," he admitted, before reaching for his brandy to take a sip.

"And I'm your first date after the breakup," she stated, as if it was a known fact.

"Actually, no. No, you're not," Anson said.

She looked surprised and then skeptical as she watched him over the rim of his glass. "And no one compares, right?" she asked, settling back in her chair to cross her legs.

Not a one.

"So, Anson, here's what's going to happen," Diana said with a kind smile. "I'm not up for being the rebound girl. So I'm going to enjoy my wine and you are going to ask the maitre d' to call me a cab, and this first date with the already awkward beginning *must* come to an end."

"I understand," he admitted. "But I will take you home."

"No, I don't want you to," she said. "And I will deal with Jade later for setting me up with a man who is still hung up on his ex."

"It was nice meeting you, Diana," he said, rising to his feet.

"Same to you," she said, taking her wineglass to sit at the bar.

As he walked from the table, Anson actually felt relieved. The last month of his life had been a series of first dates set up by well-meaning people convinced that a new relationship would help him get over Mona. They had all been wrong.

He did indeed ask someone to call for a cab and paid the bill for their drinks. He was halfway to the door when he turned and headed back to the rear of the restaurant, where Mona had disappeared.

She was sitting in the center seat at a long row of tables pushed together to accommodate all her guests. Her face was animated and lively as she leaned this way and that to talk to everyone. When she flung her curls back and laughed, Anson's gut clenched from wanting her so much. Missing her so much.

He looked on as she lightly tapped her glass with her fork and rose to her feet. The dress she wore was a killer. *But it still doesn't do justice to her naked body.*

"I just wanted to take this time while we are waiting for our drinks to sincerely thank you all for being here tonight. It's wonderful to sit among all this beautiful black love and take pride in the role I played in bringing together really good people who deserve to be happy," she said, looking at the faces of the couples at the table with her.

His heart skipped when she glanced up at him and then did a subtle double take. He started to retreat, but decided to remain there leaning against a pole to watch her.

Mona looked down at the glass she was holding before looking back up. "I believe in love, and in happily-ever-after, and that's what Modern Day Cupid is all about. And that's what life is all about."

She looked over at him. "Finding the one person made just to love you," she said, her eyes serious. "Flaws and all. Who wouldn't want to have that in their life?"

Anson knew the question was truly meant for him, but it also confirmed that Mona still did not understand or respect his point of view on their relationship. Allowing himself one last look at her, he turned and walked away.

One week later

Mona couldn't sleep. She tossed and turned and punched the pillow like it stole something from her, but nothing brought her comfort. Seeing Anson on that date had sent her world into a spin. Seven days later and she still hadn't recovered.

It had been a performance worthy of a reality TV show to keep a smile on her face throughout that dinner. And late that night when she was home alone in her bed, she couldn't escape assumptions of just who was in Anson's bed.

She still couldn't.

Mona sat up in the middle of the bed and flung her pillow across the room. *So he's dating. Replacing me. Forgetting me.*

The rationale that it would work out in the end could not outweigh the jealousy and anger she felt that Anson was moving on with life. For the last month her life had been Modern Day Cupid and nothing else. She made her business her focus while she waited on her personal life to pan out. That didn't stop her from missing him and wanting him and continuing to fall headfirst in love with him.

Pulling her bent legs up to her chest, she rested her head on her knees and tried to breathe through all of the emotions clawing at her. Tugging at her.

Reeba was right. It was better not knowing. Since their breakup, Mona had replayed the missteps that led to her life being in limbo. Carina walking into Modern Day Cupid for a love match was one, and her going out to search for Anson to warn him about being injured was another. She wouldn't have hit him with her car or been in his house to meet or accidentally read his brother—the start of it all. Instead fate would have led to her meeting Anson at another place and time and falling in love without this drama in the middle.

"My drama. *He's* fine," she mumbled, reaching for another pillow to throw.

It hit a picture of her and Anson during one of the better days of their relationship. She climbed off the bed and picked the frame off the floor, walking over to her bedroom window to look down at the picture by the moon's light.

It was from the day Anson and she were at lunch and he got an emergency call to one of the construction sites. She went along for the ride, and one of the workers thought the sight of her—in a construction hat that dwarfed her head while dressed in a full satin skirt, T-shirt, and heels and riding on Anson's back— was photo worthy. She agreed and had him forward the photo to her phone, which she later printed off.

She smiled sadly. *We will have these fun times again. Question is when?*

Car lights flashed into her room and Mona looked out her bedroom window to see Anson's BMW just as it stopped in front of her house. Her heart pounded as she raced from the room and across the living room to peek out the curtains.

His car was now double-parked in front of her home. Shielded by darkness, she looked on as he climbed from the car and then leaned against it as he gazed thoughtfully at her house.

Mona froze. *What's he doing? Is he going to knock? Why is he standing there?*

She caught her breath as he pushed up off the car where he had been leaning and walked down the drive. Her pulse was racing and she felt lightheaded. Every bit of anger she had about his date earlier was fading fast as she became hopeful that he would be returning to her life.

Finally.

He stopped. Beneath the yard light she could see the struggle in his face.

"Still, Anson? Really? You're *still* conflicted?" she whispered.

Mona moved to the door and reached for the handle, feeling the cool metal in her hand. She didn't turn it. She refused to beg him. He had to come on his own. He had to set things straight.

With a swoop in her shoulders she released the handle and stepped back from the door. She moved back over to the window. Disappointment slumped her shoulders lower. He was gone.

One week later

Anson picked up the floral wedding bouquet from where it hung off the corner of his drafting table. After he and Mona had argued and he dropped her off at home, she left it behind. When he found it on the floor of his car the next morning, he hadn't had the urge to throw it away nor the courage to return it to her.

For him it was a reminder of the day they were their happiest and their saddest. He smiled, remembering the look on her face after she'd caught it at the reception.

"I wonder if this many people will come to our wedding. . . . I meant, you know, if we work it out and if . . . you know, if we . . . if we get married."

"What's up, bro?"

Anson looked over his shoulder to find his brother standing in the doorway.

"I really need to get that key back from you," Anson joked.

"No haps," Hunter said, walking into the office to claim a seat on the lone sofa. "And why do you have *that?*"

Anson shrugged and hung the bouquet by the wide white ribbon back on the edge of the table. It swung and hit the leg, and several dried leaves and roses dropped off to land on the floor. "Just a reminder of what was," he said.

"You mean of what could have been . . . with Mona," Hunter added.

Anson glanced at his brother before rising to grab two beers from the small fridge near his desk. He tossed one to his brother. "I don't want to talk about her," he said, the sound of him opening the beer echoing in the air.

Hunter held his beer, but did not drink as he looked down at the unopened can. "Do you ever think about them?" he asked.

Anson took a deep sip of the ice cold beer. The serious tone of Hunter's voice was a clear clue of whom he spoke. "No," he lied, hating that familiar ache at the mere mention or thought of their parents.

"Well, I do."

Anson dropped down on the opposite end of the sofa. "And what do you think?" he asked, letting his brother's desire to dwell in the past outweigh his desire to leave it be. It was the very last conversation he wanted to have at the moment.

"That we're lucky they didn't really mess us up," Hunter said, setting the beer can on the floor by his foot. "There's a lot worse things we could turn out to be than commitment-phobes."

Anson looked pensive.

"I'm greedy about women. I see—and want—them all," Hunter admitted with a charming grin.

Anson gave him a half smile.

"And you are loyal to one at a time, but you find a way to keep them from getting too close."

Anson's smile disappeared. "And we're back to Mona, huh?" he asked, his voice dry.

"You don't think it's odd that you were engaged to a woman you admit you weren't in love with, but the one woman who made you happier than you have ever been is the one you end up running away from?" Hunter asked.

"Who said I loved Mona?"

"Are you saying you don't?"

Anson looked down at his can of beer. No other woman had ever been close to piercing the barrier he put around his heart. "So I'm wrong to want to make sure she loves me for me and not just because of some stupid vision?" he asked, confused by the tightness in his throat as he spoke his fear.

"But wasn't she feeling you before the vision?" Hunter asked. "Didn't the vision cause conflict in her because she wanted you?"

"But she admitted that if she believed the vision had continued to mean that she would be with you, then she would have left me alone," he said, swallowing over a lump in his throat.

"And you don't want that to happen again?"

Hunter said in a low voice that Anson barely heard. "Do you?"

Anson looked confused. "What are you talking about?"

Hunter just locked eyes with him and said nothing. The silence was profound.

"Look, Hunter, I'm not in the mood for amateur psychiatry," he said.

"They were our parents and they chose drugs over us," Hunter said. "They left us a long time before the state took us."

Anson closed his eyes at the memory of walking in on their mother getting high. He shook his head to clear it. He took a breath to free the pain that rose in a rush. "Leave that shit off, man," he said, rising to reclaim his seat at his drafting table.

"I think we've left it off for too long," Hunter said, rising to his feet.

"Enough, Hunter," Anson said, his voice sharp and tight with anger as he snapped the drawing pencil he held in his hand.

"You can't let what they did mess you up so bad that you're afraid—"

Anson turned in the chair and jumped to his feet to snatch at the front of Hunter's shirt. "Enough!" he roared.

Hunter locked eyes with him. "No. I love you and I appreciate you giving up so much to raise me because they wasn't shit, Anson. But I'm all grown, and the truth is the truth and I can speak it if I want."

Anson released his shirt and smoothed the wrinkles he'd created with his hand. Hunter swiped his hand away and pulled his brother close to embrace him. "I love you, bro," he said.

Anson lifted his arm to break the hold.

Hunter held him tighter. "That shit was about them, not you. Not me. Them. They didn't know how to love, but it doesn't mean that we don't *deserve* to be loved, bro."

Anson bit his bottom lip hard as myriad emotions flooded him while locked in his brother's embrace. He held his body stiff and shook his head as he fought to remain stoic.

It was hard. It was hard as hell.

Every child deserved to be loved and to feel that he was loved. He didn't get that growing up. Not at all.

His parents made him feel like he was a hindrance to their drug activity, and his various foster care mothers had made him feel like he was just in their lives for a check. He couldn't remember once being held. Not once being told he was worthy. Not once feeling loved. Not once.

Pain, anger, disappointment, grief, and frustration punched him in the gut and then radiated out across his body. Was he wrong to protect himself from the pain of rejection all over again? He felt the tears well up, but he swallowed them back as he finally twisted free of his brother's embrace. He closed his eyes as he sought and found control.

"Mona loves you. Mona wants you. And Mona is the one you should be with," Hunter said.

Anson shook his head. "I just want to be loved for me and no other reason," he said with conviction, revealing it all to his brother. "And I'm not sure that's the case with Mona. And until then? No, I won't risk my heart if she's decided to be with me based on superstitions and such. I can't."

Hunter reached out his fist to his brother for a dap. "Then I respect how you feel, big brother. I got your back. Always."

With a smile that was more sad than happy, Anson dapped his brother.

Mona strolled out on to the porch of her little cottage before she called her sister.

"Hey there."

Mona laughed at her sister imitating their aunts. "Well, hey there to you, Shara," she said. "Did I wake you?"

"No, I've been up. It's a little after ten here in Australia."

"Good, good," she said, her eyes shifting up to look at the towering pine trees surrounding her little house. The early July southern heat was thick and pressing even at night.

"Sooo . . . any sign of Anson yet?" Shara asked.

"Not yet," Mona said lightly, pulling her foot up onto the swing. "But I was thinking maybe I should be inspired by my baby sister and see some of the world before I settle down. . . ."

"And avoid seeing Anson?" Shara asked gently.

Mona rested the side of her face against her knees. "That too," she admitted softly, with a small smile.

"My hotel suite is big enough for two," Shara said.

"That's just what I wanted to hear."

* * *

Millie and Winnie sat on the swing under the huge oak tree, each with a pot on her lap. One peeled potatoes and the other shucked corn for the night's dinner.

Millie paused with her knife in the air as she closed her eyes briefly. When she looked over to her sister, she saw Winnie was doing the same. "So we gon' have some company soon, hey?" she asked with a side-eye look to her sister.

"Looks that way, sis. Looks that way," Winnie agreed with a wink.

The twins went on swinging, humming, peeling, and shucking.

Chapter 15

Mona sat on the covered balcony of their hotel suite in Perth and looked out at the rain pouring down on the large city. "No harm, sis," she called over her shoulder. "But this looks like Detroit to me."

Shara laughed as she stepped out onto the balcony and handed her a glass of champagne. "Well, I'm sorry you didn't join my expedition when I was in the Outback. There are no koalas in the city."

Mona accepted the drink and took a sip. "Who knew it was the middle of winter in Australia?" she said. "You could have told me. All of those bikinis and summer clothes are a waste."

"I'm glad you're here even if you're not," Shara said.

Mona felt bad. "I'm sorry, RaRa. I bombarded your trip and now I'm whining just one day in," she said, reaching over to playfully tweak her sister's nose.

The sisters fell into a comfortable silence as they listened to the rain beat against the building.

"You've been seeing the world since Daddy died,"

Mona began. "When are you going to settle back down again?"

Shara shrugged. "I don't know. I guess I'll be like Forrest Gump, who kept running 'til he just didn't want to run anymore."

"Are you running?" Mona asked, looking over at her above the rim of the glass.

Shara shook her head. "I'm just having fun. Daddy left us a good bit of money and I just decided to spend it doing what I want most in the world. Am I wrong for that?"

Mona shook her head. "No. I put a big chunk of it into moving my business back home. So, no, it's yours to do as you see fit," she said with honesty.

"Well, Reeba thinks I'm wasting it."

"Sometimes I think Reeba disagrees for the sake of—"

"Disagreeing," they said in unison before touching glasses in a toast.

"She needs to get some," Shara said.

"She ain't the only one," Mona said into her glass before she took another sip.

Shara made a mocking sad face. "Well, I'm getting enough for you both. While I'm seeing the world I am seeing *all of the world*," she said.

Mona looked shocked. "Don't wear it out, girl."

"And if y'all don't use it you'll dry it out," she countered.

Mona looked off at the skyline. "Anson and I had the best sex ever," she said, releasing a breath that she wished released some of the pressure built up in her. "It was just like amazing on a whole 'nother level. You know?"

Shara raised her glass in a toast. "To great sex," she said.

"But it was more than that," Mona said, feeling a shimmy of electricity chase over her body at the memory of what she shared with him. "I don't know how I could ever think that he wasn't the one for me. I didn't need a vision to know that. It was already in my heart and my soul."

"Isn't that what you told me he wanted to hear?" Shara asked. "Is that what Anson wanted you to say?"

Mona looked over at her. "Huh?"

Shara rolled her eyes. "You have to respect that he doesn't believe in our gift. And you know what? To me that's cool. He can't see what you see, and he wasn't brought up and spoon fed to understand the way it goes, Mona," she said.

"But I am the one patiently waiting—"

"For him to come around to your point of view," Shara interrupted with ease.

"So what was I supposed to do?" Mona asked, feeling her annoyance rise. "He ended it. Should I chase him?"

"No, but just a little fight for your love wouldn't hurt either."

Mona waved her empty glass in the air.

Shara playfully snatched it from her as she rose to walk back inside their luxury suite to refill it. "Have you ever told him you love him?"

"No," Mona begrudgingly admitted, taking the glass offered.

"Hmph."

Mona took a sip. A deep one.

"This ain't all on Anson, and maybe a part of your fate is fighting for your man instead of sitting around on your ass waiting for him to see it your way," Shara said. "There are two sides to a street for a reason, sis."

Mona eyed her sister as the rain continued to pour. "When you'd get to be so smart?" she asked.

Shara pretended to smoke a cigarette and flicked the imaginary ashes. "I've seen the world, darling. I've *lived*," she said in a false haughty tone.

Mona playfully rolled her eyes and they laughed.

Anson used his hand to wipe some of the sweat that soaked the neck of his tee as he and Hunter walked up Bourbon Street in the heart of the historic French Quarter in New Orleans. "I don't know how I let you talk me into this," he said.

"The Essence Music Festival is just what you need," Hunter said, turning to look at a bevy of big-boned beauties stroll by them. "Good food. Good music. Good people. Damn good time."

"If you say so," Anson grumbled, reaching in his pocket for his cell phone.

"She ain't called you, man. Put that phone up," Hunter said, taking it from him to power off. "Let's soak up the sights, eat some good food, and then rest up for the concert tonight."

Anson gave Hunter a long stare and held out his hand without saying a word.

Hunter wordlessly slid the phone back into his brother's hand.

They continued along the street infamous for its

all-night partying. The area was flooded with people, so they had to bob and weave and twist their bodies to make their way down the street. The brothers laughed at some of the drunken high jinks as they went in and out of clubs and burlesque shows, intent on soaking up the scenery.

"Palm reads for five dollars."

Anson looked at a short white woman with a hunched back in her midsixties. As soon as they made eye contact, she grabbed his hand and traced his palm with her age-spotted finger. He pulled away from her touch. "No, thank you," he said, shifting to the left to move beyond her.

She grabbed his elbow.

Anson turned to stare down at her.

"Your happiness lies with the woman still waiting on you," she said.

Anson's heart pounded and he felt like everything around him went still for a second. Shaking himself free of the fugue created by her cryptic message, he stepped back from her. "No, thank you," he said again, even as his heart continued to pound.

Hunter reached in his wallet and pulled out a crisp twenty-dollar bill to hand to her. She snatched it quicker than a swift pickpocket and licked at her thin lips as she glanced up at him with eyes as silver as her hair.

"You know she's right," he said to his brother.

"She could have guessed that," Anson said.

"Maybe," Hunter said. "Or maybe not."

Anson thought of Mona and how beautiful she looked when she flung her hair back and laughed like she didn't have a care in the world. Longing for her stung him like a deep ache.

He stopped and turned there in the middle of the bustle of Bourbon Street and his eyes searched the crowd for her. She was gone.

As the soft refrains of Robin Thicke's "4 the Rest of My Life" began to play, Anson planted kisses along Mona's jawline as he pushed the red satin gown she wore from her shoulders. She sighed and tilted her head back to gasp hotly as he dragged his fingers up the front of her thigh and then across her belly before going back to softly cup her buttocks and draw her body close to his.

"Anson," she whispered as she lifted her head to lightly lick at his lips before she blew a cool stream against them.

His entire body shivered as he captured her mouth.

She melted against him as she clasped his buttocks and arched her back.

Anson dug his fingers into her buttocks and slowly gyrated the soft flesh as he enjoyed the feel of his hard dick sandwiched between them, being stroked by both of their brown skins.

"For the rest of my life you know I wanna be yours. . . ." They both sang along with the music as he lifted her body up for her to wrap her legs around his waist.

They smiled softly and kissed again. Slowly. Deeply. Passionately.

They were lost in each other.

He walked her over to the bed in the center of the candlelit room. She purred from the feel of the red satin against her skin as he spread her legs and climbed on the bed between them. She reached her arms above her head to tightly grip the sheets as he planted kisses on one knee and then up her thigh.

The next few minutes she released sighs, soft giggles, and heated gasps as he kissed his way over her entire body, missing not one peak, not one valley, in his quest to please.

Anson lay on the bed on his side and wrapped his arm around her waist to pull her back against him. Their limbs tangled and she bent her head back on his broad shoulder as he massaged her from her knees to her shoulders with delicate twirls of her nipples that caused her clit to swell and ache.

And she was moist and ready when he used his thigh to lift her leg and guided the thick tip of his dick inside her from behind. He thrust forward with a spin of his hips that united them ever so deeply. She gripped the sheets and pulled at them. Anson bit her shoulder and winced as he fought against the explosion rising fast in him from the very feel of her.

Every stroke stoked a fire and they didn't mind the burn as they made love slowly, with no shame. Their hands were everywhere, their mouths panting and gasping. Their bodies moved in a sweet and hot unison as he continued to stroke her from behind as she met him stroke for stroke with her hips.

Mona looked back at him over her shoulder as he pulled her hair from her face so that he could look down at her as he brought his hand between her thighs to thumb her clit.

"Promise you won't leave me," he whispered
against her cheek.

"Promise you love me," she countered, her eyes
glazed with desire.

*With his hands twisted in her hair as he circled his
hips to drag his dick against her walls, Anson let all
of his feelings for her show in his eyes. "I will always
love you," he swore, his pace quickening as he felt
that sweet anxiousness at the rise of climax.*

"I will never leave you," Mona assured him just as
she closed her eyes and bit her bottom lip as her body
trembled from her core outward with her release.

Mona awakened with a gasp and looked up at the
ceiling of her room in their suite at the ski resort. She
lay there cloaked in darkness with her entire body
pulsing and alive with desire. The dream had been so
vivid and her climax so real that her clit still throbbed
between her thighs. She spread her legs a little to
relieve some of the pressure. It had all felt so real.

All of it.

"I will always love you."

His promise in the dream replayed and she rolled
on her side and curled her body as she hugged the
pillow close. It was a sad replacement for his strength
and heat.

Anson's eyes opened and he cleared his throat as
he awakened. The afternoon sun was still high and
blazing, basking his bedroom at their hotel suite in

light. After his shower he had lain across his bed hoping for a brief nap in the coolness of the room.

He'd gotten that *and* the most vivid dream of his life. He had been making love to Mona with all of the passion she evoked in him. They'd been surrounded by red satin sheets and a sexy Robin Thicke song filling the heated air.

Anson turned over onto his back and his erection stood up thick and strong. He put his forearm over his eyes as he waited for the hardness to ease.

Knock-knock.

"I'm up," Anson called out, knowing it was Hunter waking him up for them to head to the Superdome.

He sat up on the edge of the bed.

"I will never leave you," she had promised.

The words filled a need in him. But it was only a dream.

Mona sat in the lodge decked out in form-fitting ski apparel as she sipped hot chocolate blended with brandy, topped with cream whipped by hand and stacked tall as the snow-covered slopes surrounding them. The fireplace crackled and the warmth felt good near her feet after a day of skiing.

"I skied today," Mona said to herself, enjoying her adventure with her sister.

Over the rim of her cup her eyes sought out Shara and found her by the bar talking to a tall, rugged-looking blond who couldn't take his eyes off her. And Mona knew her sister well. Shara was in full flirt mode.

"Care for some company?"

Mona looked over her shoulder to find a handsome man with jet black hair and green eyes standing behind her. "Actually I'm good, but thank you," she said politely with a warm smile.

He gave a respectful nod and walked away. She allowed herself to enjoy his walk away. He was fine, but no Anson. And her body was tuned for only him.

She took another sip of the hot chocolate and lay her head back on the leather recliner. Her thoughts were never far from that dream.

"Promise you won't leave me."

"Promise you love me"

"I see you sent another one on his way," Shara said, looking like a true ski bunny in all white as she sat on the arm of the recliner next to Mona.

"I think you were right, sis," Mona said.

"About?" Shara asked, taking Mona's hot chocolate from her hands to take a sip.

"I need to go home and fight for him," she said.

Shara looked alarmed. "I didn't mean today," she said. "At least enjoy the rest of our week here at the ski resort."

"Hypocrite," Mona chided her playfully, signaling the waitress for another drink.

"I just miss my sisters," Shara admitted, gazing into the fire. "Maybe you're right too."

Mona leaned back in surprise. "You going to stop running, Forrest?" she asked.

"Yeah," she said with a nod.

Mona accepted the cup the waitress brought up to her and the two sisters toasted to that.

* * *

"Jill Scott is dope as hell," Hunter said close to Anson's ear, trying to be heard over the roar of the crowd and the music filling the Superdome.

Anson glanced up from his phone in their spot on the floor just a few rows back from the stage. "I love her music too," he said, searching through his hundreds of saved contacts,

"Huh? Uh yeah, her music is good too," Hunter said, snapping his fingers as he swayed to the music and watched Jill's every curvy movement as she strutted across the stage.

Anson found Malik's e-mail address and shot him a quick request. Although his office manager was off the clock and not at all obligated to answer him, Anson trusted he could get the info he'd requested.

"Man, get off your phone," Hunter said, reaching for it.

Anson held it away from him. "This is important," he said.

"How important?"

"Mona important," Anson said.

Hunter looked surprised. "Oh, word?"

Anson nodded as he looked around at the crowd. A lot of people were coupled up and, as much as he liked spending time with his brother, he would much rather be listening to Jill Scott with Mona by his side.

Through the rest of the concert Anson tried his best to enjoy himself, but he really just wanted to get back to the hotel, order some room service, and leave the frolicking to the rest of the visitors to the city.

As they followed the herd of people out of the Superdome, Anson checked for incoming e-mails or missed calls. He was disappointed to see he had neither.

"Excuse me, sexy."

Anson looked up as a curvy cutie in a sundress with a plunging neckline squeezed past him far closer than she really needed to be.

"He's taken," Hunter said next to him.

The woman shifted her eyes over to his brother before shifting her body that way as well.

Anson shook his head. He was not cut out for the chase of the single life. Never was. Never would be.

He kept slowly shuffling forward with everyone trying to leave the crowded venue. Hunter nudged him and held a hotel key card in his hand between his index and middle fingers. "Did she just give you that?" Anson asked, his face filled with judgment and displeasure.

Hunter nodded as he turned the key card over and showed him a gold foil Magnum condom taped to the back.

"So she just had that ready to hand out to some-body?" he asked.

"Just my type of one-night stand, bro," Hunter assured him, sliding the card and condom into his pocket as they finally exited the Superdome and weaved through the crowd to walk toward their hotel.

Back in their suite, Hunter was showering for his one-nighter at a neighboring hotel and Anson was awaiting his room service when his phone lit up.

Bzzzzzz.

He answered the phone. "What you got for me, Malik?" he said, skipping the pleasantries.

"It wasn't easy to find . . . especially this time of the night, but I got the info you wanted. I'm e-mailing it right now."

"Good. Thanks, Malik," Anson said, walking out onto the balcony.

The time had come to make a move either toward or away from Mona once and for all.

"Your destination is on the left."

Following the GPS directive, Anson made the left turn down the long drive lined with oak trees. As the home came into his view, he briefly wondered if he had the wrong address. The white two-story residence with black shutters was sizeable and grand in its design. Pulling to a stop in the rental car, he picked up his iPhone from the passenger seat and double-checked the e-mail Malik had sent him last night.

"Hey there."

Anson looked up through the windshield at two silver-haired ladies standing on the porch, one with one hand on her hip and the other waving him over. "Aunt Winnie and Aunt Millie I presume," he said, driving forward and parking.

He climbed from the car and walked up to the foot of the steps to look at them. "Good morning, ladies," he said, seeing Mona's resemblance to them and missing her all the more.

"Mighty fine, ain't he, sis?" said the one in the "Baton Rouge or Bust" T-shirt.

"Yes, yes, yes," the other said.

Anson smiled and looked down at the ground before looking back up at them.

"Come on in," one said.

"We been waiting on you."

Waiting on me? About to walk up the steps, Anson paused as he watched them go into the house.

They both noticed his hesitation and turned in the foyer to wave him in.

Chapter 16

Anson took a sip of his coffee as he sat across from Mona's aunts in the living room. One was slicing a coffee cake and the other was eyeing him with plenty of scrutiny. He couldn't help but shift uncomfortably under the gaze.

"What's you name again?" she asked, passing him the saucer with the cake as she waited for her sister to cut another piece.

"Anson. Anson Tyler," he said. "I guess you're wondering why I'm here."

The aunts shared a glance.

"Do *you* know why you're here?" the one cutting the cake asked before sitting back in her seat. She took a bite from her slice before rubbing her fingers together to free them of crumbs.

"Yes, ma'am," he said, sitting up on the edge of the sofa as he placed the coffee and saucer on the table.

The other one held up one hand and shook her head.

He closed his mouth as his eyes went from one to the other.

"You don't believe, huh?" she asked.

"Believe?" he asked.

The aunts nodded.

"It's just not my type of thing," he explained.

"It's Mona's type of thing," one said.

"And ours, too," the other added.

He nodded. "I guess I just wanted to know more about it," he said.

They both shook their heads and chuckled.

"That's not why you're here."

Each held out a hand to him. "You want to believe, eh?"

Anson eyed their hands warily. "No, I just wanted to understand more about it," he said.

Shaking their heads in unison, Millie and Winnie rose to come around opposite ends of the table to sit beside him on the couch. Each took one of his hands in theirs.

"You ready?" one asked him.

Anson felt nervous as he looked from one to the other as they closed their eyes.

"Aw, poor boy."

"Yes, yes, yes," the other said.

As each opened her eyes to look at him with pity in their depths, he freed his hands and stood up to move from between them. "Maybe it was wrong of me to come here. Mona and I aren't even together anymore—"

"You love her," the one in the print tee said with clarity.

"Yes, yes, I do," he said. "But—"

The twins chuckled. "Hey there, we not asking you, boy. We telling you," she said.

"And you deserve the love our niece has for you," the other said, rising slightly to reach for her cake. "It will make you forget all that hurt your parents poured into your soul."

Anson slid his hands into his pockets. "I think I better go," he said. "I'm sorry I came without calling. I—"

"She didn't mean it when she said she never wanted you."

He froze as he was about to walk out of the living room.

"She looks down on you from heaven."

Anson turned and eyed them; they were comfortably sitting back eating cake as if they weren't delving into his life, seeing into his life story.

"She's sorry about the cigarette burn on your wrist."

Anson felt a cold chill race over him. He looked down at his wrist and pushed back his sleeve to look at the scar still there. It was indeed a cigarette burn from when he was five or six. His mother had been so high that the cigarette fell from her lips and landed on his wrist as he sat beside her.

"You believe now?" one of them asked.

"Or you want more?" the other asked.

"Your happiness lies with the woman still waiting on you."

The palm reader. His dream. Their knowing. It was all too much.

He moved back over to the sofa and sat down on it as he eyed them.

Their eyes were loving and patient. He found comfort in that. "I don't—"

"You must," they insisted together, cutting him off gently.

"Why?" he asked.

"Because it is such a big part of Mona's life and as she gets older her gift will grow," one said. "She will be able to see things. Know things."

"Just like us," the other added.

Anson squeezed his eyes shut and pinched the bridge of his nose.

"Your happiness lies with the woman still waiting on you."

"You believe now?"

"Or you want more?"

Anson rose to his feet. "I'ma take a walk. Can I take a walk? I need to take a walk," he said, pointing toward the entryway of the living room.

"No," they both said calmly. "No running."

"Your happiness lies with the woman still waiting on you."

"You believe now?"

"Or you want more?"

"Who wants to live with someone who can see things?" he asked, almost to himself.

"It shouldn't matter, if you are where you say you are and you're doing what you say you're doing," one said.

"Hey there. Bye there," the other said by way of agreement.

They winked at each other before one rose, lightly patting his shoulder as she walked by him to leave the room.

"Your happiness lies with the woman still waiting on you."

"You believe now?"

"Or you want more?"

"I came to Louisiana with my brother. He's back in New Orleans waiting on me," he said, rising to his feet, determined to get the space he needed right then. Without it he would never find clarity.

Mona's aunt rose to her feet and came over to put her hand in his. He fought the urge to flinch away from her. "Not yet. You gon' spend some time with us and have lunch before you head back," she said, patting his hand as they strolled out of the living room.

"But—"

"Be lucky we like you," she said, her voice no nonsense.

"Yes, ma'am," he said, wondering just what the twins had in store for him.

As she and Shara sat in the airport waiting for their connecting flight to Charleston, Mona yawned. "I am dog tired," she said, shifting her body to rest her head on Shara's shoulder. "We won't get back to Holtsville 'til morning."

Shara chuckled. "You inexperienced world travelers are lightweights," she said, playing a game on her touch screen cell phone.

Bzzzzzz.

Mona dug her own cell phone from the back pocket of the jeans she wore with gold wedge sneakers. "Probably Reeba still feeling left out," she joked, turning the phone over in her palm.

"We coming home, sis. Dang," Shara said.

"Oh, shit," Mona said, looking down at Anson's handsome face on her screen. She showed it to Shara with her eyes widened in surprise.

"Answer it," she said.

Mona shook her head.

Shara rolled her eyes. "No fight, huh?"

Mona's heart was pounding.

I will always love you.

She answered the call. "Hello," she said, swallowing over a lump in her throat. *Or is it my heart?*

"Hey," he said. "I thought we needed to talk."

"I agree," she said, waving away Shara, who was trying to tilt the phone so she could listen in. "There's a lot I felt that I didn't say. Things I should have said."

The line remained quiet.

"That's right. Fight, fight, fight," Shara said in urgent whispers.

Mona closed her eyes and pressed the phone closer to her ear. "I should have told you that I loved you. That I wanted you. That you are the one for me. You are what I want."

Tap-tap-tap.

Mona glanced over at her sister tapping a pen against the back of a magazine.

"Tell him what you told me," Shara mouthed, nodding emphatically.

Mona closed her eyes, trying to remember. "I . . . I . . . I don't know how I could ever think that you weren't the one for me," she said.

Shara snapped her fingers like she was at a poetry slam.

Mona turned her back on her. "If the vision didn't

happen it wouldn't have mattered, because I already felt you were special to me. Everything between us happened so fast and that's because we're right for each other," she said, drawing her sneakered feet up onto the chair and settling her head on her knees.

"I love you and I want you and I will fight for you. You are in my heart and my soul, Anson," she admitted to him. "And I can't go another day without loving on you."

The line remained silent.

She licked her lips. "Hello. Hello. Anson?" she said, pulling the phone away from her face to look at the screen.

It was jet black.

"What happened?" Shara asked.

"My phone went dead and I didn't even realize it," Mona said, looking around for a spot to charge it.

"It's time to board," Shara said, rising to her feet and gathering things into her tote bag. "You can tell him when you get home."

Mona nodded and rose to her feet as well. "I wonder how much he heard before it cut off," she wondered aloud.

"I just hope you can remember it all," Shara said dryly.

"Me too," she said, lightly biting her bottom lip as they moved forward in the line to board.

Anson tried Mona's cell for the tenth time in the past three hours since their call dropped. And again it went straight to voice mail.

He smiled at the thought of her words.

"I love you and I want you and I will fight for you. You are in my heart and my soul, Anson. And I can't go another day without loving on you."

He had called her to begin their reconciliation and instead she had slid right in and put her heart on her sleeve for him. His heart hadn't stopped pounding during the ride back from Baton Rouge.

Dropping the phone onto the bed, he peeled off his shirt.

The door to his bedroom suite opened.

"Dude, where you been?" Hunter asked.

Anson shook his head. "I told you when you called me I got up early and rented a car to drive to Baton Rouge," he said, sitting down on the edge of his bed as he kicked off his dusty and now well-worn leather loafers.

"All day?" Hunter asked, coming over to pick up the black square wicker basket sitting on the bed.

"Man, Mona's aunts put me to work around there," he said, stretching his arms high above his head.

Hunter laughed. "Not a honey-do list," he said, lifting a bar of soap from the basket to raise to his nose.

Anson just shook his head. "Inside and out," he muttered.

"Well, I'm glad you hauled ass without me," Hunter said, picking up a jar of strawberry preserves.

"You weren't back in time for me to take you anyway," Anson said, standing up to grab the jar from his hands.

"Long nights, early mornings," Hunter said with two thumbs up.

"What's her name?" Anson asked.

"Huh?"

Anson just shook his head and walked to his adjoining bath. "Let me grab a shower and a nap and then we can enjoy our last day here before we head out in the morning. I'm ready to see Mona."

"About damn time," Hunter said over his shoulder.

And Anson agreed.

He finished undressing and climbed in the shower, still shaking his head at all the hard labor the aunts flung at him that morning. He had become their handyman. But they were adorable and so he knuckled down and proved to them that he was worthy of their niece. *Now I just have to prove it to Mona.*

Anson lathered his rag with the homemade soap from the basket of goodies they sent with him on his way—after a lunch of the best gumbo he'd ever tasted. He inhaled of the cleansing scent and washed himself.

When he had arrived there he was still a skeptic, but by the time he left and they handed him the basket already stocked full of homemade goodies and wrapped with a large black bow, he knew they had had the gift prepared before he got there. He was a believer. Not that he was comfortable with it all, but he was accepting.

Knock-knock-knock.

Anson frowned. "Man, I'll be out in a sec," he shouted, peeping his head out of the shower as he did.

Knock-knock-knock-knock.

"Hunter, stop playing, man. Damn," he roared,

glaring at the door to the bathroom as he paused with the sudsy washcloth cupped against his privates.

Knock-knock-knock-knock-knock-knock-knock-knock.

"Oh, hell no," Anson said. Stepping out of the shower and grabbing a towel to wrap around his waist, he snatched the door open. "What the hell do you—?"

Mona stood there beaming at him with a smile almost as wide as her face.

The sight of her made him lose his breath, and he stood there still sudsy and wet from his shower as he devoured her with his eyes from the top of her curly head to her gold-sneaker-covered feet.

"Hello, Anson," she said, waving her fingers at him.

"You surprised me," he said, feeling bashful.

"My aunties called my sister's phone to let me know you were in Louisiana and had just left their house and I hopped out the line and bought a ticket here to New Orleans," she explained, her face beginning to fill with concern. "I told you I didn't want to—"

"Go another day without loving on me," he finished for her, smiling and biting his lip as he looked down at her.

Her eyes opened a bit wider in surprise. "So you did hear me?" she asked.

"I did," Anson admitted. "So let me finish my shower and then I'll come and say what I have to say. Cool?"

Her eyes shifted past him to the shower and he

thought she was going to offer to join him, but instead she stepped back and nodded. "Cool," she agreed, turning to leave the room with just one last look at him over her shoulder.

Anson rushed through the rest of his shower feeling as excited as a child sitting by the Christmas tree waiting for the clock to strike midnight so he could get to the presents. He couldn't believe she was here. He was anxious to get to her. To talk to her. To touch her. To kiss her.

To set things right again.

He dried off and dressed in linen shorts and a white V-neck tee that clung to his athletic build. He almost tripped over himself leaving his bedroom and stopped to find Hunter sitting before a loaded room service cart alone.

Did I dream that?

"I offered her my room to shower and change," Hunter said, taking a bite of a crispy beignet dusted with sugar.

Anson glanced at the closed door before going over to sit at the table. He selected a shrimp, crab, and lobster omelet.

"You a'ight?" Hunter asked, glancing up at him as he reached for a fresh strawberry.

"Yeah, I'm good," he said. "I'm damn good as a matter of fact."

"That girl flew here to see you," Hunter said, leaning back in his chair. "What more does she have to do?"

"I get it," Anson said.

"Too bad you didn't get it two months and ten terrible first dates ago," he said.

"I love her, man," Anson said, letting the feeling flourish in his chest.

"I know," Hunter said with the utmost seriousness. "Now tell her."

When the bedroom door opened and Mona stepped into the living room, they both rose from their seats.

"It's hotter here than it was in Australia," she said, smoothing her hair upward.

She's so beautiful. Her hair was in her beloved messy topknot and she was dressed in a white fitted tank with a mint green pencil skirt that hit her just at her knees with metallic gold wedge heels.

"Good-bye, Hunter," Anson said, never taking his eyes off her as she came to him and lightly touched his arms before she sat in the chair he held for her.

"I knew it," Hunter said, grabbing a plate and piling it with sausages, beignets, and more fresh fruit before he headed to the door. "You guys have an hour before I get back. And that's an hour to do *everything.*"

Anson and Mona laughed lightly before glancing at each other and looking away.

"It's been a long two months," Anson admitted.

"Yeah," Mona agreed, sitting back in her chair and crossing her legs.

His eyes dipped to take in the innocent move that she made all the more sexy by not even trying.

* * *

Mona bit back a smile at the way Anson's eyes were on her legs. She reached for a piece of cantaloupe and shifted in her seat, crossing and uncrossing her legs again as she bit into the fruit. She smiled again when his eyes went from her legs to her lips as a small trickle of juice ran down her chin.

He reached out to catch the juice with his finger before she could pick up a napkin. She arched a brow when he sucked the juice instead of wiping it away. "Thank you," she said with more calm than she felt as her heart beat wildly.

He cleared his throat and shifted in his seat to cross his ankle over his knee.

Mona had the distinct impression he was hiding a growing erection.

"I want to start over. I want to be with you. I want to show you that I love you, and I do. . . . I love the hell out of you, Mona Ballinger," he said, uncrossing his legs and leaning forward to take both her hands in his.

Mona closed her eyes as a tear fell.

She gasped at the feel of his finger against her skin as he wiped the tear away. "I have always wanted to be in love—you know that. But I need you to know that this is isn't about that. I love you, Anson. I truly love you and you have to believe me."

He pulled her over into his lap and wrapped his arms around her. "I had my head too far up my ass to see it before, but I believe you, baby. I believe you, and I love you just as much."

He tilted his chin up as she leaned down. They kissed.

Mona pulled back from him as she licked her lips. "Do I have to worry about you and my aunts?" she teased, eyes filled with love and happiness as she looked into his.

Anson shrugged with one hand lifted. "They were looking right in those leggings," he joked.

Mona poked him in the side as he laughed. "Silly self," she said, cupping the back of his head to taste his mouth again.

They smiled at each other and shared a dozen more kisses filled with love.

"So I think I should tell you a little more about my childhood," he said, his eyes serious.

"I would like for you to share that with me," she said, stroking the side of his face.

She looked at him as he turned to stare out the open balcony doors at the landscape of New Orleans in the distance. "Your aunts told me that my mom is dead," he said.

"Oh, Anson," she sighed softly, her heart aching for him. "So you believe them?"

He met her stare and nodded. "I do," he admitted.

She pressed a kiss to his brow.

"I mean I haven't seen her or wanted to see her in a long time, but it's different knowing she's dead, and we didn't even know it. You know?" he said, looking up at her.

"Are you okay?" she asked, rising to her feet to go around him and massage some of the tension in his broad shoulders.

"I'm good. I mourned for my mother a long time ago," he said matter-of-factly.

"Are you going to tell Hunter?"

Anson nodded. "When we get home tomorrow I'll tell him," he said.

Out of respect for him and however he decided to deal with the news of his mother's death, Mona squelched the desire she felt rising in her at the feel of the muscles of his shoulders beneath her fingers. It wasn't easy to release him, but she did, moving to walk out onto the balcony and look down at the historic city. "Let's meet up with Hunter and go sightseeing," she said, glancing back at him over her shoulder.

Anson agreed, rising to his feet to pull out his cell phone, and she knew she'd made the right decision. They had forever—and more specifically that night—to complete their reconciliation.

And late that night, long after they had seen as much of the city as they could and Hunter had bid them farewell and retired to his own bedroom, Anson took Mona by the hand and led her to his.

In the bathroom, once her shower was complete, Mona undid her hair and dropped the towel to the floor after she dried off. A red satin robe awaited her and she could only wonder when Anson had had time to purchase it as she slid the smooth material onto her naked skin.

She froze at the sound of the Robin Thicke song from her dream that night. She opened the bathroom door and a déjà vu sensation made her spine tingle as she took in the candles lit around the room and the red satin sheets now covering the bed. Anson smiled at her over his shoulder as he lit one last candle.

She took in the sight of him naked and waiting for her as she crossed the room to reach him. "I swear I dreamt of a scene just like this," she said, reaching up to stroke the back of his hair with one hand and the length of his dick with the other.

"So did I," he said, reaching down to cup her buttocks.

"Song and all?" she asked, tilting her head back as she slid off her robe and bent to kiss him from one shoulder to the other.

"Can you believe we're at the point where the idea of that is not crazy at all to me?" he asked against her neck.

She smiled and nodded as he kissed her pulse.

Their foreplay and lovemaking matched that of their dreams. Bit by bit. Move by move. And somehow the knowledge of it all did not kill the anticipation nor the pleasure, from the removal of her robe to Anson stroking deeply inside from behind as she lay on her side.

"Promise you won't leave me," he whispered against her cheek.

"Promise you love me," she countered, her eyes glazed with desire.

With his hands twisted in her hair as he circled his hips to drag his dick against her wall, Anson let all of his feelings for her show in his eyes. "I will always love you," he swore, his pace quickening as he felt that sweet anxiousness at the rise of climax.

"I will never leave you," Mona assured him just as she closed her eyes and bit her bottom lip as her body trembled from her core outward with her release.

Chapter 17

Five months later

Mona sat at her desk drumming her fingernails against the top of it as she leaned back in the red leather chair. She looked without moving a muscle as her sister Shara came through the door carrying a Tupperware bowl. Mona shook her head and held up her fingers in a mock cross. "Reeba is not going to blow my ass up playing taste tester for her bakery," she said.

Shara came to sit on the edge of Mona's desk and opened the Tupperware container, pulling out a chocolate chip cookie. "She wants to call it the kitchen sink cookie," she said. "There's walnuts, almonds, macadamia nuts, and peanuts."

Mona eyed the cookie as Shara broke it in half. She knew they were still warm by the melted milk chocolate chips dripping back down in the bowl. "Give me one," she said, holding up her palm.

Shara laughed and did just that before taking a big

bite of her own. "Oh my God, that is so good," she moaned, doing a little dance with her shoulders.

Mona picked up the Tupperware and rose from her seat to drop it on Shara's desk, which now sat beside her own in the center of the office. "Reeba opening up that bakery right down the street will not be the cardiac death of me," she said, rubbing her fingers together to free them of crumbs.

"Well, she wants to know what kind of cake you want for your birthday," Shara said, moving back to her desk to close the Tupperware container before she turned on her computer.

"I'll call her," Mona said, already refocusing on searching for a mate for a new client—a retired bank president whose husband recently divorced her.

Mona and Shara got lost in their work and both were surprised when Anson poked his head in the office. "Hello, ladies," he said. "Baby, you ready? I'm double-parked."

Mona glanced out the window at his new Jaguar, indeed double-parked. As they did when they first started seeing each other, Mona and Anson drove in to work together. They hadn't spent a night apart since they'd reconciled in New Orleans. Sometimes she wondered why she even kept paying rent on the small cottage she barely used.

"Shara, you want a ride home?" Mona asked, rising to her feet to retrieve both her and her sister's lightweight wool coats to help keep off the December chill.

"I can catch Reeba," she said. "You two go on home."

As Anson went back to the car to wait in case he

had to move for oncoming traffic, the two sisters moved about the building closing down for the night. Mona locked the front door and walked with Shara two buildings down to where Louisiana Sweets was set to open on the corner. The all-white decor with colorful graphic prints of desserts painted on the walls was perfect. As were the small tables and chairs suitable for a quick chat as patrons enjoyed their desserts.

Reeba came from the back as the sound of the bell over the door chimed loudly. "Is it that late?" she said, pulling her cell phone from her pocket to check the time.

"Yeah. I'm headed home and Shara's catching you," Mona said.

"Home or Anson's?" Reeba asked.

"Same difference," Mona said, and that was very true.

She turned as Anson pulled up to the corner. "I gotta go," she said.

"What kind of cake?" Reeba called behind her.

"Let me ask, Anson," she said.

"No," Shara and Reeba said in unison.

Mona jumped, startled by their exuberance. "Is it that serious?" she asked, looking at them like they were crazy.

"I want to make something just for you," Reeba said with a glance at Shara. They both gave Mona a weird smile.

Mona's eyes shifted back and forth between her sisters. "Why are y'all acting crazy?" she asked, her hand still on the door, holding it open.

"Just tired," Shara said. "Tell us what kind of cake, so you can stop holding Anson up."

"I'm sick of lemon, so maybe a strawberry short-cake, ReeRee?" she asked with a shrug.

"Whatever *you* want, sis," Reeba said.

Shara elbowed her.

They gave her those weird smiles again.

"Night, y'all," she said, after noting a few shifts of the eyes between the two of them.

Mona rushed across the sidewalk and climbed inside the warmth of the Jag. She instantly leaned over to kiss Anson with a press of her hand against his face. He winced.

"I forgot my hands are cold. Sorry about that," she said.

He grabbed her hand and turned his face into it to kiss her palm. "No worries," he said.

When he released it she settled her hand onto his thigh as Anson made short work of driving them from Walterboro to Holtsville.

The last five months of their life together had been everything they both wanted and more. Much more. She let him know that he was the love of her life and he proved every day that he cherished their relationship and her love.

As they pulled up to Anson's house, workmen were still high on ladders putting the finishing touches on the Christmas decorations. Mona clapped excitedly and barely waited for Anson to stop the car before she climbed out of it. "It's so beautiful," she said. "I don't know why we didn't hire them to put it all up sooner."

Anson came to stand beside her just as the lights of the garland were turned on. She glanced at his side profile and loved the twinkle of the lights in his eyes. She pressed a kiss to his cheek and said, "You look happy."

He glanced over at her before wrapping one hand around her waist to pull her even closer. "I am happy," he said. "The happiest I've ever been."

She grabbed his face and planted a loud kiss on his lips. He swung her up into his arms and carried her inside the house.

Mona awakened quietly, on the bed, the darkness broken up by the moonlight, with Anson's arms securely around her waist holding her body against his. She shook her head a bit to free it and turned on the bed. He grunted slightly in his sleep as Mona faced him and reached in the darkness to lightly touch his lips with first her fingertips, then her lips.

"Stop, Mo," he said, his voice thick with sleep and his eyes still closed.

"But I need to ask you something," she insisted.

"No, my dick is not awake either," he said.

"Are my aunts coming to Holtsville?" she asked. "I just had the weirdest dream."

Anson's eyes popped open. "No, but since you woke me up," he said, pushing her back down on the bed with his body.

Mona avoided his lips, twisting her head this way and that. "I didn't wake you up for that—"

Anson captured her chin with his hand and pressed

kisses to her mouth until all questions were completely forgotten. Then he slid his hand beneath her buttocks and lifted her high to slide himself inside her with one thrust.

Soon her questions where replaced with cries of pure passion.

"What are you up to today?"

Mona looked over at Anson across the island as they enjoyed a late breakfast. "Really nothing. I was just gon' lay around the house all day while you fish with the Jamisons. Why?" she asked, looking at him over the rim of her pink spectacles.

"I thought we could have a date night," he said.

Mona eyed him. He was looking everywhere—at his plate, at his phone, on his iPad—anywhere but at her. *What's that all about?*

She popped a grape in her mouth and chewed on it until he looked up at her in silence. "What's up? What's going on?" she said, her eyes on him like a hawk's on a field mouse.

"Nothing's up," he said, rising to come around the table. "We don't do date nights anymore?"

Mona tilted her head back to look up at him as he loomed over her. "Of course," she said, puckering her lips.

He kissed her as requested. "I'm heading out, but I'll be home by six at the latest," he said, already walking toward the archway.

Mona rose from the stool and walked over to the kitchen to peep through the thick wood slats of the

blinds as he eventually drove off down the driveway.
Something was definitely up.

Mona bit her lip as she reached across the island
to pick up her cell phone. Mr. Cool Calm and Col-
lected wouldn't give it up, but she knew who would.
"Reeba, hey, sis. What you doing?" she asked, leaning back against the island and twisting a curl around
her pinky finger.

Mona tensed when she heard plenty of voices in
the background. Was that a "hey there"?

"Nothing," Reeba said.

"I'm about to ride down there. Girl, I'm so bored,"
she lied with an arched eyebrow.

"No! No, we . . . uh . . . Shara and I are headed out
the door—"

Child, please.

Mona studied her nails. "Well, come scoop me up.
I wanna ride out too," she said, rolling her eyes as
she came around the island and picked up a piece of
turkey bacon.

"Well, if you must know, we were going to get
your gift," she said.

Amateurs.

"My birthday's not for another week," she said.
"Matter of fact, let me call you back and cancel this
date night with Anson. I think I'm just gonna stay
home all night and chill."

"No!"

Reeba had *no* sense of chill.

"Let me call you back, ReeRee," she said, raising
her finger to end the call.

Boop.

Mona loved surprises. Ever since she was a little girl she got the greatest tickle out of surprises of any size or nature. But what she loved more than a surprise was doubling back and surprising those who thought they were surprising her.

With a hearty laugh she walked into the bedroom to plan just what outfit she would wear to her surprise party—which wasn't a surprise at all anymore.

"You really look beautiful, Mona," Anson said as he opened up the passenger door to the Jaguar and held out his hand to help Mona from the car.

Under her coat she wore a gold strapless jumpsuit which gleamed next to her cinnamon brown complexion. Her curly hair was up in a topknot showing off the large gold hoop earrings, and her makeup was smoky and sexy. "Thank you," she said, taking his hand and standing.

He decided not to fight the urge to press a kiss to the base of her neck. He loved that he felt a shiver race across her body from that simple gesture. He had much more planned for her later that night. "Ready?" Anson asked, closing the passenger door behind her.

Mona nodded as they walked across the lot and into their favorite soul food restaurant, YaYa's. She loved the dishes that reminded her of the good and spicy Louisiana cooking she grew up on.

"Wait, Anson," she said, grabbing his arm before he opened the door to the restaurant. She removed her coat and folded it over her arm. "How do I look? Is everything where it's supposed to be?"

Anson fought the urge to chuckle in her face. "I already said you look good, baby. What are you worrying about?"

Mona released a little laugh and released the death grip she had on his arm. "I just want to look good for you," she said.

Yeah, right.

"I am dying for some of those fried gator bites," Anson said, holding the door as she entered.

Mona gave him some side-eye. "Aren't you glad I bribed you into trying one?"

"For what you were offering that night I would've tried anything," he said, his cheeks warming at the memory. Mona was just as spontaneous and free-spirited in bed. She'd taught him a few things—and that was saying a lot.

"Welcome to YaYa's," the hostess said, already holding two large leather bound menus in her hand. "Two?"

"Yes. Thank you," Anson said.

"Huh?" Mona said in low voice.

He saw the confused look on Mona's face as she looked at the patrons seated around the restaurant enjoying their food. "Something wrong?" he asked, motioning for her to precede him in following the hostess to their table.

Mona forced a smile. "No . . . no. Nope."

She led them to the back of the restaurant. They came to a stop by a set of wooden double doors. "The table needs to be cleaned. Let me get a busboy for you," the hostess said, giving them an apologetic smile before she turned and walked away.

Mona continued to cast surreptitious glances

around as she smoothed her hair upward. "The restaurant is pretty packed," she said, her expression a little pained. "We barely got a seat."

Anson pressed a kiss to her bare shoulder. "I'm going to the bathroom. Be right back," he said, before striding away.

He chuckled as he moved around the corner leading to the restrooms but instead opened another set of double doors leading into a large room filled with balloons and streamers and nearly fifty people. All eyes fell on him but everyone remained quiet as he moved through the crowd to reach the other double doors. Anson's heart was pounding in anticipation as he grabbed both handles, looked over his shoulders. "One . . . two . . . three," he mouthed before opening the doors wide.

Mona stood there and jumped a bit as her eyes widened like a deer caught in bright headlights.

"Surprise! Happy birthday!" they all exclaimed in unison.

Anson pressed a hand to her lower back to guide her into the room. "Happy birthday, baby," he told her warmly in her ear with a kiss to her cheek as all of their family and friends began to surround them. "You surprised?"

Mona wrapped her arms around his neck and hugged him close. "Yes, baby, thank you."

Mona's heart was pounding. She felt silly for correctly guessing the party and still being surprised like crazy when those doors opened. She released Anson as she felt herself pulled into a small circle of hugs made by her two sisters and two aunts.

"Hey there," her aunts said in unison, looking lively and regal with their silver hair and colorful dresses. "Happy birthday, Mona."

Mona hugged them both at once, her head between both of theirs. She enjoyed their scent and their eternal positive energy. "Thank you for coming all this way," she whispered to both. "And thanks for being the guardians of our gift. We are forever blessed by having you both in our lives."

"Hey, what did you say to them?" Reeba asked, as both aunts wiped at their eyes.

"None of ya business," Mona said, pulling her sister close and then wiggling their bodies like they were making shakes. Just as they did when they were teens.

She hugged her littlest sister next and did the same. "You're my fav, you know," she said playfully.

"I know," Shara said.

Mona turned and surveyed the room of smiling faces and bright decorations. "Oh," she said, turning back to the Ballinger women. "I knew all about the surprise."

She did a little victory dance as their faces filled with remorse.

"Who gave it away?" one of them asked.

"One guess," Mona said with a long stare at Reeba before she stepped away from them to playfully bicker.

There were a large group of people waiting to wish her well and Mona reached back for Anson. His hand slid right into hers. They both made the rounds around the room together. Everything felt right with them. Complete. Happy.

"Where's Hunter?" she asked, looking around the room once they claimed a quiet corner for themselves.

"He couldn't get time off from his residency," Anson told her. "Trust me he is crazy disappointed he is missing the chance to hand pick which of your sisters he wants."

Mona just rolled her eyes playfully and laughed.

"So you knew all about it, huh?" he asked.

She shrugged one shoulder. "I still love it though and it's the best surprise birthday party ever. My family. My friends. My favorite food. *My man*."

Mona leaned against the strength of his chest and looked up at him as she stroked his chin with her thumb. "Thank you for everything, including showing me that love—being in love—is even better than I ever imagined," she said to him softly, her eyes filling with emotion as she bit her bottom lip.

Anson bent his head enough to kiss her mouth several times—short and sweet and with the promise of more when they were alone.

Both of their hearts pounded at the thought of more. Much more.

Mona felt slightly shy at the love she had for this man and rested her head on his chest as she smiled.

Suddenly everyone began to sing happy birthday.

She looked and turned. The room was slightly darkened and the crowd parted as her sisters rolled up to her with a cake lit with tall thin candles. She gasped at the 3-D heart-shaped cake and grasped

Anson's arm after he wrapped it around her waist from behind.

"Happy birthday, Mona," he whispered before releasing her.

She stepped forward to look down at the cake and then looked up to meet the eyes of her sister Reeba. "*You* are my fav, you know?" she said.

Reeba looked bashful as she nodded. "I know."

"Make a wish," one of the aunts said.

The room went quiet.

Mona reached her hand back for Anson's. She stiffened when she felt an object pressed against her palm instead. She looked down at it as he came around to stand before her beside the lit cake. It was a bright red suede-covered ring box.

She gasped and then just as quickly released the breath as she looked up to him. "Anson," she whispered as he lowered himself before her on one knee.

"Mona, you are everything I ever needed and didn't even know I wanted. You make me laugh. You make me have fun. You make me think. You have made me believe in things I never could have imagined were possible. And you make me a better man. We have come a long way since that first time we met in your office—"

"Thank God," she inserted with a smile, wiping away a tear that raced down her cheek.

"Yes, thank God," he agreed.

The party goers lightly laughed.

"I went from wanting you, to needing you, and now loving you with everything I am. I simply want to spend the rest of my life loving you and I ask you to want the same with me." He reached for her hand

and gently took the box from her to open and reveal a beautiful three carat heart-shaped solitaire set on an intricately designed gold band.

"Good job, Anson," Shara said.

"Hey there," the aunts agreed.

The crowd laughed again before settling back into a respectful silence.

"I was meant for you and you were meant for me, Mona Ballinger. Will you be mine?" he asked, holding the ring at the tip of her finger.

She felt a slight tremble in his hand and his nervousness made her love him even more. She nodded and clutched at his hand as she began to tremble. "For forever and a day," she swore as he slid the ring onto her finger.

He rose to his feet with ease and pulled her body close to his to kiss her as everyone around them applauded. They began with light touches of their lips and it deepened with a moan as they held each other tightly and enjoyed the taste of each other without a care in the world.

They were forced to end the precursor to the night ahead as the crowd swelled forward to congratulate them.

"Oh, and your aunts told me you knew about the party," Anson said.

Mona's mouth gaped. She didn't even bother to ponder how they knew she knew.

"And your sisters tell me how you love interceding a surprise," he continued as he turned and held up his hand high in the air while holding on to one of hers with the other. "But I do believe now that the ring is on your finger, and you have said yes, that we got you. So . . . one, two, three!"

"Surprise! You're engaged," everyone exclaimed in unison.

It was Anson's turn to do a little jazzy two-step as Mona looked bashful. "It's not your birthday party it's your engagement party. You were wrong. Stop guessing. You were wrong. Stop snooping. You were wrong," he chanted.

Mona's mock serious expression broke when her aunts came around the cake to do the bump with Anson as they joined him in their chant. "You were wrong. Stop guessing. You were wrong. Stop snooping."

She couldn't do anything but laugh and turn to dance herself back into the middle of their frivolity.

"Forever and a day, huh?" Anson asked as he lay still and enjoyed the beating of her heart echoing the pulsing of her core against the hard length of him inside of her.

Mona nodded as she rubbed her legs down his calves and arched her back as she tightened her walls around his dick with a moan.

He hissed in pleasure and hotly licked the sweat from the length of her neck up to her chin before biting her lightly as he slowly worked his hips in tight little circles that sent his hardness deeper inside of her. Easing his hands beneath her soft buttocks to cup her deeply he rose up just enough on his spread knees to stroke inside of her. Deeply. Powerfully. Quickly.

Mona cried out and turned her face on the pillow

causing her hair to cover her face as she dug her nails into his shoulders and enjoyed the passionate onslaught. She shivered with an explosive climax that pushed her so far over the edge that her nails lightly scratched his back as she shifted her hands down to grip his hard buttocks, enjoying the clench and release of his ass as he delivered each delicious stroke.

Anson looked down at her, consumed by his love and desire for her. "My wife," he said thickly, enjoying the pleasure on her face.

"Not yet," she reminded him.

"But soon," he promised her, just before he quickened the pace to unleash his own climax. He released a cry from deep within his chest as he closed his eyes and stroked inside of her until they were both weak, and so spent, that moments later they were in a deep sleep.

Epilogue

Six months later

"Introducing for the first time, ladies and gents, Mr. and Mrs. Anson Tyler!"

Mona and Anson shared a brief kiss behind the closed doors just before they opened and they walked into their reception holding hands. The live band played up-tempo music and their wedding party was lined up right at the entrance and clapping. Her two sisters were looking pretty in bright red dresses. And for the groomsmen, Hunter and Malik stood out strong in their all black tuxes.

"Soul train line," Mona said, taking off dancing and pulling Anson behind her.

He resisted. "No, I don't think that's a soul train line—"

"It is now," she said, letting his hand go as she turned and did small body rolls away from him.

Anson eyed her in her white strapless trumpet gown that fit her body like a glove and made her the most regal and beautiful bride he'd ever seen as she walked down the aisle to him. But in that moment, seeing her willing to be goofy and carefree, made him love her all the more. Shaking his head, he two-stepped down toward his bride, pausing just long enough to share a dap with Hunter and Malik.

All of the wedding attendees were on their feet and were enjoying seeing a true testament of Anson's love for Mona as they playfully danced with each other. The upbeat music faded and soon the sound of their song—"For the Rest of My Life" by Robin Thicke—filled the air with the vocalist singing the words they both heard in a dream.

Anson pulled her close to him with his hand at her back as she lightly clutched the lapels of his tuxedo jacket and leaned back in his embrace to look up at him.

"We did it," she said, licking her gloss-covered lips.

"Yes, we did," Anson agreed.

"We're going to do something else too," Mona said coyly as she brought her hands up to his shoulders and then up around his neck to stroke the back of his head.

"What's that?" he asked as they gently swayed back and forth to the music.

Mona pulled in closer to him and kissed the spot just below his ear. "According to my aunties we're going to make a baby tonight," she whispered to him.

He paused and leaned back to look down at her. "Wishful thinking?" he asked after a few seconds of studying her face.

"With my aunties?" she asked. "Oh no, that is knowing not wishing."

Anson looked down at her and then his eyes searched the crowd for Winifred and Millicent. They were standing together at the very edge of the crowd of people watching them dance. There was no mistaking the happiness on their faces for their niece and their new nephew.

He smiled.

They smiled and waved back.

He looked down at Mona.

"Do you believe?" she asked with a slight arch of her eyebrow.

Anson nodded and laughed, pulling his wife back close to him and pressing kisses to her temple. "Damn right I do," he promised.

The music shifted again and the dance floor filled with people as the band began to play the Jackson 5's "(You Were Made) Especially For Me." Anson and Mona reluctantly moved apart from each other as Hunter cut in and started dancing. Mona couldn't do anything but give him the floor as he took over like he was trying to win a dance contest.

"Leave it up to you to steal the show," she called to him over the music with a laugh.

In time her love for her new brother-in-law had grown and with that love came a lot of patience for moments like this.

The crowd opened up and circled them.

"I'll stop if you make one of your fine ass sisters dance with me. Either one. I'm not picky," Hunter said, revealing the real reason he cut in for a dance.

Mona knew exactly which one she should steer toward Hunter but she was determined to let fate run the show just as she had for the last year as he shamelessly flirted with both whenever he was in town. One of them would tame Hunter Tyler but neither she—nor the aunts—were telling.

Mona looked back to see her two sisters standing there together on the perimeter watching them. She turned again and searched for her husband. Anson was off to the side holding the hand of each of his aunts and dancing with both.

She looked back to Hunter and then to her sisters and then to Anson off a ways in the distance. She smiled so big and broad that she thought her cheeks would cover her eyes.

"The vision," Mona mouthed. "This is the moment I saw in the vision when I touched Hunter. This is it."

She didn't need the reassurance but she had to admit that it was pretty damn nice seeing all of it come to fruition. To know that her gift was intact, her life complete, and her love meant to be.

Don't miss any of the Strong Family novels

HEATED

Bianca King is living the golden life—until her somewhat estranged father asks for her help in keeping the family ranch afloat. When Bianca returns to Holtsville, South Carolina, she meets the latest threat, neighboring rancher Kahron Strong, a man with knowing eyes and the body of a gladiator. But this competition may just do Bianca some good. . . .

HOT LIKE FIRE

Sexy widower Kade Strong has moved back into the house he once shared with his wife, hoping to bring some stability into his six-year-old daughter's life. He's certainly not looking for a relationship—but the women of Holtsville have different ideas. Only Garcelle Santos respects Kade's grief—and he can't help being irresistibly drawn to her. . . .

GIVE ME FEVER

Kaeden Strong is a workaholic who's allergic to the outdoors. Jade Prince is an adventuress with a vixen's body and a tomboy heart. He's wanted Jade from the moment he saw her, but so do a long line of men—including her business partner, Darren. On paper, Kaeden is all wrong for Jade—but can he prove he's right in all the ways that really matter?

THE HOT SPOT

Zaria Ali is looking to make up for lost time. Who says she can't be living *la vida loca* in her forties? And who says she can't date hot twenty-six-year-old Kaleb Strong? Zaria lightens up his serious side—and turns him on like no one ever has. But is there more between them than just explosive chemistry?

RED HOT

For Kaitlyn Strong, life has been a fun-filled free ride, all expenses paid by her wealthy father. But when her father cuts her off, a shocked Kaitlyn gets a job and an affordable apartment to go with it—where she meets hardworking single father Quinton "Quint" Wells. He's never met a demanding diva like Kaitlyn. Yet despite their verbal clashes, there's a sizzling attraction between them. . . .

STRONG HEAT

Lisha Rockmon just wants a good man. But most of the men of Holtsville, South Carolina, want to get physical a lot faster than she does—except Kael Strong. Wounded by his last relationship, Kael is hesitant to open his heart again, even to a woman as irresistible as Lisha. But despite his misgivings—and some outside interference—love just may find a way. . . .

Grab the Hottest Fiction
from
Dafina Books

Grab These Novels by
Zuri Day